THE
BONE
VALLEY

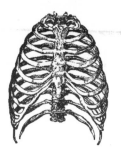

CANDACE ROBINSON

Midnight Tide
PUBLISHING

For Mallory

ONE

ANTON

Anton Bereza lay restlessly in bed with an unclothed Maryska. He stared up at the ceiling, his body still drenched in sweat from how hard she'd made him work for his money. As the morning light spilled in through the window, he knew he had to leave soon and quite possibly take a long bath to rid himself of her overwhelming scent. It was a mixture of an overly sweet orange with a tinge of something he could never name—yet didn't like—hidden somewhere in its beauty. No matter how well he washed, her smell always seemed to linger.

With quiet precision, Anton lifted his head to peer over Maryska's still form and settled his gaze on the four silver coins gleaming on the wooden nightstand beside her bed. *Perhaps I could grab them quickly and run.* But no, that wouldn't be possible. Then she would gossip to all the other village folk, which, in turn, would destroy his reputation from future work.

And he *needed* the money.

He was physically and emotionally exhausted from having to pretend to worship and yearn for these customers. Although he enjoyed the burst of in-the-moment bodily pleasure, it never felt good afterward. If he was to have a lover for his own, he didn't want it to feel like this anymore—he wanted it to be real.

"Maryska, I have to leave," Anton whispered, giving her a soft nudge of the arm.

Maryska's eyelids fluttered open, her dark brown gaze catching his. "Stay a little longer?" With a yawn, she stretched her body as she rolled to face him. She knew the whole reason behind him being there was because of the money.

Anton mentally groaned and displayed a seductive smile anyway. "If only I could, my goddess, but I need to check in on my sister and help her at the market today."

She sat up, pressing her shapely lips into a pout, then crossed her arms against her youthful light brown skin. At that moment, she appeared more like a petulant young girl than a woman in her twenties.

In answer to her pout, he tugged on his worn trousers, tossed on a gray tunic, and slipped on his boots. Rubbing the side of his jaw, he hesitated, before turning back to her. "May I have my payment?"

Maryska's chestnut-colored brows furrowed, and he knew in an instant that it was the wrong thing to have asked. Anton didn't understand a lot of these customers, but that was why he'd come there. He knew that—*she* knew that.

While holding her breath, Maryska pulled the knitted covers back and stood from the bed. She snatched the silver coins and slowly sauntered toward him, leaving her form unclothed, trying to tempt him again.

Even though his body would have considered giving in to a quick tumble, he was not in the mood for her attachment. He was done with her.

Sliding his arm forward, Anton held his palm open for Maryska to drop the money in. She released one silver coin against his flesh, then came the second, with a clang and a clack against the other. The pouring of coins stopped.

2

Anton stared at the two pieces of silver for a moment before returning his gaze to Maryska. He avoided looking at her large breasts and focused on her hard stare. "You owe me four, Maryska."

"You can have the two other coins"—a smirk spread to the left side of her cheek—"when you come back tonight."

Anton inhaled sharply, his voice coming out low. "That's not part of our bargain." He held back the growl that wanted to escape as a frown crossed his face.

"I changed my mind," she cooed. "Didn't I tell you that last night? Two coins per session." Her head tilted to the side as if Anton was a child and should know better.

"You didn't mention that." She hadn't told him anything about flipping to a new payment arrangement. He would have remembered that.

"Oh, well, it must have slipped my mind." She shrugged and inched closer to him, tapping two of her long fingernails against his chest.

There was nothing he could do about this. *Nothing.* Despite the blood boiling through his veins, he accepted the situation for what it was, and closed his hand into a fist. His grip tightened on the coins, causing them to dig into his flesh. "Fine. See you tonight, *Maryska.*"

Without another word, he turned and trudged his way out of her room to the front door, shoving the coins deep into his pocket like they might disappear. As he yanked the door open, he wanted to slam it shut, but he knew angering her would only lead to losing the rest of his payment.

"Oh, and Anton?" Her voice came out laced with false sweetness as she sauntered into the candle-decorated sitting room. The candles were everywhere, hanging on the walls, resting on the table, some fresh, others almost completely.

Gripping the golden handle in one hand, he twisted his head over his shoulder and unclenched his teeth. "Yes?"

3

"I'd watch how you act around me, or I may take it down to one silver." Maryska walked to the circular wooden table and set down the two remaining coins. One spun several times before falling over with a ping.

"Then I wouldn't return." He shouldn't have said those words, but he couldn't hold them back. Maryska knew how much his family needed the money. Everyone knew. It had only been two years since his father passed. That day never went away, the image of his father collapsed outside their cottage with his hands sliced clean off after being caught stealing at the market. Anton and his sister had done all they could to save him, but the infection had taken him anyhow, leaving them orphaned.

Maryska held it over him, continuing to taunt him more and more with each visit.

Grinning, she edged alongside the silk-covered chair, running her fingernail down the blanket resting on top. "I just might have to spread word around Kedaf about you."

Anton's heart lodged into his throat, and he pulled his face into as much of a smile as he could muster. "I'll be here right on time." If she were to spread those vicious lies—most likely that he had a spreadable sickness, or worse—they would be ones he could never wash away. No customers would want him after that.

"Good." Maryska waved him off as though he were her pet. Perhaps he was.

After stepping outside and leaving Maryska behind for the time being, he withdrew a leather strap from his pocket to tie back his disheveled blond hair. Maryska's large orange tree, full of ripe fruit for the picking, stood in front of him. He plucked a perfectly-shaped orange from it, despite the threat of a reprimand he'd get over taking her precious fruit if she saw.

He peeled the orange and ambled carelessly down the dirt path, rolling up his sleeves as perspiration gathered on his back. Anton tossed the rind to the ground as he walked toward the market, leaving a trail behind him.

A heavy gust of cold wind blew past him with an angry howl, rumpling his hair and causing a chill to race up his spine. The sound of something clacking echoed around him. He looked up into the trees, and all the birds seemed to be peering in the direction behind him. Nothing was there, not even another gust of wind. It was way too early for cold weather to start trickling in. *Very strange.* He shook his head and continued on.

Luscious green hills in the distance stood out against the foliage. He lived in the less populated village of Kedaf, full of dense forests, near the border of Verolc, where gossip grew fast and hit hard. The three territories—Kedaf, Verolc, and Narwey—were once united neighbors, then became divided by war. Peace now reigned. However, what happened on the other lands across the sea, past Huadu, he didn't know much about, besides tales of magic. But that was all they were, only tales.

Up ahead, as Anton approached the market, all the booths appeared empty. No morning breakfast smoke filled the air yet as he passed a wooden stand and table. The sun was rising higher in the sky, and the vendors should all be there soon.

A row of sellers' stations extended on each side as he walked by. Down the line, his family's booth came into view. His sister, Yeva, always insisted on getting started as soon as the sun rose. She had a good head on her shoulders, except when it came to doing things too early without getting paid. She and their brother, Pav, could show up later, and they still would make the same amount of coin.

Across the table, various shades of green herbs were sprawled out and separated into bundles. Anton searched for Pav's strawberry blond mop of hair and his sister's wheat-colored braid, but they were nowhere to be seen. He would shake them both if they'd left the herbs alone for the taking.

A heavy sigh of relief escaped his mouth when a head sprung up from inside the booth. He stilled after noticing that the girl's braid was the color of a fallen raven's feathers instead of wheat. A delicate hand of rich olive clasped a bundle of rosemary—his family's rosemary.

Anton scanned the surrounding area to see if other sellers or early customers had trickled in. None had. It was only him and the thief. *This should be amusing.*

Shuffling his feet past the jewelry vendor next to his sister's booth, he stopped directly in front of the waist-high wooden door and prevented the girl's escape.

"Good morning," Anton sang. He wished he had a hat atop his head to remove and bow to the girl, in order to sarcastically appear more gentlemanly in contrast to her thieving ways.

The thief whirled around to face him, startled. Her shocked open-mouth expression vanished, turning into something much fiercer, making her facial features sharper. He only felt tired for a moment until his eyes lowered to the bag beside her feet, stuffed with herbs. Annoyance fluttered through him and his heart started to pump harder.

"We're closed," she said, lips pursed while her fist squeezed a bundle of lemongrass.

Anton wanted to roll his eyes as he tilted his head to the front of the booth. "Sign up there says you're open." There was no sign, but she didn't have to know that just yet.

The girl stood on her tiptoes, trying to see over the edge. She appeared close to his nineteen years, perhaps a year younger.

Before she could look, Anton moved forward and shoved his open hand in her face. "I need my palm read." After all, his sister did read palms for the customers at this booth.

"What?" The girl's brown eyes flicked back and forth between his hand and her satchel on the ground. As her fingers nervously twitched, his irritation altered into gratification that she would slip up.

6

"I need you to read my palm." He wiggled his fingers in front of her and moistened his bottom lip, holding back a bemused smile.

"You want a palm reading?" Her dark brows rose, and he could tell she was trying to figure out a way out of the situation.

"Yes. Please tell me what you foresee in my future." He knew he could pick this girl up and set her outside the booth before she even realized what had happened. But he preferred to see what she would do next.

"Sure. Come inside." There was a slight hesitation and a hint of a Huadu accent within her words. She waved him in and set the lemongrass on the table.

"You look nervous." He studied the beaded perspiration that had gathered on her forehead and upper lip.

She brushed her hands against the sides of her pants. "I'm not. It's hot out here, is all."

"And you are?" Anton asked, not really interested in who she was, yet he couldn't help but enjoy the charade.

The girl's eyes angled to his and narrowed. "Why?"

"I'm just curious."

She paused as if she wasn't going to answer, then nodded and glanced away. "I'm Nahli."

Something in his chest tightened as he could have sworn he'd caught a glimpse of a hollowed expression on her face. There wasn't time to feel for someone who was trying to steal from his family, and he needed to put an end to this. "Can you tell me *my* name? Since, as a fortune teller, you know all."

Her eyes fluttered as she gently took hold of Anton's hand that had become a fist. She unwound his tight fingers, then stared at the center of his palm. With the tip of her index, she softly drew a circle in the middle of his hand. "Your name is Anton."

His body stilled, stunned by the fact she knew his name. Perhaps she *was* a real fortune teller. "And how do you know that?"

"Your reputation precedes you, Mr. Bereza." She shrugged and removed her fingers from his palm.

"You mean I'm a whore. That's what you're trying to say." Bitterness found its way into his voice, and shame seeped into his words. He told himself he couldn't care less what people thought, but being confronted about it directly instead of behind his back was more insulting.

"We all have to do what we must. You're not harming anyone," she murmured, seeming taken aback by his words.

But he *was* harming people. Himself, most of all. "What else does my palm say?"

Nahli studied the thin lines intently. "You will find a love one day that will conquer all obstacles, and you will be happy forevermore," she replied with the generic answer of most fortune tellers, besides his sister, who at least tried harder.

"Let me read *your* palm now." Anton stirred out of Nahli's grasp and clasped her wrist. "Ah, yes. Nahli, it says here"—he ran the tip of his finger softly along the curve of the line in between her index and middle digit—"that you are a thief." She tried to pull out of his hold, but he fastened his grip. He slid his finger to the center of her palm. "It also shows here that you are in *my* booth."

He glanced up and met her eyes with an even stare, a wicked smile on his lips. But she was beaming right back at him, feral. Two dimples showed in her cheeks.

"Look over there." She cocked her head in the direction of the forest behind the booth.

"I'm not that foolish." If this girl thought he would really turn his head to look at the trees so she could run off, then she needed to learn more about thieving.

"Maybe you are." She reached her other hand to his arm and pinched the delicate skin of his inner wrist with needle-like claws, even though they were only her fingernails.

Out of instinct, Anton ripped his arm back with a curse,

8

releasing her. "You have claws like a cat." He couldn't believe how much his skin throbbed, more than getting bested by his younger brother.

Before he could grasp her arm once more, she darted past him and leapt over the fence with quick reflexes, angling her head over her shoulder. "More like a leopard."

"Don't forget your bag." Anton bent down and held up her satchel, dangling it on his finger by the strap, letting it sway side to side.

She slapped the side of her thigh. "Damn."

"Be careful, you might lose both your hands if it's someone else who catches you next time." Thieves always reminded him of his father, and he didn't even know the girl's story. He didn't want to know it, either.

Nahli didn't glance back at him as she scurried out of the market. After her image faded, he grew frustrated since his brother and sister still hadn't come back. What would have happened if Yeva had come to find Nahli instead, or if it had been a larger man trying to steal their herbs?

Kneeling, Anton gathered the fallen herbs from the ground, then opened the brown leather satchel and fished out the remainder. He rolled them back out on the table where they belonged, before shoving the bag in the corner. It looked like his sister would have a new satchel.

Moments passed by, and vendors were starting to slowly come in and stock their booths—fruits, vegetables, candles, fabrics, and other tinctures displayed for all the customers. A heavy clacking of iron being struck by hammers and wood being cut pierced his ears. The fresh aroma of cooking meat filled the air, and his stomach rumbled with hunger. Anton patted the coins in his pocket, shoulders slumping when he realized he wouldn't have enough to purchase any meat. There was just enough to stop by a seller on his way out to pick up a loaf of bread and vegetables. That would have to be satisfactory.

9

"Ton-Ton, what are you doing here?" a gentle voice asked.

Anton spun around to find his sister, Yeva, opening the rickety wooden gate, her hands holding two wicker baskets flowing with herbs. Shoved under her arms were even more.

"You know you don't have to call me Ton-Ton when Tasha isn't around." Anton was used to the nickname their younger sister had used since she could first speak.

"Sorry, it's a habit—and a hard one to break, at that." Yeva smiled, closing the gate and dropping the items on the table with a sigh.

For a moment, Anton almost forgot that he was supposed to be angry with her. "Where's Pavla?" He surveyed up and down the market strip for their younger brother, his eyes settling on a customer trying to barter for thread.

"He's—"

Anton glanced back at his sister and pressed a hand against the gate. "Neither one of you are supposed to leave the booth unattended when you have all the merchandise exposed. There was a girl here earlier trying to swipe the herbs."

Yeva's smile faltered, then faded. "Sorry, but Tasha's not feeling good, and Pav had to stay home and look after her. Mrs. Evanko wouldn't watch her because she didn't want her other children to get sick."

Anton's back straightened with worry. "Tasha's sick? You could have come and found me." He would have gone home in an instant.

"From Maryska?" Yeva let out a harsh laugh. "She would have been angry with me for showing up and interrupting."

Once, his sister had stopped by Maryska's home to retrieve Anton when she'd thought Pav had broken his arm. Maryska didn't know Yeva was his sister, and she'd been furious. Even after she'd learned of their sibling connection, Maryska still resented her.

Lately, Maryska had become even more jealous of the time he spent with his family.

"You still should have come, Yeva."

She waved him off, then spread out the herbs on the counter in a precise manner and set up small display signs in front of each type. His sister's mannerisms reminded him more and more each day of their mother's. He prayed the day would never come when he recognized the same haunted sadness in her eyes. The deep depression after Tasha's birth that had driven her to hang herself from a tree. His father had told them she just wasn't ready for another child.

"I have to see Maryska tonight," Anton said, stomach sinking at the thought of it.

"Already?" Yeva threw her hands above her head. "You're supposed to have dinner tonight with us and Ionna."

"We really need the coin," he muttered while helping Yeva organize the herbs.

His sister gripped his callused hand and stopped him from setting down a bundle of thyme. "No, we don't. The business has been picking up and seeing that I'm to marry Ionna in the summer, I'd like you to spend more time with her."

Anton slipped out of her grasp. "You're too young to get married." Ionna was a good enough woman, and she had her own farm at only twenty, but he didn't want his sister to feel as if she needed to marry someone.

"I will be eighteen by then."

"No matter." Anton knew he was hitting a wall because she was set on marrying Ionna. He only wanted her to be sure about it.

"Ionna promised to take care of all of us, and I will continue to work the market. It's not only that—I love her. You know I wouldn't marry someone only for money." She paused, then clapped her hands. "Oh, and she told me she found work for you."

"What kind of work?" Anton lifted a skeptical brow. But he would take any other trade he could if the coin was right. Yeva might be all right with Ionna taking care of the rest of his family, but he wasn't. He wanted to provide for Pav and Tasha, not Yeva having to do everything.

"Gathering herbs." She smiled, though it looked more as if she were wincing.

"You mean *you* found me work." He hated to think that Yeva bothered Ionna to do this for him. *Yeva's poor brother can't find honest work on his own.*

"Just take it until you find something better. *Please?*" she begged, clasping her hands and knocking them against the wooden table.

Anton pressed his lips into a thin line. She had taken on a parental role in the family after their birth mother had died, and he just couldn't tell her no.

"Fine, but only after I get the rest of my coin tonight, then I promise I will do what you ask."

12

TWO

NAHLI

Nahli Yan had been in a bind ever since sailing from Huadu to Kedaf last winter. Though it was spring verging on summer, she could still feel her body brimming with ice, remembered the frozen chips that had been embedded on her eyelashes.

Now, only frostbite remained inside her heart from when her childhood friend, Zikri, had abandoned her in this foreign place. A frigid ache haunted her memories after she'd left her home behind to go with him. The wintry haze bound itself to her, and she would never be rid of the coldness, making it difficult to thaw and reseal her broken heart.

She hurried out of the market, attempting to avoid thinking about the coin she could have made when Daryna—the woman who she sold stolen goods to—set her eyes on all those herbs. Nahli had almost gotten them. Almost. What could she bring to Daryna now? She hadn't scavenged anything useful in days. Tired of the thieving, Nahli wanted to return home, though she wasn't sure why anymore since her parents would only punish her for leaving.

From the corner of her eye, Nahli caught a glimpse of someone walking her way. An older man, with graying hair and a receding hairline, limped up the dirt path toward the entrance of the market. A large straw basket filled with shiny beaded jewelry dangled and glistened from his left hand.

It would have to be sufficient for today. Nahli wouldn't be paid as much, but she was sure she'd get at least a few coins from Daryna. Better than nothing.

"Hello, sir." Nahli put on her brightest, trustworthy smile and straightened her spine as much as she could.

"Good day, isn't it?" the man asked, rotating the basket to his other hand. The jewelry rattled, and she took a deep breath to prevent herself from reaching in to snatch it all.

"May I have a gander at what you have to sell today? I want to rush home and tell my mother to hurry to the market before all the good jewelry is sold." She knew the jewelry wouldn't all be collected from customers. He might only sell two or three, but she wanted to boost his confidence.

Scratching the patch of thinning hair, he smiled and lowered his basket. "Only really quickly. My wife is meeting me with the rest of our goods at the market, and I don't want to have a late start."

Up close, she could see the deep pockmarks buried into his cheeks. Even then, he carried himself with the poise of a man who'd been handsome in his youth. Though he wasn't as pleasant to the eyes now, his swagger had survived the years.

Nahli knelt, her knees brushing against the dampened grass beside the path. While rummaging through the colorful rounded beads of bracelets, necklaces, and earrings, she studied the man and asked him about the market to keep his focus on her face, instead of her fingers lightly sifting through the jewelry.

In one quick flip of the hand, she slid a few pieces up her sleeve and pushed herself up to stand. She stared down at an azure-colored necklace resting on top of the other jewelry. "I think my mother would love that blue piece. Would you mind holding it for me at the market, if I come right back?" She wouldn't be returning, and he would only become another person whom she'd swiped from. Perhaps one day she would have enough coin to pay back everyone she'd stolen from, but she knew that day would most likely never come.

"I most certainly will. My wife will be thrilled that her jewelry is loved and appreciated. She spends every waking moment at home stringing them." The man tipped his head and once again limped toward the market, causing Nahli's heart to shrivel a little more.

Closing her eyes for a moment, Nahli shook away the guilt. She needed to do this. It was the fastest way to get back home to Huadu.

But there could be a quicker way to make coin...

Her thoughts turned to Anton.

There had been a time when she'd stolen from a woman at a market dance who'd been gossiping to a friend and pointing to Anton's tall frame. Then again, Nahli had heard his name roll off the lips of giggling women at a pub. Yet, she couldn't do what he did.

When she'd told him *we all have to do what we have to do*, she had meant it. But she was already empty as it was, and anything that could make her feel more barren would certainly end her.

She shook her head from the thoughts of the man who'd helped to put her in this predicament by keeping hold of her satchel.

Daryna didn't live far from the market, her small cottage merely hidden by the thick woods most people avoided.

With a flitter of her arm, she let the trinkets slide down her sleeve into the palm of her other hand. Two mismatched earrings and a bracelet. She hoped they were worth something, but she knew it wouldn't be as much as she wished for.

Taking in the warmth of the sun and cloud-filled sky, Nahli trudged ahead, the dirt crunching beneath her boots. Eventually, she arrived at the fork in the dirt road and stared briefly in the direction leading to the ocean that would take her back to home. Shaking away the ache in her chest, she took a left and crossed into the heavily wooded area. People in the village believed Daryna to be a witch, but Nahli knew better than to consider such ridiculous gossip. The woman only acted like one, with her distant and moody demeanor.

As Nahli trekked through the muddy woods, past thick moss hanging from branches, the only sounds echoing were the squish of her boots contacting the wet dirt, the rustle of branches, and the barking of foxes. Daryna's ivory-painted, wooden fence came into view, surrounding her brown and blue cottage. Surprisingly, it was a beautiful home—secluded from all eyes, no wood decay, topped with a pristine thatched roof.

The steps to the maroon front door groaned and creaked as Nahli strode up them. From the side of the cottage, a group of chickens squawked. Before she could bring her hand up to knock, the door swung open, revealing Daryna's scowling face.

Daryna was possibly ten years older than Nahli, maybe a little less. But the way she presented herself made her seem older, harder. The woman's hazel eyes stood out against her warm brown skin and black hair. Her nose was slightly crooked, and the edges of her mouth were always turned down in a way that made her appear harsh. Even without a smile, her face had a certain prettiness, though.

Jaw clenched, Daryna clamped down on Nahli's wrist and tried to tug her inside the cottage. "You know better than to show up at this time of day. We have set times. What if someone sees you?" Her thick black hair was pulled into a low bun and loose strands hung beside her ears.

Nahli twisted her head from side to side and even angled it back over her shoulder to prove a point that no one was out there but her and Daryna. "No one else is here." The woman needed to calm her nerves. *Who else would be out here this early except for me or Boda?*

"Just get inside."

She tugged her arm from Daryna's grasp and walked into the cottage. Searching around the sitting room, Boda was nowhere in sight. Boda was Daryna's 'helper,' but Nahli wasn't sure of exactly what she did.

"I'm sorry, Daryna. I only wanted to do a trade today, and I thought it would be better to arrive early."

"You should have come yesterday."

Daryna closed the door, her wool skirt swaying as she made her way to the center of the main room. The wooden rocking chair remained still, a knitted blanket hanging over its arm. Beside it rested a large settee that could substitute for a mattress. Nahli had thought about asking Daryna to use that piece of furniture as a bed for herself, would have gotten down on her knees and begged, even cried heavy tears against the floor for it. But she was sure Daryna would have denied her, and she didn't want the pity.

Nahli knew Daryna was right—she should have come yesterday. Yet she'd spent the day sulking like a child of eight instead of a woman of eighteen. "I know. But I'm here now."

The scent of sweet bread struck her nose, and her eyes drifted to the kitchen. She instantly found the honey-colored source of food sitting on top of the stove. Her mouth salivated for only one taste.

Daryna's hazel gaze fell to Nahli's empty hands. "Well?"

Returning her attention to Daryna, Nahli reached into her pocket and withdrew the mismatched earrings and bracelet. She silently prayed for Daryna to hand her a few coins so she could leave.

Instead, Daryna slapped her hand against Nahli's, causing the jewelry to plummet to the floor. "Why did you even bother wasting my time? You might as well go sell yourself with the ones who are destined for nothing better."

A fire sprang up inside Nahli's chest. She might have made a pitiful decision today with losing the herbs and bringing the

17

jewelry, but she'd made plenty of good finds for Daryna in the past. The payment hadn't been much for Nahli, but Daryna had to have made an astounding amount of coin from the stolen items.

Nahli was tired of having to search for breadcrumbs in this life while everyone else trudged ahead. She lifted her arm before Daryna could do anything, and shoved the woman out of the way, making her stumble. Without any more thought, Nahli took off in the direction of the backdoor, snatched the bread on top of the stove, and flew out from the cottage.

Behind her, the sound of Daryna's heavy footsteps pounded against the wood steps as she tried to chase after Nahli. "You give that back!" Daryna hissed.

Nahli only became more flustered. She plucked up a red-faced chicken with her other hand when she rounded the cottage. Taking one last look at Daryna, she could see her clutching her left leg as though she'd injured it. For a brief moment, Nahli wanted to turn around and help her, but she held on to the flicker of anger and fled.

"You're going to give me both of those back!" Daryna's rage-filled voice grew smaller and smaller as Nahli drew farther away from the cottage.

"Then I guess you'll have to hunt me down!" she called back with a smile, not knowing if the woman could even hear her. If Daryna reported her for stealing, then the woman would be turning herself in for knowingly purchasing stolen goods.

Nahli jolted out of the thicket, brushing moss out of her way, until she hit the fork in the road. Breathing heavily, she continued in the other direction opposite the market, following toward the large hills brushing the bright blue sky. Her lungs were finding it hard to pump, and her thirst increased as she carried the chicken awkwardly. When she reached the lake, she came to a stop, clutching her chest with the bread.

She placed the hen on the ground in between two moss-covered trees and sat on the hard earth, propping her back against the rough bark where no one would be able to see her. The chicken let out a teeny cluck and took a tiny step closer to Nahli, then plopped down beside her thigh, as it cushioned itself in the tall grass. It seemed to stare at the loaf of sweet bread resting in Nahli's lap. Feathers of black and white ruffled as if the chicken still wasn't comfortable enough. Its small red head turned, looking up at her through dark beady eyes. Her heart softened—the hen was sort of cute.

"All right, I'm hungry too," Nahli said and broke off the top of the bread. She set it next to the bird, and its small beak pecked rapidly at the crumbs.

Nahli stuffed pieces into her own mouth, satisfying her aching stomach, then drank a few handfuls of water from the lake.

She wasn't sure why she'd taken the chicken or what she would even do with it. Most villagers could easily make a fine meal out of the hen, but she couldn't bring herself to eat many animals besides fish. She had just wanted to take whatever she could from Daryna in the heat of the moment. But she still wouldn't bring the chicken back to Daryna's cottage.

After finishing half the loaf of bread, she went to place the remainder of it into her satchel then remembered she didn't have one anymore. She would have to find another ... or steal one.

Nahli ignored the swell of emotions that built inside her and leaned her head against the tree, closing her eyes to stop the thoughts of her wrong choices from creeping in.

A rustling, followed by a splash of water, grabbed her attention, and her eyes fluttered open. She'd somehow drifted off, but for how long, she didn't know.

Nahli peeked around the tree as more movement came from the lake. At the edge of the water, in a heap, were a pair of boots, trousers, and a tunic. Her gaze flickered to the lake and narrowed on a blond head poking out of the water. She knew that head.

Anton.

Scooping up the chicken—who she was surprised hadn't roamed off—in her arm, she grabbed the bread in her other hand and rushed to the edge of the water. Dirt crunched under her boots as she hurried to the clothing and lifted them to see if her satchel was buried underneath. It wasn't.

"Where's my satchel?" Nahli yelled out toward Anton. She kept her distance to make sure she'd be able to run from him easily if she had to.

Anton faced the other direction, but his body froze when he heard her voice. He quickly turned around, wet hair brushing against his broad shoulders. The smallest of smiles played across his face, though she might have been imagining it was there at all.

His blue eyes locked with hers, but he was too far away for her to see the faint scar beside his eye. "I did tell you it was going to be gifted, didn't I?"

Nahli placed the hand with the bread against her hip. "I want it back."

Slowly, his gaze lowered to her hands. "Is that a chicken?"

With a proud grin, she peered down at the hen in her arm. "Why, yes. Yes, it is."

"All right..." A brow quirked its way up his forehead.

Nahli examined the clothing on the ground and decided to return the favor. She plucked up the trousers and tunic. "I suppose I have gifts to give away now, too."

Anton cringed and released a loud curse. "Come on, you can't take my clothes."

"I left your boots ... as a gift." She smiled even wider, taking off with her hands full and Anton shouting at her to come back. It was the most enjoyment she'd had in a while.

She continued to smile the rest of the way until she made it home—the decaying wooden bridge she lived under. It looked as if it were meant for trolls but they didn't exist—she did. Her face fell as she neared the wide opening. Some of the planks were missing on top, others were cracked or broken. It wasn't that terrible living there, now that winter was over…

Who was she kidding? It was horrible.

Slowly, Nahli padded her way to the hidden area. No one drifted that way or used the dilapidated bridge anymore. It was the place where she felt the safest … and the loneliest.

She set down the chicken, and it followed her like a puppy to her already sprawled out blanket. A musty aroma wafted off from the cloth, and it would need to be washed in the lake soon.

After taking a seat, she broke off another piece of bread and shared it with the hen. She grabbed her silver flask from the edge of the blanket and drank all the water inside, which wasn't enough to sate her thirst.

Why did I ever come here? Oh right, Zikri's bright idea. Zikri. She couldn't stop herself from thinking about him.

"Zikri, my parents are forcing me to marry," Nahli said, *sobbing softly into her hands. She was conditioned to handle her parents' emotional abuse at home but being betrothed to someone she didn't know affected her more.*

He ran a hand through his dark hair before wrapping his gangly arms around her, his golden-brown eyes studying her. "They can't do that."

"They're sending me off in two weeks."

"I have an idea," he whispered in her ear.

His idea had involved the both of them stowing away on a ship across the ocean. The idea had been brilliant … until it wasn't.

Zikri convinced Nahli to steal as much coin as she could from her parents, and he'd promised her they could send money when they had enough to pay them back.

He had been her childhood friend, her best friend, the one she'd fallen in love with. When they'd arrived in Kedaf, they found rest at an inn. Zikri then told her he loved her, and so she gave him the two things that were truly hers … her heart, her body. He'd been gentle as he entered and moved inside her, even though she didn't find the blissful release he had. She hadn't cared.

The next morning she'd woken to him opening the door to leave.

"I'm going to get breakfast," he'd said over his shoulder.

Something in his voice had sounded off. Yet she'd still waited.

She shouldn't have waited.

After getting dressed, she sifted through her pack, finding her coin bag missing. He'd left her with nothing and never returned.

Tears streaked Nahli's cheeks when she thought about the last words he'd said, and she hastily wiped them away. She didn't want anything else to be for Zikri, including her tears.

The breeze picked up and Nahli threw on Anton's shirt, which smelled of a combination of herbs. She allowed the comforting aroma to wash away the lingering thoughts of Zikri.

A soft nudge pushed at her ankles as the chicken curled up beside her. She scooted closer to the soft feathers of the hen and tried to drift to sleep so she could dream of somewhere better.

The dream that washed over her was of a place filled with bones.

THREE

ANTON

Anton could not believe it. No, he *could* believe it. The girl—Nahli—with the black braid and dimples from the market had stolen his clothing. He wasn't surprised she'd taken his clothes, but more so at the fact he'd seen her twice in the same day.

He knew he wouldn't be able to catch up to her to swipe his things back. By the time he swam long strokes to reach the edge of the lake, she would already be long gone. Instead, he decided to finish bathing, then think about what had occurred with Nahli. He'd come to escape for a little while, to not think about Maryska, to not think about his family.

Leaning back, Anton dipped his hair into the lake and let his mind clear. With his eyes tightly shut, he floated down into the lukewarm water, as far as his body would go.

When he spread his arms and let himself resurface from under the blue liquid, a blast of cool wind struck his face. Just as it had earlier. But when he stood to look around, he was met with only the sun's warmth and the sight of his lonely boots. He groaned with irritation at what he would have to do.

Before Anton had come to cleanse himself, he'd dropped

off the things he'd purchased from the market, along with the satchel that would be a gift for someone. He'd given the remainder of his coin to Pav before trailing his way to the lake. If the thief from the market had stolen those things, he would have most certainly tried to track her down.

Squeezing out his wet hair, he lifted himself from the shifting water to go to what Nahli had left him. His boots. "Well, there's that," he said aloud to himself as beads of water slid down his shoulders and chest.

If he had to trudge home like a newborn babe, then so be it. It couldn't be worse than having to see Maryska that night. Anton lifted the worn boots, holding one in front of himself and the other over his buttocks, before he started to shuffle his way home.

He found himself partially smiling and half frowning at the ridiculousness of it. Nahli had been running off with a chicken of all things. Then the smile vanished when he was unable to control his thoughts from taking a darker turn. Only one more day of this life, of doing what he loathed. As vile as tumbling with strangers made him feel, it had helped his family survive before Yeva had started selling herbs and reading fortunes at the market.

Dirt stuck to his bare feet, smaller bits gathering in between his toes. Perhaps he should just put the boots on, but he didn't feel like exposing himself to the whole village.

Once he broke out from the forest, Anton scurried as quickly as humanly possible toward his home. Luck was on his side this time since no one was out. His family's older cottage shifted into view. The charcoal thatch roof needed to be repaired, but the windows were spotless from Pav keeping them clean.

As he edged closer, Mrs. Evanko was out in her garden next door, her fiery-red braid brushing her waist. He tiptoed as silently as he could, just as he used to when he was younger after sneaking about and doing things he shouldn't have been doing. But nothing ever slipped past Mrs. Evanko.

He saw it coming as her head slowly glanced over her shoulder, her eyes narrowing immediately. Anton froze in his indecision on whether he should run inside or have a nonchalant chat.

The chat it is. "Good morning, Mrs. Evanko. Tasha already seems to be getting better." When he'd dropped off the items earlier, Tasha had appeared well as she slept. However, he could still smell the lingering stench from the empty bucket sitting beside her bed in case she grew nauseated again. "We'll let you know tomorrow morning if you're able to watch her, or if she'll need to stay home again." He spoke with ease, as if she wouldn't notice that he was indeed almost as naked as the day he'd been born, despite the boots.

She glanced at his home, then back at him with a chastising look, tapping a finger against her chin. "Hmm."

"It isn't what you think."

She most likely thought he was coming back from making coin. More than once, her disapproval had echoed his own regarding his nightly activities.

"So, you aren't gallivanting in the village and picking up customers?"

He wanted to scratch his face in nervousness, but instead shifted his boot in front of him to make sure he was completely covered. "Not at the moment, no."

"Anton, you're like a son to me, and you need to stop this nonsense." Small creases appeared at the edges of her eyes, and exhaustion rolled off her as she let out an exasperated huff of air. "Your mother and father would be so disappointed in you if they were still here."

He wanted to tell her that he was disappointed in his mother for leaving them when she could have tried harder to stay, and at his father for not being more careful. But out of respect for her, he remained silent on the matter. Mrs. Evanko had treated them well over the years, even if she needed to mind her own damn business most of the time.

Before he gave her a response, she shook a pile of weeds in her fist in the direction of her home. "And do go and put some clothes on before Polina and the smaller ones see you."

Polina was her eldest daughter who had just turned fifteen. She used to follow him around with a childhood infatuation, until not that long ago when she'd finally noticed Pav. His brother had been practicing with the sword, more so lately, gaining strength and hoping to become a soldier one day.

With a final nod at Mrs. Evanko, Anton hurried to the front of his cottage. When he reached the offset door that needed adjusting, he kicked it softly several times with the heel of his foot.

The bolt unlatched with a hard click and Pav opened the door. A brow arched, and his lips twisted to the side as his green eyes quickly skimmed over Anton. "Where in all of Kedaf are your clothes?" He chuckled.

Anton strode past his brother. "Taken by a thief."

"While you were wearing them?" Pav shook his head and closed the door.

"That's exactly how it happened, Pavla," Anton said with sarcasm. "A thief held me at knifepoint and stripped me bare, only to leave me with my boots to cover myself and come home safely to tell you this most magnanimous story."

Pav's eyes widened, his freckled cheeks drawing upward. "That is quite a story. How did you manage to barter to keep the boots?"

Anton released a huff of air, his gaze drifting to the roof of the sitting room. "You know that isn't what really happened."

"It did sound like quite a tale, but you never know with thieves. One did threaten to cut my hair at ax-point once." He shrugged with a smirk.

"Pav, stop being ridiculous. We both know that never happened. Also, it wasn't a he, it was a *she*, and a very small she at that."

Pav gently patted Anton on the back. "Poor Anton, growing weaker and weaker by the day."

"I was in the lake, and she wasn't. I'm not a fish who can glide through water."

"Should have grown wings and flew like a bird."

"What?" Anton shook his head. "I'm done with this conversation, and I'm going to find something to wear." He inspected the tiny sitting room and the two empty chairs. "How's Tasha?"

"Still in bed asleep. There hasn't been any more retching."

Pav looked like he wanted a pat on the back, but Anton was still holding his boots. So he headed to his bedroom while his brother continued to prattle away about nothing. When he closed the door behind him, Pav was still talking to air.

At the market when his brother worked with Yeva, Pav did more talking than trying to sell anything. But for some reason, people were charmed by him and would continue to come back and chat with him while buying herbs. There were several customers who had asked to get their fortunes told by Pav, and it ended up being absurd, yet the people loved it. His brother was going to be a handful for the women when he was older—Anton was sure of it. That last thought brought another unwelcome one on its heels. Pav wasn't a child anymore—he would be sixteen in a few days.

Anton set the boots on the floor and drew open a dresser drawer, pulling out a pair of trousers and a tunic. He threw them on and took a seat on the edge of the bed he shared with Pav.

He rested on the flattened pillow, his partially damp hair touching his cheek as he closed his eyes for a little while.

A knock at the door stirred him out of his slumber.

"Yes?" His voice came out groggy as he sat up, rubbing the heel of his hand against his eye.

The door swung open with a soft couple of squeaks. Yeva stood in the doorway, her hair at her forehead soaked with

27

sweat. "Did you decide to stay for dinner?"

Anton's shoulders stiffened. "I already told you I can't, Yeva."

"You can." Her lips pursed together in agitation.

"All right, I can." He let his shoulders relax.

She leapt on the bed and wrapped her sweaty arm around his shoulders, giving him a quick kiss on the cheek. "Ionna will be thrilled. She should be here soon." A broad smile crossed her face, showing the two slightly-crooked teeth that he used to tease her about when he was smaller. He used to tell her it made her look as though she was part wolf. Though her personality was never fierce, she was more like a gentle deer.

His thoughts turned to Maryska. "I won't be able to stay the entire dinner."

"I will take whatever you're willing to give us. A little time is better than no time."

"Ton-Ton?" A soft voice entered the room.

"Tasha, did you grow already?" he asked his younger sister as she tiptoed into his area. Her complexion was no longer pale but a healthy hue. "You look taller than yesterday."

Tasha's spine straightened as if she were trying to make herself appear even taller. She was still small for her age, and she was the only one out of the four of them who looked exactly like their father. Tan skin, black hair, and bright green eyes, but the wild curls in her hair were from their mother.

"My feet do seem bigger today." Tasha padded toward the bed and took a seat on the other side of him, then placed her foot in his face.

Yeva giggled, and Anton wrinkled his nose, pretending to appear disgusted while shoving Tasha's foot back down. "It smells like goat," he said.

Tasha lifted her foot to her face and took a long sniff. "It does not!"

"While you two are talking about feet, I'm going to go and finish up dinner," Yeva said before giving Tasha a hasty tickle to the ribs.

Anton turned to Tasha. "Are you feeling better? You don't appear sick anymore."

"Yes, but oh how it was wretched, and I kept feeling nauseous."

He remembered the smell from earlier. "Such big words. You seem to have a larger vocabulary than I do." Anton smiled and shook her foot.

"That's because you need to read more." She tapped at the book in her hand that he was only now seeing.

"Pav doesn't read often, either."

"Pav could do with expanding his vocabulary."

A roar of laughter escaped Anton, and he glanced up to see Pav standing in the doorway, leaning against the frame.

"Are you two talking about me?" Pav asked, cocking his head. "I know everyone here can't help but enjoy my presence."

Anton nudged his younger sister. "Tasha here said you needed to expand your vocabulary."

"My dear lady, what an *atrocious* discussion to be allowed." Pav squinted his green eyes at Tasha. "There. Is that better?"

She held up her hand, sliding her index finger and thumb close together. "A little."

Pav rushed to the bed and rustled Tasha's curls, making them even wilder. She patted his hands away while giggling.

Anton stood from the bed. "I'm going to see if Yeva needs help with anything in the kitchen." He inhaled the scent of the herbs, spices, and meat brewing from inside the other room. His stomach ached with hunger for just one single taste.

"Where did you get the meat?" he asked Yeva when he strode up beside her.

"I made a good amount of coin at the booth. People like to tip extra after having their palms read, and there were more customers than usual today." She shrugged and stirred the

29

liquid in the large pot on the stove, tapping the wooden spoon on the edge before setting it down.

The meat didn't smell like the scraps they generally had or the tough jerky that was always too hard to chew.

A sense of pride washed over Anton for his sister. She had done this mostly on her own, besides using herbs from Ionna's farm. But she'd made sure to pay Ionna back each time she took them to sell at the market.

Yeva nodded in the direction of the vegetables sprawled across the table. "If you want to help and slice up those, you can work on that."

Anton grabbed a knife and a carrot from the table.

She looked at him and smiled warmly. "Thank you for the vegetables and bread, by the way. The meal wouldn't be the same if you hadn't gotten those today."

Nodding while holding his emotions back, he chopped into a carrot. Unlike Yeva being content with how she'd bought the meat, there was nothing pleasing about the way he'd paid for the other things. But he was satisfied nonetheless that his family would be able to have a proper dinner. That was good enough for tonight.

A heavy knock at the door arrived right as Yeva was pouring the meal into ceramic bowls. "Can you answer that?" she asked Anton.

Pav had gone next door to borrow *something*, but he had really gone to most likely flirt with Polina before dinner. Tasha had returned to her room to rest and read, to make sure her condition kept improving.

"Sure." Anton walked across the wooden floor and pulled open the door to Ionna's beaming face.

The yellow tunic she wore complimented her dark skin.

Her tight black curls seemed to bounce, and her wide brown eyes automatically flicked over his shoulder toward Yeva, before falling back to him. Anton could understand why Yeva had fallen in love with her, especially when she gave him a genuine smile that highlighted her cheekbones. He hoped that love would always be enough.

"It's nice to see you, Anton."

He opened the door the remainder of the way and motioned her inside. "Likewise."

"I'm coming!" Pav's loud voice shouted from the direction of Mrs. Evanko's cottage.

Ionna stopped and turned around to wait beside Anton.

"Sorry, it took longer than expected." Pav's breaths came out heavy from his sprint, and his cheeks were reddened. Oddly, so were his lips.

"So, what did you have to go and borrow exactly?" Anton asked, the side of his mouth quirking up.

Pav chewed on the edge of his lip. "I got distracted and forgot to ask."

"Sure, you did, Pav."

Ignoring Anton's comment, Pav ran a hand through his curly hair. "Lovely to see you again, Ionna." Grasping her delicate hand, Pav lifted it to his mouth and brushed a soft kiss against her skin. Anton had to stop from rolling his eyes.

"You are so sweet." Ionna patted Pav's head even though she was a bit shorter than him. Pav had grown over the winter months, and his shoulders had broadened. He was now more muscular than Anton but not quite as tall.

Ionna drew her hand back and smiled, before turning and heading toward Yeva. His sister wrapped her arms around her fiancée and kissed her.

Pav attempted to shuffle past Anton, but he tugged his younger brother back by the tunic. "You better not be doing more than kissing, Pavla," he whispered close to his ear.

"I wouldn't dream of it." Pav smirked, flicking Anton's

hand from his shirt.

"I'm serious," Anton said through gritted teeth. Pav was too young to have a child of his own running around. He already took care of Tasha a lot of the time.

"So am I." His brother plucked a piece of string from his tunic and avoided eye contact.

"Pav?" Anton asked in a serious tone.

"It's only kissing, I swear."

A huge weight lifted off Anton's shoulders. "All right. Keep it that way as long as you can."

Pav pursed his lips and nodded, then went inside to sit next to Tasha on one of the wide chairs. She had quietly made her way into the sitting room, toting a book which had been read so many times that sheets of paper were practically falling out.

Closing the door, Anton approached Ionna, who was already seated at the cramped dining table. His father had crafted it himself, and he'd made almost everything inside of their house. Dabbling in woodwork was no easy task for Anton, though. When he'd tried, the outcome was always off. He was better at carving and sculpting areas than aligning to make sure parts were sturdy and even. His focus and detail were more suited for smaller objects, and he didn't understand why he couldn't do the same with larger furniture.

Anton turned to Ionna. "So, I hear you're going to help take care of my sister."

"She can handle herself." Her eyes brightened when she glanced at Yeva, who was putting the last of the meal together. "But we'll watch over each other."

Perhaps his sister wasn't too young to get married, as he'd previously thought. After all he and his family had been through, Yeva already took care of everything well enough. Besides, he did like Ionna.

Yeva was near, but he could tell she wasn't even listening, too consumed with pouring hot tea into petite cups.

"I hear you decided to help gather herbs. After our

gardener passed away, I've been needing someone." Ionna smiled. "Yeva just knew you would be thrilled about the work."

He wouldn't have used the word *thrilled*, but it would do well enough. "Thank you so much for the opportunity."

"Anton made you a gift in thanks," Pav said as he reached for something in his pocket.

What is he doing now? Anton furrowed his brow in confusion, knowing he hadn't made anything for Ionna.

Pav took out a tiny barn owl and displayed it in his palm. Anton's cheeks heated with embarrassment. His brother had swiped the owl from their shared room. It made a soft clack as he pressed it to the table in front of Ionna.

"You made this?" Ionna's lips parted as her fingertips roamed over the feathered wings, tracing each delicate curve.

"It's nothing," Anton rushed the words out. "I only do it to try and improve my woodwork." It wasn't really nothing, but he didn't want to say how much it relaxed him and made him feel like he was doing something worthy. Even if it only pleased himself.

"It's beautiful," Ionna gasped. "Have you thought about selling these at the market? You could even add paints to bring out the texture."

Yeva seemed to be listening now as she plopped down beside Ionna. "I've told him he should, but he insisted on doing other things for money."

Ionna set the owl on the table, keeping one hand folded around the carving. "But you could make more money with these."

"You think so?"

Anton hadn't put much thought into trying to sell the small figures. He had mainly used them for practice to perfect his skill on larger furniture. Now, something blossomed in his chest, akin to hope and possibilities. Those emotions were hard for him to let take shape because they were easy to split and break apart.

"I do. You could still start by collecting herbs while selling these at the market and see what happens." Ionna grinned wider, straightening in her seat.

It was an idea. An idea that was starting to make him feel like maybe he could become something, better than who he was. Not for himself, but for his family.

While they ate dinner, Ionna, Yeva, and Pav did almost all of the talking. But mostly it was Pav asking about Ionna's farm.

Apparently Yeva and Ionna had run into each other at the market one autumn afternoon, and connected on the subject of herbs, quickly agreeing to a partnership. Something bloomed after that, and every day Yeva had come home, Anton would notice her smile growing brighter and brighter from each interaction with Ionna.

Anton watched out the window as the day darkened to night, and he knew he didn't have to go and visit Maryska. Yet he was still frustrated and too proud about not getting his full payment from her earlier, and needed to finish what he'd started.

"I'm sorry to leave like this, but I have to go to work," Anton said, not looking directly at his sister or Ionna.

Yeva closed her eyes and sighed. "You really don't have to go, Anton."

He stood from the table and brushed a kiss against her soft cheek. "Last night. I promise."

"I know it's none of my business"—Ionna rubbed a finger against her lower lip—"but I can give you whatever payment you would have received tonight."

His chest swelled at the possibility of taking her money, then deflated knowing the shame that would follow if he actually carried through with it. "I'm as stubborn as my sister about things like that, but thank you."

Tasha had gone back in the sitting room, eyes closed with

a book in her left hand. Anton gave her a kiss goodbye on her plump, delicate cheek. Her lids fluttered open for a brief moment. "Bye, Ton-Ton."

"Goodnight, baby bean."

She half-smiled and drifted back to sleep.

"Where's my kiss and nickname?" Pav asked from the floor, where he was playing a game with a deck of cards.

Anton leaned down and gave him a wet kiss on the cheek. "Goodnight, my darling."

Pav grimaced and wiped his cheek. "It was only a joke, Anton."

"I forgot you already had your share of *kisses* today."

"That, I did." Pav smirked.

Chuckling, Anton headed out of the house. His laughter subsided and his chest clenched as he walked in the direction of Maryska's cottage.

When he stood in front of her home, a blast of cool air struck him, making him shiver. A wind chime clacked above him. He looked up at the new object, and it appeared as if it were made from bones. Holding his breath, he touched the shell of what had to be some sort of animal piece. A warmth from the wind chime seemed to caress his fingers, and he dropped his hand.

The night felt off as he studied several candles burning through the window, thoughts swirling in his head about how Maryska had cheated him. One more night. Only one to touch her, to taste her, to be inside her. *Only one.*

Raising his clenched fist to the door, he knocked rapidly, harder than he should have. Maryska took her sweet time answering, and he knew she would be furious he hadn't arrived on time.

"You're late." She sneered as she yanked open the door. A sheer nightgown clung to her body, showing every inch of Maryska's skin—her rosy pink nipples, the dark curls between her thighs.

He had to be polite for now. "I know, I'm sorry. My sister made dinner and wanted to have a family meal tonight since her fiancée was coming over."

"Yeva, Yeva, Yeva. It's always about your sister. Are you sure *you're* not in love with her, Anton?" she spat.

The fact that Maryska's thoughts were that deranged disturbed him, but he said nothing. After tonight, he would never have to see or speak to her again, or worry about the rumors she would spread.

Anton steeled himself for what the night would bring, avoiding her gaze and keeping his on one of the chairs. A wave of something hit his senses, and he inhaled deeply. It wasn't just the usual scent of oranges but something else, something heavier, something he'd never quite breathed in before. "Do you smell that?"

Maryska didn't respond to what he'd asked as she slipped the gown from her body, only reached between his legs, cupping his manhood. "Now strip," she demanded like he was her personal slave.

And for the night, he supposed he was.

FOUR

NAHLI

Cluck, cluck, cluck. Nahli's eyes flicked open at the unfamiliar sound. For a moment, she didn't understand why there was a hen in her home—the old bridge she considered to be her shelter for the time being, anyway. Then she remembered the day before: Daryna, the chicken, and the tunic she was still wearing.

Tugging the thin fabric of the shirt over her head, she set it aside and stared at her new acquaintance. "I can't give you a name since I'm going to find a home for you today."

The chicken stared back at her, as though it were listening intently before preening its feathers.

"I know. I know. You wish you could live here, but this is no place for a chicken." She laughed then wrinkled her nose. This was her life—talking to a *bird*.

Standing from its sitting position, the hen scuffed its feet and moved away to reveal a wonderful surprise.

A lovely tan egg.

Nahli's chest fluttered at the sight. While she couldn't bring herself to eat a chicken, she had no qualms about having an egg. "You left me a gift?"

As expected, no response came from the guest, so she

snatched the branches she stored under the bridge to start a fire. It had taken her a while to learn this technique. Teaching herself to start a fire was a tiresome thing she didn't want to revisit, and the memories of the blisters that had coated her palms were proof of that.

After rubbing her hands together down the twig multiple times, a hint of gray smoke curled upward, and the woodsy scent invaded her nose. She quickened the pace while smoke continued to drift skyward until a flickering orange flame caught its fiery paws onto the other branches. On top of her stash, of what most villagers would consider garbage, was a meager pan she'd taken from a bakery.

While the egg cooked, Nahli collected a cracked ceramic bowl that was buried beneath a broken candle holder. Running the tip of her tongue along her chipped bottom tooth—a gift from her mother when they'd been practicing with swords— she watched most of the egg slide from the cast iron pan into the bowl with a soft plop. The rest she had to scrape out.

Nahli brought her lips to the ceramic and blew several soft breaths over the top. "Egg?" she asked the hen who quietly studied her. As she thought about it, she cringed. "Sorry, perhaps I shouldn't have asked you that." She didn't believe a hen would be too eager to eat something that could have potentially been its baby chick. With dirty fingertips, she stuffed bits of egg into her mouth and tried to figure out the plan for the day.

A gurgling rumbled from her stomach, and she was already aching for more food. Back home, Nahli hadn't ever had to starve. But here, in this foreign place, she was always hungry.

The plan she decided on would be to drop the hen off somewhere, bathe, then steal something to eat while figuring out another way to get coin. Without Daryna purchasing from Nahli anymore, she'd have to find another way to make money from thieving. It would be easier if she could stick to only stealing coins directly from villagers, but most of the time she found out they didn't carry around as much as she'd thought.

Despite feeling like the world was against her, Nahli went down on her knees and clasped her hands in prayer, then bowed her head like her mother always did when she prayed to the gods. Nahli didn't have the candles with her or the silver rings, but she tried anyway.

"I know I haven't spoken to you in a while, but please, please help me get through this day, this life, because I have no one."

She didn't even know if she had the gods. Her home wasn't a secure place to go to. Once she finally scraped up enough coin to return to Huadu, she would be beaten and married off to someone, even when she paid her parents back. It wasn't like in Kedaf where the villagers could choose what they wanted to do. In Huadu, whether male or female, it was the parents who chose. Perhaps she should just cross the sea to somewhere else.

Nahli slid on her boots, caked with mud from the previous day. She then scooped up the chicken and brushed dirt off her pants with her free hand.

The sun hadn't found its place fully in the sky yet. As it drifted upward, rising above the verdant hills, it seemed to follow and watch her in judgment as she headed in the direction of the village. She passed rows and rows of beautiful homes with sturdy shutters, straight roofs, and maintained gardens. While staring at the wealth that these villagers must have, she came to the realization that this wasn't the brightest idea she'd ever had.

As she ventured farther away from the well-groomed and pristine homes toward the poorer ones, she hoped someone who seemed in need would want the hen. She stepped over a fallen tree—its roots sticking out and twisting in all directions—then followed the curved path downward.

A twin set of cottages poked out from the flowering trees when she reached the bottom. One appeared to be more wilted and possibly tilting. The closer she got, the harsher it looked. A frail girl with messy dark curls sat on the uneven porch steps with a book in hand. When she studied the girl, she knew she'd done the right thing and had found the perfect person. Perhaps it was a good idea, after all.

The little girl must have felt Nahli watching her because she closed her book and glanced up at her.

Nahli smiled and held out the hen in front of her. "Do you need a chicken?"

"What?" The girl blinked rapidly while staring, as though she couldn't believe the offer. "We can't afford to buy a hen."

Doing a good deed wasn't something Nahli had done in a long time, and her fingers twitched in nervousness. She took a few hesitant steps closer to the girl. "I'm giving it away."

The girl frowned. "Well, why are you giving it away?"

"Because I live on my own and can't take care of it."

There was a brief pause before the girl shut her gaping mouth and set the book on the steps. She practically radiated as she ran closer to Nahli and the hen. Not the least bit afraid, the small girl reached upward and stroked the black and white feathers. "I'll have to ask my brother if I can keep it."

"Tasha!" The girl twisted her head around to the male's voice. Nahli looked up to see a boy around fifteen or sixteen with blond curly hair, but not as disheveled as the little girl's, marching down the steps. "You aren't supposed to speak to random strangers."

Nahli understood that—she could have been anyone, and the little girl had run right up to her with no way to defend herself. Perhaps she *was* someone Tasha should be avoiding since she was a thief.

She scanned the boy and the freckles sprinkled across his cheeks while he frowned at his sister. Nahli steeled her spine. "I was seeing if she wanted this chicken ... I ... uh ... found it."

The boy shifted his attention away from Tasha and focused

his green eyes on Nahli. "Oh, you're a girl."

Tasha tugged on the boy's shirt sleeve. "Pav, do you want this chicken? Or should we ask—"

"*Of course,* we want this chicken." Pav lifted the hen out of Nahli's arms. "And you are?" he asked, giving her a soft smile and holding out his palm.

She stared at his hand, unsure what to do. "No one, really."

"No one has to have a name." He brought his empty hand back and pointed at his chest. "My name's Pav."

"So I heard."

"And your name is?" He held out his palm again, letting it dangle in the air.

"Nahli." She brought her hand forward to shake his since it was still shoved toward her.

"Lovely name for a lovely girl." He brought her fingers to his lips and gave it a gentle peck. "Or should I say a woman?" His eyes roamed her up and down.

Pav continued to lightly hold her hand, so she pulled it out of his grasp. "Let's not think about that."

"I'll be sixteen soon," he said with a warm smile.

"Right." Her eyes squinted of their own accord as she studied him. He looked ... familiar, strong jaw, perfect nose—

"Are you sure Anton and Yeva want this chicken?" Tasha asked Pav.

Nahli choked and her shoulders tensed at the name. "Anton?"

That was why Pav looked so familiar. He was broader, had freckles and green eyes, but his facial structure was incredibly similar.

"Our brother," Pav answered, flicking his wrist as though he was the one in charge of the decision making.

"Shoulder-length, straight blond hair?" She wanted to confirm it, even though she knew what Pav's answer would be.

"Why yes, that describes him perfectly," he said, brushing

41

away his locks of blond curls from his face.

She was wrong. Her decision wasn't a good one. "I think I'll find someone else to give the chicken to." She reached forward to take back the hen, since Anton did have her favorite satchel.

Pav pushed her hand away with his index finger. "Tasha, go inside and ask Yeva if she wants this gift before we drop you next door and head to the market."

Tasha nodded fiercely and ran inside the rickety cottage.

Cocking his head, Pav put on a smug grin and winked. "Are *you* one of Anton's ladies?"

"What?" she asked, incredulous, stumbling back.

"When I mentioned Anton, you made a face and then wanted to take back the chicken."

"No, I'm not one of his ladies and would never be anything of his," she shot back.

He pursed his lips, holding back a laugh. "Mm-hmm."

A door squeaked from the porch, and a tall willowy girl, with a long blond braid down her back, strolled down the steps toward them. She wore a plain dirt-brown dress similar to Tasha's tattered one. Tasha was right on the girl's heels but then sat down on the porch and picked up the forgotten book from earlier.

"We appreciate the gift," the girl said with a thankful smile. "Tasha explained to me how you found the hen and have no need for it."

"Don't worry, Yeva is Anton's sister, not a lover," Pav whispered so only Nahli could hear.

The veins at Nahli's temples throbbed from the situation, and she needed to leave before Anton was the next one to slip outside from the cottage.

Pav petted the red comb of the chicken's head and gestured at Nahli. "Our new friend here is also a friend of Anton's."

"Oh." A scarlet flush crept up Yeva's neck and deepened on her face.

"No. *No.* Not that type of friend." Nahli hurried to get the words out. "Not even a friend. I just know him."

She wasn't going to mention that she'd tried to steal from them at the market. Perhaps she did owe the chicken after what she could have taken from them. If Anton hadn't shown up, she would have had a satchel and hands full of herbs.

Pav elbowed Yeva in the upper arm. "Her name is Nahli."

"I'll tell him you dropped this off"—Yeva's eyes fell to the hen—"and I'm sure he'll be most grateful for it. We sure are."

"All right, well, I must hurry off. I have work to take care of myself," Nahli said, turning to rush away.

"You can always stop by later when Anton's home," Pav called as she took off down the path.

She ignored Pav's remark and continued to scurry from the family who she now wished she had never met. She couldn't let herself feel any regrets about what could have happened if she'd stolen from them. It wasn't as if she hadn't tried to find work—she had. The bakery—no. The market—no. The only thing she hadn't attempted a hand in was selling herself, and perhaps Anton and others could, but she would rather feel ashamed about stealing.

As she headed up the pebbled path toward the lake, the hills in the distance now glistened a bright green, not quite the shade of emeralds, but close.

She peeled back a thin branch budding with tiny leaves and ivory flowers to reveal the sparkling lake. With haste, Nahli removed her clothing, stepped into the tepid water, and let out a sigh at how good it was to remove the filth from the day before.

She didn't have any soap left but as she scrubbed away the dirt and grime the best she could, she felt a thousand times lighter, her mind free.

Lying back and closing her eyes, she floated for several moments and tried not to think about anything besides the water swishing back and forth against her ears, creating a calming song.

Above her, she opened her eyes and stared at the blue sky. The puffy clouds tinted with gray were fattening themselves up with water to bring down the rain. She'd have to hurry since the village would be consumed by a storm soon.

She rolled over and swam until she reached the edge of the lake, then pulled herself out to squeeze the water from her hair.

Nahli stepped into her clothing, and it clung uncomfortably to her damp skin. She slipped on her tattered boots and noticed the tip of the sole flapping. "Great," she muttered to herself. "Just great."

While in the middle of braiding her hair, someone shoved her from behind, knocking her to the ground. Before she could pick herself up, a hand yanked her by the braid and pressed a cold blade against her throat. Nahli released a small gasp and froze. A rusty dagger was hidden in her boot, but she was unable to reach it at the moment.

"Don't even think about moving, little girl," a low female voice purred in her ear. "You're going to return Daryna's loaf of bread and her chicken. But first, you're going to choose two things for me to remove from you."

Boda. The woman was Daryna's helper. What she knew about Boda was that the woman had no intelligence. She was what most would consider stupid. Nahli would get herself out of this situation, or else, Boda might have to die.

"Sorry, I ate Daryna's chicken," Nahli taunted.

Flipping Nahli over to her back, Boda's muscular arms had her pinned with the knife at her throat again. Boda was a large woman, and even so, Nahli could have already had her dead on the ground if she hadn't been taken by surprise.

"Do you want me to choose which body parts to remove?" Boda panted. "Because if you don't choose, it will be both your hands, and I'll remove each fingertip until I reach your wrists."

44

"That would be more than two." Nahli should have held her sharp tongue. A fear then washed over her of how heavy this situation was getting. She wouldn't be able to survive in a world without her hands. But she could still get out of this—she always did.

Boda's eyes narrowed, her gaze like razors. "Answer me! Which parts do you want me to take? *Now.*"

"Two toes," Nahli answered quickly, knowing the woman's attention would focus downward, giving her the chance she was waiting for.

As soon as Boda peered toward her boots, Nahli headbutted the woman. Boda shouted and clasped her forehead. Chest heaving, Nahli thrust her hands against Boda's shoulders and pushed her backward. Nahli sprung up and sprinted toward a cluster of weeping willow trees.

But Boda was faster than she looked, and Nahli was soon slammed violently from behind, thrown into the nearest tree trunk. Everything spun as Nahli stumbled back. Boda clenched Nahli's tunic collar in her fist and smashed Nahli's head into the trunk. Bark scraped the side of her forehead, breaking open the skin. Vision blurring, Nahli swayed side to side. She tried to catch her balance so she could find a way to escape.

"You think you're so clever, don't you?" Boda's stale breath smelled of rotten lemons. "But don't worry, little girl. You won't live to waste any more of our time."

Before Nahli could contemplate the last sentence, the strong pressure of the dagger dug in at her throat, tearing it open, followed by an unbearable pain as the weapon plunged into her chest. She couldn't breathe, couldn't speak, couldn't even let out a single squeak.

Exhaling, she dropped to her knees. The ache inside her chest grew, like her heart was expanding and cracking open her rib cage, as though the organ was trying to take in a deep breath itself.

She looked up at Boda's haughty face and fell to the side,

her head smacking the dirt with a heavy thump.

Is this really happening? Am I dying?

Nahli shut her eyes and awaited the darkness to sweep her from this horrible life that she had to wake to over and over again—endlessly hungry, endlessly tired, with no home, no rest, no end in sight. Perhaps one of the gods who she prayed to earlier would be waiting to take her away and bring her into oblivion.

She expected a serene feeling to emerge as an unfamiliar scent nestled around her, but it didn't come as the darkness embraced her into a full cocoon. Her heart didn't speed as it sat dead in her chest—her lungs didn't pump as they disintegrated.

What did come was pain, a pain so fierce and so harsh it lit up the darkness into a glowing orange beneath her eyelids. It was as if her skin was being ripped from her body, muscles torn away, organs removed, and her bones being broken and snapped apart. Unconsciousness did come then, and the only choice she had was to be content with it.

FIVE

ANTON

Anton awoke to an empty bed and a white light with a hint of blue shining brightly through the glass window. The blanket swaddling him was restraining. He tossed off the fabric and sat up, knowing he'd overslept. A biting throb pulsed at his back from the scratches Maryska had left behind as her marking. Dried blood lingered where she'd dug her nails into his skin as hard as she could, as if she knew how badly he wanted to get away.

With swift motions, he picked his trousers up from the floor and slid them on. Maryska must have heard his shuffling because she sauntered into the room wearing an almost see-through cream nightgown, different from the night before. Carrying two white cups, she set them down on the nightstand. Anton lifted the one nearest him and inhaled the peppermint, letting his nostrils drink in the intoxicating scent. He drank the tea, not only to quench his thirst but to satisfy her, though the drink left his mouth slightly dry.

"I shouldn't have slept so late," Anton said. "Do you have the rest of my payment?" He didn't want to beat around the bush—he needed to let her know that he was finished with this type of work.

"Why the rush?" Her tone was light as she tapped her long nails against the nightstand from pinky to index finger, twice.

"I'm beginning a new craft, so this was my last shift, Maryska." She only stared at Anton's mouth, her gaze steady, as if waiting for more words. He hurried on, "I'm sure the other customers can refer someone else to you."

She tilted her head from left to right, making a popping noise come from somewhere within her long neck. "Is that so?"

Her voice continued to stay light, but the way her eyes darkened told him she felt otherwise.

"I'm sorry. It's been … well, it's been." He wouldn't tell her that their time together had been wonderful because it wasn't. It always left him despising himself.

"Let me guess, you think it ends when *you* say it ends?" She paused, leaning toward him so she was only a hairsbreadth away from his lips. "It ends when *I* say it ends."

His body flinched back from the anticipation of her touch. Perhaps, as much as he would have hated doing it, he should have taken Ionna up on her offer about giving him the coins, then paid her back. He could see now that the choice would have been the right one.

The previous night, Anton had decided he would use the coin to purchase pieces of finer wood for his carvings. But from the way Maryska's brown eyes drilled into his with anger blazing, darkening to a shade that almost appeared black, he wouldn't be getting his payment.

As Maryska's tightened fists trembled, the cottage seemed to do the same. But that had to be his imagination.

Anton stood from the bed, a dizzy spell striking him. He lifted a hand to his forehead, letting out a small sigh. "Maryska, I need to leave. I'm not feeling well, and if you aren't going to pay me, then there's no reason to stay. It was a mistake coming here."

He strode past her, his legs and feet heavy, his shoulder

bumping into hers as he headed for the front door. From behind, bare feet stomped against the wooden floor, cracking throughout the cottage, radiating with a boom off the walls.

Swallowing, he peered over his shoulder to tell Maryska to calm down, but she yanked him back by the arm. "You are *not* going anywhere."

He'd had enough of this woman, and the spinning of the room was only making everything worse. *What is going on?* "I don't know what delusional fabrication of love you've built, but I"—he pointed at himself—"am not your permanent lover. I let you spread your legs for me only because you give me coin for it. You know this. If I don't want to tumble for money anymore, then I don't have to. You don't own me."

Suddenly, his dizziness turned into something else, splitting everything apart. His vision doubled. Two Maryskas, two fur rugs on the wood floor, and two doors. He pressed his fingertips to his temples to try and make this unfortunate world stop and pull back into one.

"Are you sure about that?" Maryska's grin grew into something monstrous. She flicked a long lock of hair over her shoulder—the both of them.

"I'm sorry, but I'm done here." Anton turned and reached for the doorknob, his hand passing through the false exit. He tried again and shakily clasped the real handle, but he was already falling as his knees buckled. Falling, falling, falling— a never-ending plunge to nowhere.

"No, I don't think you will ever be finished, my sweetest Anton," Maryska purred in a silky voice edged with hidden spiked maces.

Even in his weakened state, he attempted to tell her to go and find a goat for a lover, but his vocal chords wouldn't spew out a single word. He attempted to peel himself from the floor but only collapsed back down.

The drink. She'd slipped something into that damn tea. It should have been clearer, that she would have sensed he

49

wouldn't return … and now she had poisoned him.

Three innocent faces flashed before his eyes—Yeva, Pav, and Tasha. Yeva would take care of her siblings—she always did. Despite a murky cloud starting to consume him, he smiled in relief that his siblings would be all right. Then a heavy crack of thunder, followed by a familiar gust of cold wind, forced him into darkness.

Anton struggled to open his eyes as a wave of grogginess hit him. When he finally did, his gaze met a pair of bare feet, the color of gray with a slight sheen making them closer to silver.

"Finally awake, my sweetest Anton?" Maryska's voice boomed from above him, echoing in a way that proved she had a hidden agenda.

"What did you put in the tea?" he rasped. It couldn't have been poison like he'd originally thought, because he wasn't dead. His eyes focused as he struggled to bring himself to a sitting position. Catching his breath, he scanned his way up her form, and his body stilled when he truly saw her. "Why are you dressed like this?"

It wasn't the light causing her skin to appear silver—*all* of her exposed flesh was the shade. Her fingernails came to prickly fine points, the color of charcoal. No longer the light brown, her irises were now the hue that mirrored her nails, all the way to where the pupils lay hidden.

Two inky-colored antlers protruded from her forehead, an eye-width apart. Around her head was a coiled thick braid, and a sparkling silver crown resting atop. The gown she wore was a sheer black, hugging each and every curve of her body. A cuff bracelet, matching the crown on her head, was wrapped around her wrist.

"It was the only way to bring you to my home, Anton."

Her charcoal lips broke into a wicked smile.

Heart pumping and body shaking, Anton brought himself to stand and swept his gaze across the room. They were no longer in Maryska's cottage. He didn't know where he was, but it couldn't be Kedaf. The room seemed to be made of onyx with ivory embedded like stars in its shining dark surface. They glistened and blinked, as though watching Anton. In front of him was a small body of water, unmoving, sparkling with colors ranging from a pale white to the darkest of browns. Directly above him, giant colorful orbs floated and lightly swayed.

Anton rubbed his eyes several times and inhaled the sweet scent of the unmoving air. "I don't know where in the bloody moons we are, but I'm leaving." He didn't know which way to go to get home, but he turned and walked away from Maryska and the strange lake.

"You cannot go back home if you are not alive, my sweetest," she cooed, her voice tickling his eardrums in an uncomfortable way.

Her words caused him to stop in his tracks. Everything shifted when her hand curved around his shoulder. They were no longer in the area with an unmoving lake, but in a new room forming a circle or, to be more precise, a sphere. The pitch-black floor beneath his feet dipped low in the center and curved upward.

Anton wasn't one who scared easily, but the peculiar things that were happening around him had his heart thumping harder and harder. His breathing increased, and he ran the tip of his tongue along the center of his lower lip, pulling it between his teeth as he observed the rest of the room. Flaming orange orbs floated near the ceiling, and their light shone on the dark walls. He silently studied the walls as they shifted like the waves of an ocean.

As he turned around, his gaze slowly leaned to the right, taking in red steps leading up to someone.

Maryska.

She was seated on a throne of alabaster bones—an antler connected at the top on each side, coordinating with the ones jutting from her forehead. Except hers were dark as night, as if they'd been burned to charcoal, and Maryska herself a creature straight out of the flames of death's abyss. An empty seat, incredibly similar, but with no antlers attached, stood beside her.

Inhaling and exhaling in an uneven way, he spoke softly, "You're not covered in paint, and this is you." *All of this isn't a nightmare, or is it?*

Scraping a fingernail against the bone armrest, Maryska eyed Anton with what looked to be pleasure, her tongue swiping the curve of her top teeth.

"And I'm dead," he whispered, but she most certainly heard him.

"And you are mine." Her hand lifted, pointing to the empty throne. "My king."

The surreal part of it struck him through the chest, the feeling of being trapped, the sickness at being trapped with *her*, the coldness of defeat. There wasn't a way he would be able to escape this … death.

"King of *what*? The *dead*?" he shouted with a growing frenzy.

Maryska rose from her seat and descended the scarlet steps toward him with nonchalance, until she stood where her antlers almost kissed his face. "Over time, it has gotten lonely down here. No one pleases me, except for you. The hate in your eyes I relish even more, my sweetest Anton."

"You took me away from everything … my family, my home. Now you want me to sit beside you in a chair made of bones forever?" He gripped his hair tightly, on the verge of storming past her, up the steps, and breaking the throne to pieces. "And do what?" It was a question he didn't want an answer to, and one he should not have asked.

She reached for him, and he flinched, taking a step back. "You will be *my* king. You will bow down to me. You will please me in any way when I ask it. You *will* do what I say."

His heart had calmed a bit, but his blood was beginning to stir with fury. "I will do nothing of the sort," he whispered. "You can either choose between returning me to Kedaf, or I will sit here for an eternity and never be your property. I will *not* be anyone's king, least of all yours."

Maryska's dark eyes narrowed, her shoulders lifting and falling as she breathed deep, violent breaths. She made a grab for the collar of his shirt, but he moved before she could grasp it. Jaw clenched, she slapped him hard across the cheek. His face fell to the side, and he didn't even bother to bring it back up as he listened to her sharp words near his flesh.

"Even if I were able to restore you, I never would. You now belong here in Torlarah, not Kedaf." She leaned forward, her mouth beside his ear. "Is that your choice? To not do as I say?"

Anton didn't have to think about it—he knew without a doubt what his answer would always be. "Yes." He didn't bother to drag his gaze up to meet hers.

When she pulled away from his ear, her hand touched his shoulder, nails digging in with such strength he could feel blood beading to the surface. Gritting his teeth, he finally brought his gaze back up, finding that they'd returned to the room with the earthy-shaded lake.

Waves in the unmoving liquid appeared, rustling before his eyes. A tug, or possibly a pinch, pulled at his skin, his clothing growing tighter. It was something he'd never felt before. In a way, it was like when Tasha would give him a hard pinch, only this was dozens and dozens of sharp pricks covering his entire body.

An abrupt rip yanked at his body, as though his skin was being peeled away. He moaned in agony at the sharp spasms. His body hunched forward from the anguish, and he stared down at his arms to see the peach of his skin and clothing were missing. To his horror, what covered his body was the color of blood … muscle.

An incoherent stutter of words escaped his lips.

"Who else would truly want anything from you, Anton? You were lucky enough to have my offer," she spat.

His gaze flicked to Maryska's, trying to not let her words affect him, even though a part of them did. She didn't say another thing, only clacked her front teeth against her lower ones as she watched him with animosity. Then the harsh discomfort, leading to extreme pain and his screams, came again and one by one, parts of him ripped away. Muscle, organs, almost everything that made him who he was, until he was nothing. The nothing he always felt he was had become his reality.

But he was not nothing because he was still there, in a place that could only be one from his worst nightmares.

Anton brought a quaking hand to his face, and it was the alabaster white of bones. Bones matching the queen's throne.

The room shifted once more when Maryska firmly pressed a hand against his skeletal body. His eyes adjusted to a new place that wasn't the lake or the thrones but somewhere entirely different.

Bones trailed over the dirt and piled up in endless hills— real, human or animal remains. Tall trees without any life left in them appeared to be sucked dry to the bare bones.

Anton pressed a hand to his chest. He should have been feeling his heart about to explode from a speedy dance, but nothing thumped inside. Only emptiness lingered there. As he stared at his unwelcoming purgatory, he wanted to hyperventilate but couldn't.

SIX

ANTON

Anton studied the bone yard that lay before him and brought a hand to his skull. He couldn't quite contemplate what had happened. Maryska had taken away everything about himself, except for his skeletal remains. The sensation of touch still swirled within him, though considerably dulled from its original strength. Anton's hearing and sight were still intact, but his sense of smell remained missing. Although he could still draw in breath to lungs that were no longer there. This should have been impossible, but somehow it wasn't. As he shifted his lower jaw back and forth, adjusting to the absence of his tongue, Anton was hit with the realization that there would no longer be the bliss of taste.

Lifting his chin, he focused on Maryska's dark eyes and antlers. "What did you do?" The last two words came out shaky with the understanding that he could still speak, even without a tongue.

In response, she lunged forward and pushed him to the ground. She hovered above Anton, watching him as if he was worth nothing. "I stripped away all but your bones and added your other pieces to the Lake of Flesh." Maryska stroked the crown cuff on her wrist. "You will remain here until you decide to be my king. For now, you will be King of the Bone Valley," she taunted and lifted her hand up, flicking it in the direction of a tall mountain of remains.

A loud crack from the gray sky roared and opened to a sliver of luminous white. Anton squinted as several things poured down like rain, hitting the ground with a heavy clack. With venom burning inside of him, he started to rise. She slammed her foot on his sternum, preventing him from sitting.

"People die every day, Anton. Prepare to be welcomed by new guests at any time, any moment." Maryska ran a hand over his forearm, and he recoiled from her.

"How long are you planning on keeping me here?"

He couldn't comprehend what was going on inside this woman's head. But she wasn't really a woman... He didn't know what she was. A demon?

"As long as it takes until you decide to become my king. I'll come back whenever I feel like it's been enough time … to see if you've changed your mind. I do enjoy having a man to work for my affection, and you will have to work harder since you did not choose to be mine the first time," she cooed, finally releasing her foot from his rib cage.

Anton would not work for this—his siblings were safe in Kedaf. There was no leverage to make him do a damn thing. "No," he answered simply, bringing himself to stand.

"As King of the Bone Valley, the only company you will have is *bones*." Maryska released a high-pitched laugh, her antlers bobbing. "I think you will be highly disappointed."

Anton gritted his teeth and didn't speak a word as she sauntered toward a large tree with gnarled branches that had possibly once been an oak. In the middle of the trunk rested a gray, oval door.

Maryska looked over her shoulder after opening it. "This is all but a challenge for me. Eventually, you will change your mind. You will see." She faded away behind the closed exit, perhaps sitting back on her throne of bones.

Anton stormed up to the tree and attempted to yank open the door, only to find it locked. Propping his foot against the trunk, he tugged as hard as he could on the knob, but it wouldn't budge. Cursing, he slapped his hand against the bone that should have been bark. The pain didn't strike, instead an odd vibration played through his remains, oddly satisfying.

Worried. That was the only word to describe what he was currently feeling. Anton turned around to stare at the Bone Valley, his gaze settling on rows and rows of what had to be empty cottages. Each home was formed by bones that must have been merged together to create the style and texture.

"Hello?" he called out.

Silence.

In the distance, he made out the low clack of bones descending from the ever-changing opening in the gray sky. After the skeletal remains landed at their destination, the sliver of white closed. Jaw agape as he peered at the bone cottages to his left, Anton finally made a decision and started toward them. He followed a rocky path with broken bits of pebbles and dust rising beneath his feet. Farther ahead, a large lake caught his attention. He continued in that direction, passing bone after bone after bone. Some were alone, some cluttered together, and others half buried in the ground. Everything was dead. No grass, only jet-black dirt. Nothing in this pit of a place had any bright colors. It was as though the colors themselves had died, all melting into shades of black, gray, and white.

Madness. Anton would grow mad, and it would not be a temporary delirium. Shaking his head, he stopped in front of the gray lake and looked down into the water where he caught a glimpse of his reflection. He squinted, but it wasn't with eyes. Glowing white flames inside his eye sockets narrowed instead. This whole time he thought he still had his eyes, but they were something else.

With the shock of seeing himself this way, the flames

widened. He stretched them open and closed, just like he would have done his eyelids. From what he could tell, nothing was recognizable besides his square jaw, cheekbones, and his straight hair brushing his shoulders—no longer blond, but white.

As he stared deeper, past his reflection in the lake, he could make out something bony and pale within the cloudy liquid. Fish without skin, unmoving. They lay at the bottom of the lake, no thoughts swimming in their minds. *But what did fish ever think about before?*

"Stop it," he said aloud, lowering himself to the dirt. "I've barely been here any time at all, and I'm already becoming delusional."

Anton rested at the lake's edge for a long while, glowering at his image and the surroundings, trying to shut out his thoughts until he couldn't take it anymore. He decided to have a look inside the nearby cottages to see what he could unveil. With his arms stretched out to the sky, he lengthened his spine, twisting it side to side. Popping sounds echoed through the dead landscape around him. Whatever Maryska had used on him must have been some form of magic, allowing him to do these things as a skeleton. He was curious, and perhaps a little haunted by it.

The gray sky sat empty of clouds but in its depths, it held a white moon. Or perhaps it was a pale sun? Anton couldn't be sure.

Most of his hesitance started to wear off as he marched toward the first cottage. The closer he got, the more the bones didn't appear to be human, or at least the skulls. The remains were fused together, leaving no gaps. It was as if the outer shell of the home was somehow one whole, connected piece.

Anton was sure Yeva would be sickened by this cottage, but he knew Pav would be in awe. Both feelings washed over Anton.

Sprawled across the front of the cottage, underneath a

window, were small white bone flowers sprinkled in the dirt. A crack from top to bottom lined one of the four glass panes. Nearby, ornate, bone picket fences closed in a few of the other homes.

Anton swung open the door with a bang, and several loose bones clinked together. Holding himself steady, he walked inside the darkened cottage and wished for light. About a hundred candles flickered on with white flames bobbing, and an orb, like the ones from Maryska's throne room, appeared in the center of his palm. The orb shone of a glistening white hue, with a hollow, black flame burning in its belly.

He stood in astonishment as his gaze roamed over the room, discovering that within the cottage's interior there were no bones, yet the color was still missing. In the middle of the room sat a drab velvet settee with wooden legs. Across from it rested a table and two white chairs to its left. Somehow, the flames atop the surrounding candles weren't melting the wax, yet they continued to burn.

Anton didn't have the energy to go into any of the other rooms, so he took a seat on the settee and closed the flames in his eye sockets for a moment before reopening them. In the corner of the cottage was a fireplace with firewood set aside.

Pushing himself up from the settee, he headed toward the stack. His fingers twitched as he picked up a narrow piece of wood, then carried it with him to a dining area. He sifted through the drawers until, to his relief, he stumbled upon two knives—one smaller, the other larger—that would be useful as tools.

Anton sawed down the firewood. It took all his strength, but in the end, he managed to cut the wood into four sections. Lifting one of the smaller pieces, he began to carve, for what very well might be his eternity.

SEVEN

DARYNA

Daryna hovered over her cauldron and examined the bubbling liquid. Boda, her helper, had told her how the villagers gossiped about Daryna being a witch, telling stories about her strange ways. They didn't realize how right they were.

Pulling a wooden cutting board across the table, Daryna took the plump dead toad and sliced it into thin slivers. She had no qualms about chopping up creatures when necessary if she needed them for a brew, but the act of killing them herself sickened her, so she used a special remedy to put them into a permanent sleep before the deed. It still took their life but in a more humane way.

Daryna brought her ingredients to the boiling water and let the frog bits plop into the liquid. One of the legs stuck to the wood, so she shoved it off with the tip of her knife.

She lived by herself, and she preferred it that way. Never had she been in love. After watching customers act like fools over one another, she never wanted to be like that, either. She loved herself, and that was good enough.

A knock at the door interrupted her thoughts, and her nerves were rattled by the sound. The noise was followed by three soft taps, and she calmed herself. It was only Boda, letting Daryna know she was back from her errand.

And she had better have the chicken.

Daryna needed the heart for this particular concoction. One of the love fools in Verolc, the territory next to Kedaf, wanted to break what he still harbored for a woman after she had found a new lover. The dolt had his answer right there— she'd found someone else, so their love should have then ended. But he was paying greatly for this tonic, and Daryna would gladly accommodate him for the price.

Her bulky boots thudded over the floorboards as she walked to the door, swinging it open to reveal a sweaty Boda.

Daryna still had the knife in her grasp when she peered at Boda's empty hands and asked, "Where's the damn chicken?"

"I didn't get it." Boda sighed, and her massive body stepped over the threshold.

Boda was an imbecile, but she transported things for Daryna to villages in Verolc, mostly stolen goods she'd purchased from thieves, which she in turn sold for a higher coin. But customers also wanted concoctions, whether to make their skin appear younger or to heal someone of an ailment.

Daryna would never do it out of the goodness of her heart—there was always a charge. It wasn't that she wouldn't help if she were face to face with an injured person, but she needed money to keep herself breathing. Venturing outside of her home to find work, and being around a group of villagers, heightened her nerves. Her hands shook uncontrollably every time she thought about it, so that was a quest she would have to avoid.

"And why didn't you get it?" Daryna cocked her head, remembering Nahli's quick reflexes from the prior day.

Nahli wasn't supposed to have come yesterday. Daryna had been struggling with a remedy and had needed to be left to her thoughts, so she'd taken it out on Nahli.

Perhaps she should get rid of Boda and use Nahli instead.

At least the girl had a brain, but she wasn't sure if Nahli would listen to her. For the right coin, Daryna believed she would.

"No, the girl didn't have the chicken anymore." Boda brought a hand to her shorn hair and plopped down in one of the wobbly chairs at the dining table.

Damn, I really need to get a new table or fix that leg. She then focused on the more important matter at hand.

"I needed the heart of the hen for this remedy." Daryna nodded at the bubbling cauldron. "I didn't want to have to use one of the other chickens, but Clary will have to do."

A hint of remorse struck her of what was to come. Clary liked to follow Daryna around, but she was the only one out of the other hens that wouldn't lay any eggs. Daryna understood, she would prefer to remain childless, too.

"I can steal you another one." Boda shrugged.

"We don't have time for that." She flicked her hand at the door. "Can you go remove Clary's head?"

"Let me grab the ax." Boda scooted the chair back and stood from the table, taking a step away.

Daryna's gaze fell to a splatter of red on Boda's tunic sleeve. "Wait. What's that on your sleeve?"

Boda's eyes shifted to her arm and she released a sigh as though she'd been caught doing something wrong. "Blood."

"What did you do?" Daryna knew Boda had done something stupid by the way her eyes kept darting side to side.

The woman's mouth opened and closed like a fish. "I got caught up in the moment by the lake out in the woods."

"What did you *do*, Boda?" Daryna barked, standing from her chair, inching closer to the tall beast of a woman.

Boda slapped the side of her leg with a fist. "I killed her, all right? The girl wouldn't listen to me and kept trying to run off. The only option was to take care of her."

"So you killed her? Over a chicken?" Daryna shrieked, anger lacing her words.

With wide eyes, Boda pointed a meaty finger at Daryna.

"You're the one who told me to slap her twice and retrieve your things."

"Or to *replace* them." Daryna had never once told Boda if she couldn't find her things to kill the girl.

"She wasn't keen when I told her I'd cut off her hands for stealing." Boda examined her fingernails instead of looking Daryna in the eyes.

"You imbecile!" Daryna roared, gripping her knife. "I didn't send you out there to hunt her down like a huntsman, you oaf!"

The room was spinning. It would mean people from the village would come to her doorstep searching for answers about a murder that was never supposed to have occurred. Her fingers fluttered, and she had to dig her nails into her skirt to get them to stop.

"I was caught up in it all, and it didn't turn out the way we'd hoped. What else can I say?"

Daryna's gaze locked onto Boda. "How did you kill her?"

"I stabbed her in the heart." There wasn't a single ounce of remorse in Boda's voice.

With the knife clenched in her fist, Daryna thrust it directly into Boda's chest and twisted it in her heart's center.

Boda's dull eyes bulged in surprise as her face lost its color and she tried to speak, only she made a sound like a choking horse.

"I don't take murdering people too kindly, especially over something that can be pinned back on me." Daryna may not have been one to kill an animal, but she didn't have a problem stabbing a pathetic human who murdered for no reason.

Boda's large body slumped to the floor, her ragged breaths drawing to an end. Daryna had to think about what to do now. She cursed to herself because now her kitchen was a mess. The brew would have to wait, and she'd have to retrieve the girl's body from the woods before anyone else discovered it. That meant she had to leave the cottage.

Daryna hurried to the woods, wishing witches could ride on broomsticks like in the stories. More times than needed, she looked over her shoulder until she reached the edge of the lake where Nahli's body lay lifeless and covered in blood. No one had found her.

Rage still lit a fire inside Daryna from Nahli stealing her things, but perhaps Daryna could have been a little gentler. *No*, she changed her mind quickly—the girl shouldn't have brought the pathetic jewelry on a day she wasn't supposed to.

Nahli was a wisp of a thing, but she didn't feel that way as Daryna hauled her across the grassy area, all the way back to her home. Daryna was as tall as Boda, but she wasn't as muscular.

When she made it to the cottage, Daryna removed several of Boda's organs that she could use instead of an animal's for future tonics, since her body was already there. She didn't do the same to Nahli because as irked as she was with her, she knew it was her fault for sending Boda to do the task.

Even though Nahli most likely thought Daryna hated her, she really didn't. The girl was lost, just as Daryna was, only she always kept that to herself.

Nahli had once told her she'd come from Huadu. Daryna didn't know any of the prayers that they would recite to their gods, so she made up one of her own.

Now Daryna would have to finish the load by slicing off Clary's head, then bring the tonic to Verolc. Eventually, she would need to find someone who would listen to her directions and know how to follow them correctly.

Her hand twitched again, and she became nauseous as she thought about having to venture out from the safety of her home.

EIGHT

PAV

Nahli's chicken—gifted to the Bereza family—squawked in Pav's arms as he walked with Tasha to Mrs. Evanko's. He thought about Nahli and how pretty she'd looked. But there was Polina, Mrs. Evanko's daughter. Pav wasn't sure if she even truly fancied *him* or if it was because he looked like Anton. She acted as though Pav hadn't existed one day and then the next, she was kissing him. He didn't understand women.

"Pav, can I hold Juju?" Tasha asked, stroking the red head of the hen.

"Juju?" He arched a brow.

"Well, she must have a name." She pulled the chicken from his grasp while trading him her book.

"How do you even know it's a female?" He was clueless when it came to taking care of animals.

There was a cat that used to come by the cottage often but hadn't in a while, even then it was Yeva who played with it. Anton hated the thing—it bit him every time.

"Oh, it was just a little love nibble," Pav had said.

"Love nibble, my ass. That thing is ferocious," Anton had replied.

Interrupting Pav's humorous thoughts that had drifted somewhere in the clouds, Tasha replied to the question he forgot he'd asked.

"Roosters look nothing like hens, Pav," she said. "Roosters are much fancier—no offense, Juju. They're larger, louder, and they certainly don't lay eggs."

He patted the top of her head, fingers interlacing with her tangled dark curls. "Thank you for that lesson, little sister. Now I will be most proficient in knowing the difference in genders of chickens."

Angling her head to the side, his younger sister turned serious. As did the chicken, or he thought it would have, had it understood humans.

"You can at least laugh at my wit!" he exclaimed, tickling Tasha's ribs until she let out a high-pitched giggle. Her grip held the chicken firm, but its head bobbled.

They both came to a halt when they stood on the decaying porch steps to Mrs. Evanko's cottage. Pav tapped the door in a musical knock, and after a few moments, Polina answered.

"Polina," Pav greeted her, acting as if it was any normal day and nothing new had happened between them.

"Pav," Polina replied and blinked, appearing bored. She hadn't looked too bored when she'd kissed him senseless the day before, her hands clenching his hair.

Her red locks fell right below her shoulders, and her gray eyes seemed to alter every time she had a different emotion. She wasn't thin like Yeva or Ionna, but instead had curves in all the perfect areas. Something Pav hadn't been able to ignore.

Pav pressed a hand against the doorframe. "I'm here to let your mother know we have a chicken today, along with our adorable Tasha. I needed to make sure it was all right with Mrs. Evanko to leave the new guest here."

"Oh. That'll be fine." Polina's lips parted in surprise, but he could have sworn her shoulders slumped a little in disappointment as her gaze fell to the hen.

Tasha handed Juju to Pav, took back her book, and headed inside the cottage. Pav was left standing uncomfortably with Polina.

"I'll be leaving, then. I'm going to drop Juju, this chicken"—he held up the hen for her, like she hadn't already seen it—"in the back of the house with the other animals."

She nodded, and he didn't know what else to say. He descended down the steps and scuffed his feet around the cottage to the back. Soft footsteps sounded from behind him.

Grinning to himself, he continued walking, then hunched over to place the hen on the grass beside a metal watering can. When he straightened, Polina stood behind him with her palms planted on her hips.

"Well?" she asked, holding her hands up.

"Well, what?" He held his hands up right back at her.

Polina released a loud huff and snaked a finger around a lock of hair. "Nothing, Pav."

"All right, I have to go and help Yeva at the market. See you around."

"See you around?" Her brows drew together.

What he'd said made perfect sense to him, so he didn't understand the confusion. "Yes, I'll see you around. You do live next door to us, after all." He pointed from his cottage to hers.

"Pav, you can be so frustrating, you know that?" she grunted.

He shrugged, his gaze unable to stay focused on her eyes as it dropped to her mouth. "I can be a lot of things."

Before he could walk around her, he was backed up against the cottage, and she pressed her lips softly against his. "I like you, okay."

Bewildered by her kiss with no warning, he couldn't help but ask, "Not Anton?"

"What? I never liked your brother."

Lie.

"Yeah, all right, yet you followed him around and stared at him all the time with deep and endless longing."

"I did not!" Her cheeks turned a bright shade of crimson. He found it cute, especially since it closely matched her hair. "Fine." She sighed. "I did, but that was a long time ago."

"I'm not just your second choice because you're too young for Anton, am I?" Pav smirked, and she was smiling, too.

"You're so infuriating."

"But you apparently like it."

As she leaned into him, he drew her close to kiss her again.

"Pav?" Yeva's voice called from next door, interrupting the almost kiss.

"I have to go, but I'll come by later." He wiggled his brows and hurried to help Yeva carry the supplies to the market while the kiss lingered in his mind.

The day at their booth had been good for Pav and Yeva so far. Five people had gotten their palms read by Yeva. One woman had come for a bushel of lavender and wound up with seven other types of herbs, with a little persuasion from Pav.

It had looked like rain all day with the overinflated clouds floating in the gray sky, but it hadn't started to pour yet. Pav handed Yeva a strawberry-filled pastry that he'd gotten a few booths down. He'd talked to the older woman and told her how beautiful she looked, and she handed him two desserts for free. In return, he gave her a kiss on her lovely wrinkled hand.

"You should possibly begin a craft in talking, Pav." Yeva plucked the sugary pastry from his fingertips and took a large bite. A low moan escaped her at the divine taste of the fluffy pastry.

"That's how I felt when I ate mine. Finished it in two bites."

"You can go ahead and leave." Yeva waved him off in the direction of their cottage.

"Are you sure?" He didn't mind staying for as long as she needed him to. His mouth never grew tired of talking.

"Go on." She shooed him away with a smile. "You can get a little rest."

With a tug on her braid, Pav headed out past two older women and winked at them as they painted clay pottery.

Once he made it to the old cottage, out of the heat of the day, the inside of the house felt empty. Not a single sound. "Anton?" he called. "Tasha?"

No reply.

His brother should have already picked up his sister from Mrs. Evanko. A strange feeling crawled over him, and he blew out a breath. Pav didn't like odd feelings. The last time he'd had one, his father's hands had been cut off and those nightmares had never gone away. He kept those thoughts hidden deep inside himself, and he would cover them up with humor to try and feel normal.

Closing the front door behind him, he darted across the weeds to Mrs. Evanko's and banged on the door a little too rapidly and a little too roughly.

Mrs. Evanko swung open the door with a scowl, a deep line etched in between her brows. "What in all of Kedaf, Pav? You only have to knock once and not hard either."

"Sorry, Mrs. Evanko." He couldn't even put on his usual smirk or offer her a compliment about how gorgeous she looked. "Has Anton come by to pick up Tasha?"

"No." Her brows lowered even more. "She's still in the back either playing with the girls or reading them a story. Do you want me to get her for you?"

He couldn't bring Tasha to where he would need to be. "Can you watch her a little longer? I need to go and find Anton."

"That's fine. I'm cooking dinner already, and she can stay.

Feel free to come back and join us."

"Yes, that sounds great," he said hurriedly. Whirling around, he raced down the steps.

"And knock less intensely once you come back!" she yelled.

He didn't answer her.

His chest tightened. It wasn't like Anton to be late, and if he was going to be, he would have stopped by the market to let him or Yeva know. In fact, Anton hadn't come by to see them at the booth on his way home.

Pav didn't focus on that as he ran the whole way to Maryska's. He avoided passing through the market because he knew his sister would insist on going herself to find Anton and for Pav to return home to wait on them.

It would be a terrible idea for Yeva to go and retrieve Anton anyway. At least Pav could put on a flirtatious smile and offer Maryska compliments that would entice some answers from her.

Crows cawed from a broken branch of a wide tree as Pav rounded the trunk, revealing Maryska's cottage. Besides the crows, there was no other sound as he drew closer to the door.

The home was cozy with earthy tones of green, brown, and white, and covered by a dark thatch roof. Verdant bushes were planted to the right of the door, sprouting flowers of blue, white, and yellow. Above him, a wind chime, of what could only be bones, rattled. Maryska didn't seem like the type who would have such a macabre thing.

Pav reached to touch one of the sharper bones when a loud caw pulled him from his distraction. Clearing his head, he lifted his sweaty fist up to the door and knocked. Beads of perspiration had gathered behind his ears and slid down the back of his neck.

No one answered.

Not caring if it was a bad idea, Pav reached for the handle and found it unlocked. As soon as he pushed open the door, he

70

spotted something that made his entire body freeze. On the floor rested a body—a male's body—his brother's body.

"Anton!" he shouted, dropping to his knees beside his brother.

Anton lay on his stomach, eyes closed, and blond locks of hair splayed across his mouth. Rolling him to his back, Pav pressed two fingers at the base of his neck where the pulse should have been.

"Come on. Come on!" he pleaded.

Nothing.

Pav inspected Anton for any visible wounds, but he couldn't find any. He couldn't be dead. Couldn't, couldn't, couldn't. This was Anton—the one who would do anything for someone. The one who would sell himself to help his family have food on the table.

Hand shaking, he slapped Anton across the cheek. "Wake up! Please!" Hot tears streamed down Pav's cheeks, dampening his brother's tunic.

Maryska.

Where was she?

He stood, tears still falling as he searched around the cottage, unable to find any answers to his brother's inexplicable death. Inside the bedroom, there was no Maryska either—only a rumpled bed, a large dresser with a mirror, and a nightstand with two cups on it.

He rushed toward the cups and noticed one full of tea, the other empty. Staring at the empty ceramic, then shifting his gaze to the open door that led to Anton's body, Pav picked it up and brought the cup to his nose. A lingering scent of peppermint assaulted his nostrils, and he pulled the ceramic back to inspect the minuscule amount of brown liquid sloshing along the bottom.

When he brought the empty drink back to his nose, he drew in another long inhale. A second smell hit him that he couldn't name, light, with a bit of a flowery odor to it. One that could secretly kill.

Pav would find Maryska, question her, then murder her for this. Without a doubt, he knew it was her who did this.

Setting the cup back on the nightstand, he searched through all of Maryska's possessions. Clothing, money, and her satchel—all her belongings were still there. Perhaps he was wrong and someone else had poisoned Anton and kidnapped Maryska.

No, that would be madness—he knew about her obsession with his brother. Pav was good at reading things, and that was why he wanted to be a soldier one day, not just because he could wield a weapon.

Anton had either told Maryska he was finished with her, or she knew he was planning to. Then the bitch had fed him some tea and took off. That was also madness. Either way, he knew she was the one responsible, and she was gone.

Pav didn't know what else to do when he entered the sitting room. He didn't want to leave Anton's body there, but he needed to find Yeva.

He lifted Anton's arms and placed them on his still chest in an X, as was their custom. "I'll be back, brother, and I'll figure this out."

Something else permeated the air, a light unusual scent entwined with oranges. It was an odor he'd never smelled before. He shrugged off the odd feeling creeping up his spine and sniffled as he left the cottage.

Despite wanting to curl into an infant position and sob, he hurried to the market, where he found Yeva packing up their belongings. It looked as though almost everything they'd brought had been sold.

"What are you doing back, Pav?" Yeva smiled, opening the creaking gate to approach him.

Pav couldn't get the words out—he always had something to say, having never experienced this choking inability to speak. But his throat was dry, his chest hollow, and his heart a brittle organ on the verge of erupting.

"It-it's Anton. He's gone, Yeva ... he's gone." Pav's legs gave out beneath him, and he fell to his knees with a sob, just as cold rain began to pour from the sky.

NINE

ANTON

Anton had lost track of how long he'd spent sitting and carving objects. It could have been days, weeks, months, years. Realistically, it had to have been only a few days. He'd been closed off to everything. The only activities that consumed his days were carving and sleeping, besides sifting through the closet to find a pair of trousers and tunic to wear. The clothing made him feel more comfortable, not having to see himself as only bones.

Before him in a cluster was a carved dragon to represent Tasha's favorite book, various animals, and a chicken that somehow made him think of the thief who'd run away with his clothing while carrying the feathered creature.

Setting down the knife and peering at the bones of his hand, he was no longer dismayed at seeing the alabaster skeleton parts of himself.

The thing was, Anton had never minded being alone. Rather than feeling lonely, it recharged him, helped him to find himself. But then there would always be someone to talk to or to interrupt him. And now there was no one.

No one. Only him.

Anton had a decision to make—remain in the colorless

home or explore more of what was outside. After losing track of time on the former, he reluctantly decided to try the latter.

Leaving what he could only describe as comfort, Anton stepped outside into the vacant valley. Bones rained down in the distance as a crackle came from above. The bright orb in the sky hovered, guiding Anton's way while he walked in between the rounded hills of bones. He wondered about their past owners and how they would feel to be scattered about like this. If he so chose, there was enough time to see how far the Bone Valley stretched and find out if it was larger than Kedaf.

Beyond a winding path, Anton caught sight of a garden filled with flowers shaped by chalky-pale bones of all sizes, sprouting from the soil. He plucked what looked to be a rose from the dirt, brought it to his skull, and inhaled. There was nothing to smell, only the flutter of a breath against the part of his skull where his nose should have been. That was his reality now, an existence spent impersonating a human.

Tossing the flower back into the garden, he sat down on the pebbled ground even though a bench made of various sizes of bones blocked his full view. A pile of skeletal pieces rested not far away from him. It felt wrong, after dying, for them to have to stay and be a fraction of what they'd once been. He wasn't sure if it was better than what he'd become, though.

His bones made a scratchy crack as he stood from the ground and went to the nearest pile of remains.

As King of the Bone Valley, the only company you will have is bones. Maryska's insulting words echoed through Anton's thoughts. Perhaps he would put a person back together just to spite her. If anything, it might help him feel less lonely.

Examining the white skull with specks of dirt, he found the ivory hair to be pleated in a long braid. All the skulls he passed displayed white hair, the life being sucked from that as well. By the shape of the rounded pelvis, he could tell this one was female.

Anton practically knew the names of every bone, mainly from Tasha teaching him from one of her books. Perhaps his youngest sister would be a healer one day.

"All right, my queen," he mocked aloud. "Let me bring you back to life." He knew she wouldn't be able to walk as he did or move the way he could, but at least she would be whole and not a pile of forgotten pieces in a lonely, dead garden.

Anton loathed solving problems more than anything and that was what this felt like, building a frustrating puzzle. Holding four phalanges in his hand, he already wanted to give up. But when he found the right piece that connected to them, the bones molded together with a soft sizzle, as if by magic.

Many attempts ended in failure as he made his way to the femur. But when the pile of bones lessened, the picture became clearer, and his determination stayed true.

As he reached the pelvic area of his project, he knew if he still had his skin it would have flushed a blazing red, even though a woman's body had never unnerved him. But the thought of being so many layers deeper into the place that was truly untouchable to another human, made it feel all that more vulnerable.

Proceeding on, Anton finished the spine after attaching the rib cage. Not exhausted in the slightest, but wanting to take a break anyway, he admired the beauty and curve of each bone of the skeletal body standing before him.

His attention wavered to the glowing orb in the sky as he lay on the pebbled ground and placed his hands behind his skull.

The sky had altered to a darker shade of gray than earlier, almost a slate. A hazy fog formed around the valley, coming out to play, even without a single cloud in sight. It was haunting, breathtaking, though Anton still longed for the colorful world where his family was.

Closing the blazing flames where his eyes had once been, he thought of home—living trees filled with apples, dances with breathing villagers on special days in the market, working with real women or men, feeling his slick skin against theirs, and pleasuring the part of himself that was now missing.

He opened his flames and turned back to the female who was still incomplete, her skull on the ground watching him with an empty stare. "I know, I know. You want me to finish building. I promise I'll sit here for as long as it takes until you're restored."

The clavicle and scapula came next. Things were moving along quite well when he made it to the radius and ulna, until the pile of phalanges and metacarpals came upon him.

He sang a made-up song to keep himself calm and occupied as he fit the pieces together. When all he had left was to connect the skull to the vertebrae, he sighed in satisfaction.

Kneeling, Anton placed the female's skull in between his hands and studied it for several moments. "You didn't deserve to end up this way." He placed the skull on the tip of her spine to complete her skeleton. Anton didn't know until that moment how much he'd hoped she would magically come to life. But her eye sockets remained empty.

For two days, Anton ventured into the garden, spending most of his time there. It had become easier for him to know how much time had passed based on the fog. During the earlier parts of the day there would be little to none, but as the day grew, the heavier the fog became.

At night, he tried to rest on the settee inside the cottage, but he couldn't stay asleep. He knew he was mad for conversing with a skeleton who couldn't move or talk back, but he did it nonetheless. He'd wondered who the clothing inside the cottage had belonged to, but whoever it was must have been scattered somewhere out in the Bone Valley.

From one of the closets, he took a velvet ebony dress accented with embroidered white flowers at the hem. Pearls and lace stitched the neckline and cuffs at the sleeves.

After Anton adjusted the dress on the skeleton, it molded to her body, falling right at her ankles. She looked positively enchanting. And he was delirious just thinking about what he was doing.

Plucking several bone flowers from the garden, he placed the smaller ones into the braid of her hair for decoration. He lifted her hand in between his, staring into her empty eye sockets. "Awake, my queen," he murmured with mockery. "Would you like to dance?"

He released her delicate fingers and spun around in a circle before stopping to face her once more.

And his jaw fell open.

Two white flames matching his burned brightly inside her eye sockets, the light lengthening when she stared at him. Her lower jaw fluttered, and she stumbled backward.

Anton reached forward to grab her as she fell, but missed. The female struck her arm against a stone at the edge of the garden. She howled in agony as Anton rushed to her side, pulling her into his arms.

"Are you all right?" he asked, noticing the small hairline crack at her ulna.

Ripping herself from his arms, she scooted back. "Does it look like I'm all right?"

"I suppose not." He watched her jaw chatter from fright.

"You're—you're made of bones, and you're *talking*," she whimpered. "How's this possible?"

Anton winced, knowing what was to come, but not wanting to leave her in the dark. "Have you looked at yourself yet?"

Shakily, she brought a skeletal hand to her face. The female stared at it for several moments before releasing an ear-shattering scream.

He covered the sides of his skull, where his ears should have been, and it muffled the wretched sound. Anton wasn't sure why or how he'd handled the situation better than her. *Perhaps not better, but more quietly.*

The girl peered down at herself then back at him, flames wide. "What am I wearing?"

"I dressed you."

"Like a doll?" she asked, agitated.

"Better than leaving you without any clothing on, isn't it?"

Anton studied his own trousers held up with a belt. He'd added an extra notch in the leather to prevent the pants from falling. Shiny gray buttons lined the center of the white shirt he had on today, which his finger was absently rubbing.

She didn't answer. The female's hands drifted up to her skull and her flames disappeared before widening again. "I died."

"As did I." He had tried to do everything in his power to avoid thinking about what Maryska had done, but there it was.

The female's arms fell back to her sides. "I remember being stabbed in the chest, followed by what felt like parts of my body ripping away."

Anton remembered that, too, about himself. The unbearable pain that had occurred, then vanished as if it had never happened.

"Did Maryska do this to you too?" he asked.

"Maryska? No, it was a woman named Boda who stabbed me," she ground out.

That was a name that wasn't common in Kedaf. "Boda who works for Daryna?"

Her flames blazed harder and lengthened. "Yes."

He had never seen Daryna, or at least he didn't think so, but his father would sell stolen goods to her. "And your name?"

She didn't answer at first, and he thought she never would.

"Nahli."

Inhaling sharply, bewildered, he blinked his flames. This couldn't be the same girl he'd seen at the market and by the lake. Could it? "Are you a thief?"

She again took a long time to answer, but her flames narrowed. "What's it to you?"

His bones raked with laughter and a rare deep sound escaped past his teeth. It wasn't humorous how things had ended, but he couldn't contain himself. Because out of everyone in the Bone Valley he could have brought back to life, he'd chosen *this* girl.

"Apparently, you're my *queen*." The sentence would have tasted sour if he'd had a tongue and could have truly felt the words.

She crossed her arms over her rib cage. "I am no one's queen."

"It was only something that appeared to have brought you back. I didn't mean it figuratively." He paused. "It's me, Anton. Remember, you tried to steal from me at the market?"

Her jaw opened and closed, then she took a step away. "And then I took your clothing beside the lake."

"While running away with a chicken in your other hand."

"That I gave to your family." She moved toward him.

"What?" Nahli had given the chicken to his family?

"I didn't know it was your family when I gave it to them." She pointed at him. "I met your younger sister outside and then handed the hen to your brother."

Anton held up his hands and shrugged. "How quaint. Now we're the best of acquaintances. You've met my family, and now we can live in the Bone Valley together forever and discuss our two meetings over and over."

He didn't know what he was expecting when he'd built the skeleton. It sure wasn't her being able to come to life, and it sure wasn't that she would have been Nahli. His emotions of pity for the nameless skeleton withered and died.

"I'm not staying here with you," she spouted. "I'll find someone else to talk to or some way to get out of here alone."

"You say that only because you don't know where you are. I'm not really sure you can traipse out of here, unless you find a way to open the tree with the door, then head straight to Maryska."

"What's so bad about Maryska? Who is she?"

"Did you not hear about her in Kedaf? Always overdressed when out and about, had one of the nicest cottages in the village?"

"Wait. She died, too?" Nahli blurted.

"No, she did not *die* too," he ground out slowly. "Maryska is the ruler of this afterlife known as Torlarah and where we are is the Bone Valley. She murdered me out of jealousy in an attempt to make me her king."

"And?"

And Anton decided to tell her the whole story from the beginning. For one thing, there had been no one else to talk with in days, so it was liberating. He started from when Maryska had poisoned him and continued with the liquid of different skin and bodily organs known as the Lake of Flesh, the throne room, and the ruler's obsession of making him her king.

"Why didn't you go? It sounds as though she would have returned the rest of your body if you had left."

He couldn't tell if she was ridiculing him or being serious. "I would rather remain like this." It would be his preference to stay a pile of broken bones mixed into one of the mountains rather than be Maryska's lover for all eternity.

Sighing, Nahli's shoulders dropped, seeming to understand. "Perhaps we can find another way out of here and get to the skin lake."

"The Lake of Flesh? What is that going to do?"

"Well, if you say your skin, muscles, and organs are in there, perhaps mine are too."

Anton didn't want to go on some endless journey to where Maryska could be. He would rather head back inside the cottage where he'd been staying and carve something. But what would happen when he ran out of wood? He looked out toward the lifeless trees that were all bone, twisted limbs. They offered nothing. Tearing his gaze from the trunks, he turned his attention to Nahli, and studied her white braid hitting the middle of her spinal cord.

Without her olive skin, she didn't seem like herself. The dimples were gone, but the stubborn curve to her jaw was the same as that day in the market. Perhaps there was a reason he'd found her.

"All right, you may have a point. We should have a look farther out," he decided.

Her flames fell to the rows of bone cottages. "Are there any weapons inside there?"

"Most likely. But I also have this, which may work," he said, holding up his hand. "Light." When he murmured the last word, a glowing white orb with a black center appeared.

TEN

DARYNA

Daryna carefully slid down from her horse, Lilac, and ushered the mare into the stable. Lilac still had plenty of water, but Daryna brought her a pile of hay before leaving.

Teeth clenched, Daryna stomped back into her cottage. She hadn't felt like going to Verolc and delivering tonics and remedies, but she'd done it anyway. Her satchel was now brimming with coin. Over the past couple of weeks, she'd made herself do things she hadn't thought she could do.

Her left leg throbbed as she headed toward the chair at the dining table. Halfway there, she almost fell to her knees and crawled the remainder of the way. But she managed to hold onto her dignity as she took a seat, removing the satchel from across her chest.

Hiking up her skirt, she saw her skin had swelled where it met wood, and she hissed, unlatching her false limb from just below her knee. The skin was rubbed raw, dark pink blisters already forming along the surface, the pain heightening. Standing from the chair, she hopped to the cabinet next to the stove and leaned against it for a moment to catch her breath.

Once she found a minimal amount of relief, she opened the cabinet door and filtered through empty jars and containers.

Failed concoctions. Until her fingers finally brushed the healing ointment.

Hopping back across the room, Daryna collapsed into the chair and hurried to apply the salve. She sighed in relief as the pain faded to a dull ache.

She blamed Boda for this as well. Her leg wouldn't be hurting if the woman had done as Daryna had asked. Perhaps she would rip her old helper from the ground just to stab her in the chest again.

Leaning forward, Daryna opened her leather satchel and pulled out the pouch of coins that made the journey worth the pain.

She studied the wooden leg for a moment, resentment and torment pulsing through her. This was what had caused her to spend her life being so bitter, and she didn't know the reasoning behind how it had happened.

In the territory of Verolc, where she'd lived before coming to Kedaf, Daryna had awoken with no recollection of anything—nothing of herself or anyone from Verolc.

A man had stumbled upon Daryna bleeding to death with her leg sliced off. He mended it for her and asked her endless questions to which she had no answer. The only thing she'd remembered, or thought she recalled, was how to make concoctions and remedies.

Desperation consumed her at one point to be whole, to the point she'd even attempted to stitch on a recent corpse's leg. All that did was end with the attachment becoming rotten, and Daryna having to cut it off herself. She was good at what she did, but she wasn't good enough to create a new leg.

She had thought her savior was a decent man, at least until she had healed. He then tried to force himself on her. His mistake. She glowered as she recalled the result of his actions—losing both eyes by her hand. She trusted no one after that. One evil man didn't mean they were all that way, but to her, it was safer to keep them at a distance.

A hard knock rapped at the door. She had just come back and already someone was either wanting something from her or trying to sell her items. It was one of her days where she allowed villagers to come out into the woods to perhaps make a trade.

Daryna strapped her false leg back on and tried hard not to limp as she moved toward the door. No one knew she was lacking a part of herself, and she wanted to keep it that way. It was more than just her leg that she was missing—her mind wasn't whole, either.

She opened the door to a short man with peppering of black and gray hair surrounding a bald spot on his head.

"Yes?" she asked, folding her arms across her chest.

The man peered around, sweat dripping down the sides of his thick neck, watching her as if she might bite him.

If he tried to do anything funny, she just might.

"I've come by the past few days, but you haven't been home."

"I know. I wasn't here." That was the only answer she was willing to give the nosey man.

"I was wondering if you wanted to purchase this clock, I ma-made." She could tell through his stuttering that he, in fact, had not created the clock. It was a stolen good like most of the items she encountered, but she did not question the lie. It wasn't as if she'd stolen the things herself.

"Let me see."

He held out the clock. She took it from him and held it up to examine, flipping it around. The wood was well crafted with engraved leaves across the top, gears appearing to be made from real gold—she wasn't sure if he knew that. Daryna could get a lot of coin for this if she found the right person to purchase it.

"How much are you wanting?" she asked, not handing back the clock.

"At least ten coin, Miss."

Daryna would be able to get ten times that, and she felt generous. "How about I give you twelve coin, since I wasn't here when you came last?" This would keep him returning, thinking he'd made a miraculous deal.

She turned to retrieve her coin pouch from the table when the man took a step inside. Whirling back around, she pointed at his chest. "You can wait out there, unless you want your eyes ripped out."

His face paled and he moved back, twitching nervously.

Keeping a close eye on him, she went to collect her bag. With quick fingers, Daryna unraveled the pouch, poured twelve silver coins into her palm, and handed them to the man.

He continued to stand there. "You hear about the Bereza boy?"

"No?"

She recognized the last name. A man named Artem used to come by to sell things to her, until she'd heard he'd been caught and died.

"Maryska's whore, Anton?"

Anton had been one of Artem's children. She remembered Artem would sell her trinkets and discuss his children, and all Daryna had wanted to do was tell him to stop talking so she could be alone. She wouldn't have called him anything close to a friend, but perhaps one of the more decent villagers she'd encountered.

Daryna wondered how Anton could have died. Boda had mentioned once that she could use her own coin to bring Anton out to the woods to pleasure Daryna. She'd responded by telling Boda she could go choke on a goat head.

"What of him?" Daryna focused on her nails with nonchalance.

"She poisoned him with something in his tea and fled."

Daryna's chest tightened, then her stomach dropped. "I had no idea."

"Yes, no one knows where she—"

"Sorry to end this discussion, but I have to take care of something," Daryna rushed the words out and closed the door in the man's face.

Something vile coursed through her bones that she didn't like to feel—remorse and regret. And now anger.

A few weeks ago, Maryska had come by begging Daryna to help her. Daryna was not taken with murdering for the sake of it. Anytime someone wanted a revenge concoction, she turned them away unless it was with cause.

She had refused her at first, but then Maryska must have fabricated her story.

Tears streamed down Maryska's face as she spilled out a story about a young lover she'd fallen for, but an older ex-lover wouldn't let them be together. She had escaped him once with cuts and bruises, but he was still able to locate her. If she didn't go back with him, he promised her the gift of murder.

"Being with Anton was only supposed to be a way of getting over my old lover." Maryska sniffed. "These are the scars my old lover left me with." She pulled her collar down from her shoulder, and Daryna could see the pink scars across her chest and arms.

Daryna's fists shook with fury, as she remembered the man who had tried to force himself on her once upon a time. "I can mix you a poison that can be slipped into a drink. It would be hard for most to detect."

"Oh, thank you, Daryna. I can pay you double if you fill a cup with tea and the poison in it now."

The request was strange, but Daryna couldn't turn down getting double the coin. Perhaps Maryska wanted to easily dispose of the cup afterward.

Daryna prepared the mixture and handed the cup to Maryska. "Here you go. You can reheat it on the stove before serving."

"I appreciate your gift for him," she said.

Daryna had thought Maryska had meant the ex-lover, but

now she realized it was a gift meant for Anton.

Her hands clenched with outrage, so much so that her nails punctured the skin.

She knew what she needed to do—find the deceitful woman and murder her.

ELEVEN

NAHLI

Nahli stood, unable to speak, mesmerized by the lit orb inside Anton's palm. It was like pure magic, white with an obsidian flame in the center.

"How did you do that?" she murmured.

He shrugged. "I don't know. I've managed to learn a few things here. I say the word 'light,' and it chooses to appear."

What should feel like a nightmare in the Bone Valley was more of a strange dream. She should be panicking again because she was skinless, without muscles, and missing organs. But Nahli had somehow calmed herself.

Perhaps it is a dream. She poked at a bone of her arm because there was no skin to pinch—she didn't wake.

As she scanned Anton over, she wasn't sure if she even liked him. However, his presence was better than being alone—probably.

Holding out her palm, she commanded, "Light." No magical orb appeared, only an empty skeletal hand stayed in sight. She wiggled her fingers and said the word again, but her palm remained bare.

Anton reached to touch her empty hand. On instinct, she pulled it back to her side.

"May I try something?" he asked in a soothing manner.

Nahli cocked her head, then slowly slid her hand in front of him. "Just please don't take it." She had tried to steal from him at the market, and it could be possible he wanted her appendage for that.

"What would I do with a hand if there are plenty of others around that I could build?" Annoyance was etched in his voice as he peered at the pile of bones behind her.

"Perhaps you like delicate ones." She focused on his hand, seeming delicate as well.

"I find *nothing* about you delicate." He inhaled. "Now, may I see your hand?"

Reluctantly, she placed it in his because if she had to admit, she was envious of the orb adhered to him. He flipped her palm over so it faced up once more. It reminded her of the market, when he'd stroked the lines of her hand to read her fortune.

With gentleness, he moved his other hand containing the bright orb and placed it on hers. For a brief moment, her fingers and palm tingled at the contact as she pressed each digit around the sphere, then gripped it tighter. Her reflection arose in the orb, and her body stilled when she discovered flames rested inside her sockets instead of two brown eyes. But the apprehension faded as she continued to stare.

Tearing her gaze from the orb, she lifted her head to look back at Anton. "It's amazing."

"I'm glad it entertains you," he said. "It amused me for a little while, then I grew bored again."

She went to hand the orb back to him, but it stayed attached to her. Panicked, she shook it above Anton's open palm. It wouldn't budge.

"Get it away!" she cried.

A huff of air released from his jaw area. It took her a minute to realize he'd sighed, as she had no idea how that was possible since he did *not* have lungs. Placing his hand on the orb, he said, "Off."

Nahli should have felt embarrassed by her reaction, but she was more flustered. With her flames wide, she looked down at her hand in determination. "Light." And the orb appeared. "Off." The orb disappeared. "Light."

"Off," Anton muttered after he scooped it back into his hand. "We have established that we can turn a light on and off." He turned and walked away in the direction of the cottages.

Is he really wandering off?

She hurried in his direction, the skirt of her dress swishing, and easily caught up with him. "Where are you going?"

"I thought you wanted to get weapons. Or … we can stand around and play with orbs all day. We do have plenty of time for that." His tone came out light. If he had his skin and a mouth, Nahli thought he would be smiling at her.

"Oh yes, sorry."

"No need to apologize."

He led her down a path with tiny fragments of rocks until they stopped in front of a cottage. Or was it even one? Bones and animal skulls were fused together to create the outside barrier.

After he opened the door, she stepped inside to a candle-lit room. Everything was black, white, or gray. Her gaze swept across a stove, square dining table, settee, another table, bare walls, and a wooden floor.

"There's no color here," she whispered, staring up at the ceiling, then toward the lit candles.

"Black, white and gray *are* colors," Anton pointed out. "And I haven't seen any others. I don't know why this place is like this, but Maryska must have drawn life away, even from the colors."

Nahli shivered at his response and surveyed the rectangular table in front of the settee. A knife and carved wooden objects lay on top.

91

"Look," she said, picking up the knife and pointing it at the dragon.

He took the blade from her and set it back down. "I was bored."

"You made these?" The pitch in her voice rose an octave, impressed.

"You'll find out there isn't much to do here, so I hope you have a hobby."

"But you also said you didn't venture out, so how do you know that?"

He stood silent for a moment as he stared at her. "I don't."

"I suppose we're about to find out, then."

She left him standing there and headed into the first entrance she found. It must have been a bedroom because inside sat a large bed with a floral blanket thrown across. A rocking chair rested in the corner, and next to it was a wooden desk with sewing supplies strewn atop, where a pair of unfinished trousers dangled halfway off the table.

Kneeling, she lifted the gray cloth blanket and peered underneath the bed, stumbling upon a sheathed sword and a collection of daggers. Finally, something to be jubilant about.

"Take your pick," she called to Anton, spreading the weapons out on the bed.

"Are you good with a sword?" he asked, examining one of the daggers.

"I am."

"Then you take it. My younger brother is the one great with a sword. I'm better with small knives and throwing them."

"Really?" She grabbed the sword, remembering his brother's muscular build, as well as Anton's. "You look like you would be great with a sword."

He glanced down at his frail skeleton body.

"At least, you did before, with your toned body and height," she rambled. "You know what I mean."

"If we're basing it on height, then wouldn't that mean

you'd be horrendous?" He chuckled.

"Do you dare find out?" She dropped her jaw into a smile and watched him slide the daggers between his belt and trousers. "Is there a shirt and pair of pants in here that I can wear instead of this bulky dress?"

Anton strode to an open closet and thumbed through clothing items until he stepped back with dark trousers and a light tunic.

Nahli stretched her arm forward and quickly hugged them at her chest. "Thank you." He continued to stand there. "Can you go into the other room?"

His head tilted to the side. "When you were only bones on the ground, I touched every single one as I put you together."

That answer sounded more intimate than it should have, but the words affected her somehow. Her heart was gone, yet she swore there was a ghost of a beat. "That was before I was moving around, though."

"I suppose that's true. If you need me, I'll be in the other room." Anton closed the door behind him and left her standing alone.

Pearl buttons ran up along the back of the dress that she could have asked Anton to loosen for her. Instead, she grabbed one of the extra daggers he'd left on the bed and slit it open from neck to waist, effectively shimmying her way out of the overbearing garment. Before pulling on the tunic, she tugged out the bone flowers that were entwined with her hair.

The tunic was like a dress itself as it swayed at her knees. The pants were a little long, so she took scissors from the sewing table and cut them until they brushed her ankles.

Once finished, she found Anton in the sitting room, lounging at the settee and etching into an unfinished carving of a cat.

"Ready?" he asked without looking up, thin wood shavings floating to the floor from his fingertips.

"I am."

93

Nahli headed out the front door with the sword sheathed at her side. If she thought too much about how she arrived in the Bone Valley and what the place was exactly, she would frighten herself again. But she was tired of being scared, finished with trying to figure out how to get somewhere without anything, and done with trusting people who were supposed to have cared about her. She didn't trust Anton, but he was in the same ship she was and right now, he was all she had.

The first place she stopped was the wooden door at the tree trunk. She wanted to try and pry it open herself, only to find it was locked, just as Anton had said.

She wondered if it would really be so terrible to venture through if it was unlocked. What could Maryska do that was worse than this? A chill raced up her spine as monstrous images drifted through her mind. One with creatures baring long teeth, tearing her bones to shreds, blood pooling from the remains. She shook off the dreaded thought.

"Let's try going that way, right in between the hills," Anton said, gesturing farther to their left.

Turning in the direction of the uneven hills, they moved through a light fog, past mounds piled with skeletal remains. A bang came from the sky, and a thud reverberated at the top of a hill as a bone struck the tip like lightning before rolling down it. From the sky, the narrow opening rained down more skeletons, the sound of bones hitting the rocky ground was like a hammer to stone as they fell apart on impact. The piles of remains grew even as she watched.

"People die every day," Anton whispered.

Nahli shuddered at the thought that she too, had fallen from the sky. "And this is their new life? Do you think it's always been this way?"

"Maryska didn't tell me much, only what I've told you."

She noticed the daggers were now in his hands. "Do you want to keep walking in this direction?" It didn't matter which way they went, did it? On every side of her were crooked bushes, contorted trees, and the vast array of hills and mountains.

"Sure, why not." He glanced around one last time before quickening his pace.

Nahli matched his stride, even though his legs were a lot longer than hers. As they drifted farther away from where they'd started, the ground still remained bare of grass with an endless amount of dirt, rocks, and pebbles. The hills became taller and wider, forming broader mountains of skeletal pieces. Her skull reclined as far back as allowed, while she strained to try and see the tops.

The surrounding trees reminded her of the winters in Huadu, with branches covered in snowy white, except these were all bone. Some of the gnarled limbs resembled withering hands, large enough to pluck them up as they went by.

Anton and Nahli pushed past the trees and skirted around the mountains, walking mostly in silence. Below her feet, she could feel every pebble, but oddly, it didn't hurt.

Trees became less sparse until they didn't see any more signs of human bones, except in the distance behind them. Everything blurred, and Nahli squinted her flames to try and see more clearly. It only became worse.

"Can you see past the trees?" she asked, gripping the handle of her sword. It was as though they were in a tomb of foliage.

Anton stopped in his tracks and craned his neck. "No, but listen," he said quietly, finger pulled up to his teeth.

She tilted her head. "I don't hear ..." Then, she heard it—the sound of soft, padding feet. A snapping and a crunch, as if the feet were breaking brittle bones. She unsheathed her sword, stepping forward again. Her mother had been an excellent swordswoman and had taught Nahli the tricks from an early age. *If only my parents had decided to send me off to be a soldier instead of attempting to betroth me to a stranger for more coin.*

Anton inched closer to her, daggers closed in his fists.

A low growl erupted behind a thick trunk covered in tiny holes at its base. Nahli was prepared to decapitate whatever animal it was.

And then, from behind a leaning tree, a darkened head peeked forward. Nahli's flames widened. It wasn't quite an animal, yet it was a creature of some sort with the body of a tiger and the head of an enormous snake.

She held her ground and didn't back away—neither did Anton. Lifting his weapon, he threw it with perfect precision, and it struck the center of the beast's head. The beast didn't back down as it let out a deafening growl and lunged for them.

Nahli leapt forward, swinging the sword at an angle to connect with the scaly neck. The creature's head shot off, then landed with a sickening plop as it hit and rolled across the ground. The thing was eyeless, only a large mouth with rows and rows of sharpened triangular teeth. Thick, black blood oozed from the opening.

"I'm not sure that worked, Nahli." Anton's voice cracked on her name.

"Hmm?" She was breathing hard, her gaze falling to the beast's large body.

Eyes blinked at her from all over the entire thing, where they shouldn't have been. Hundreds and hundreds of eyes were openly watching them now. With hunger? With rage? It could have been both as a new head pushed through the bloody wound.

Anton thrust the other dagger, meeting its mark in one of the glowing eyes at the beast's front leg. Screeching a shrill and horrible growl, the creature faltered, then dove for Anton's leg, teeth piercing and latching onto it. Anton howled while bellowing out the word, "Light."

The shimmering orb appeared in his hand, and the beast released his leg, seeming entranced by the illumination. Nahli didn't hesitate—she brought down the sword, splitting the beast into two once again. Dark blood sprayed her as she watched the creature's body and head strike the ground.

"Flame," Anton panted, the orb morphing into a luminous fire with pitch-dark at its center.

"You didn't show me that," she said, noticing how the flame sizzled without burning his palm.

"I told you I knew a few things." He paused. "Only these two, though."

Both portions of the beast twitched, trembled, then full-on shook as another body and head grew back, turning them into two. She searched for the head she'd decapitated earlier. Only now, it had become three beasts.

Anton hurled the flame at the creature on the right, and smoke rose from the beast's head as if his magic had been doused in water. The blow had done nothing, the creature unaffected.

"That was useless," Anton muttered, staring at his hand.

"Time to run." Nahli barreled forward as quickly as she could, Anton directly behind her.

They stomped through the woods of skeletal trees, thorn-covered bushes, and shriveled vines. Ahead, the blur became clearer as white hills in the distance took shape. The pound of paws striking earth sounded behind them, drawing nearer. If Nahli had a heart, it would have fallen from her rib cage from fright. But they were already almost out of the woods, closer and closer.

She jumped over a protruding tree root and onto a dirt path that led them right back toward the center of the Bone Valley.

TWELVE

ANTON

If there was blood at all pulsing through Anton's bones, the movement would have been desperate and enraged. What lay before him was quite unexpected, but it shouldn't have been. He didn't say a word to Nahli, not until they were all the way out of the dead woods.

Angling his head over his shoulder, he met the hungry gaze of the three ghastly beasts, watching with their hundreds of eyes, and waiting for Anton and Nahli to return. But the creatures didn't step out from the twisted trees.

Anton came to a halt near a round cluster of bones and breathed hard, ragged breaths.

Nahli lifted her skeletal hand in the air and made a spherical motion. "It's wonderful to know this place wraps around in one large circle. So now we have that particular riddle figured out," she spat with sarcasm.

Anton's bones grew heavy, and he took another deep breath to relax himself. He already missed having a weapon in his hand for defense. "Now we know not to attempt that fate again, either."

The fog around the Bone Valley had thickened, pressing itself to their bodies in a blanket of sorts. A heart-stopping crack sounded from the sky as new skeletons plummeted to the hills and ground, breaking apart.

Anton moved forward, but gasped and stopped when a sharp throb came from his leg.

Nahli's flames lowered as he touched his trousers. "You're hurt!"

"I'm fine. It's only a little … *black* blood." Like the beasts' wounds, tar-colored liquid coated and stained his pants.

He pulled up the trouser leg, and eight puncture wounds bled from his bone where the beast had torn into him. The injury had come in a wave of pain that he didn't know how to describe. While it had stung like death, it wasn't nearly as bad as it could have been if he'd had skin, muscle, and nerves. Lifting his finger, he brought it to his leg bone and rubbed away a glob of blood.

Nahli knelt, clasping her hand around his leg to examine the injury. "It's not bleeding anymore. That seems to have stopped rather quickly."

"Could you expect anything less?" He shifted his leg out of her hold.

She wiggled her index finger and stood, her flames dancing. "You're right."

"I think I'll go wash off in the lake." Blood caked his leg, dirt covered his body, and he needed to calm himself down. He needed to do *something*.

"There's a lake?"

"Yes, let me take you on a proper tour since it looks like we'll be here for a while." He sighed and waved her on, while walking toward the lake and pointing out all the bone decorations to her. He didn't know if she realized he was being humorous or if she thought him serious. But he smiled to himself, nonetheless.

"Do you know why the fog is thicker?" Nahli asked, sweeping her hand back and forth to part it as best she could.

"It's the Bone Valley's way of telling us it's night time, I

99

suppose. The fog is less dense in the morning, then gathers more throughout the day."

"That seems logical."

They passed a mountain of remains, bones protruding in all shapes and sizes, some filthier than others. Each mound became smaller as they reached the familiar tree with the locked door. Anton was tempted to shake the handle again, but he was done with that for now.

I wonder what Maryska would think of Nahli, though she did tell me bones were my only company. He didn't know when she would come back, but perhaps she'd forget about him like she had with this entire valley of bones. But he knew he wouldn't be so lucky.

Taking a turn down a path of broken rock, he pointed Nahli in the direction of the lake, right past the cottage he'd been staying in. He might as well call it his home.

Nahli halted in front of the gray lake, surveying the water. "In a way, it's beautiful."

"Besides the dead fish at the bottom," he said, tapping his toe at the edge of the dirt and stripping off his tunic.

"What are you *doing*?" she squeaked, as though the act of removing his tunic was the biggest abomination she'd seen thus far.

He tossed the shirt to the dirt and reached for his belt. "I'm getting cleaned up."

"Without *clothes*?" Nahli whirled away from him, her voice breaking on the last word.

"Have you never seen a skeleton before?"

"Are you jesting?" she asked, sounding amused but still nervous.

As he attempted a smile and stepped into the liquid, he couldn't feel if it was warm or cool, only the gentle rippling against his bones.

"You can get in now, if you want. I don't bite … much," he called.

"That's truly hilarious."

"I'll get out, if you prefer," Anton tried again.

Dirt still clung to Nahli's bones from when he'd gathered her fragments to build her, and blood spotted her skull after she'd decapitated the creatures. But he didn't want to tell her that.

"Just look the other way," she whisper-shouted.

His flames shifted to the sky, yet he spun to face the other direction to make her comfortable. A moment later, the splash of water echoed around him as Nahli entered the lake.

"You can turn around now," she said.

He whirled to face her. Nahli pulled her braided hair loose and dipped her skull beneath the water's surface.

Tilting his head back, Anton wet his own hair and ran his hands through the tangled locks. He scrubbed his leg with the heel of his skeletal hand, chipping away flecks of the dark blood.

"What made you become a thief?" he asked, hoping to make their bathing situation less awkward for Nahli.

She didn't answer for a while as she stared past him at a cluster of razor-sharp bone bushes. "What's it to you?"

"Just curious why you were at my sister's booth that day."

It was to take the herbs, but he wanted to know more about the reasoning behind her thieving. Was it a thrill for her? Was she desperate for coin? Thieves couldn't be defined to one answer. He knew, like everyone, they each had their own unique story.

"I needed coin, and Daryna uses herbs to brew things. She would have paid a good lump for that."

"The one the village calls a witch?"

His father had never mentioned anything about her being one, but he also hadn't spoken much about what happened when he'd stolen and sold items.

"So they say." Nahli shrugged and dipped her head beneath the water once more.

That still didn't answer Anton's question as to why she'd become a thief, but he decided to let the subject rest for now.

"Why did you start doing … what you do?" she asked, not meeting his gaze.

"Become a whore?"

Nahli flinched in response. "I didn't mean that it's lowly. Only, I'm curious as to how you started doing it."

The answer was a simple one, but when Anton thought about his parents, if they had still been alive, he wondered what he would have accomplished instead. Would he have become better at woodwork since he could have spent all his time focusing on it? No matter what, he would never have been good enough with a sword to become a soldier like Pav could.

"My mother killed herself when I was young, shortly after my little sister was born. The pressure was great on my father, so he started thieving to support us." Anton paused and his flames connected with hers. "He was caught and both of his hands were sliced clean off in punishment. Later, he died from infection."

"Is that why at the market you mentioned the possibility of my hands being cut off?"

"Yes." Every time he thought about a thief, Anton couldn't help but compare their situation to his father's and feared the same outcome.

"And so, you started selling yourself to help out your siblings?"

"Yes," he said simply, but the meaning behind it was more than that casual word.

Anton didn't like to recall the memory of the first time he was paid to tumble someone. He'd just turned seventeen and had never bedded anyone, although he had kissed quite a few village girls at dances at the market.

A widowed woman in her late thirties offered to pay him coin to help her get over her husband. Because she was his only lover, she paid him double. It was an easy enough way to make money and, at first, he didn't mind the task. Later, he realized how wrong he'd been. All women and men weren't like the widow. Most thought they owned him, demanding things from him that he didn't want to do.

"That was a courageous thing for you to do," Nahli whispered.

Anton waded toward the edge of the lake as something swelled in the hollowness of his rib cage, thinking of what she'd said and not feeling courageous about it at all.

"I think I'll retire for the evening." He glanced back at her. "You have your choice of where to sleep. All the cottages are empty, as you might have guessed."

Plucking his clothes from the dirt, he made his way to the cottage and slammed the door behind him. Things were different now that Nahli was in the Bone Valley. Before she showed up, he'd only had himself to converse with, whether it was his voice or his thoughts filling the bone-clattering silence. With people came questions, and those led to memories, and that reminded him why he was trapped there. But really, he'd always been imprisoned by his own mind, condemned by his own judgment.

THIRTEEN

NAHLI

Nahli watched as Anton's figure faded away into the distance, the fog swallowing him whole. His mood had shifted from cool to cold. He'd opened up about himself, the braver of the two of them, while she had kept her secrets buried and hidden.

Around her skeletal form, the fog grew heavier, wrapping her in an unwelcome blanket. She lingered in the water for a long while, reminiscing about the last day of her life. What if she'd never gone to Daryna's? She could have stolen something well worth thieving, then have come at a later time. But she'd been impulsive and desperate to make coin. And for what? To go home to parents who really didn't even treat her well or to another new land that could have put her in a worse predicament.

She floated on her back to the edge of the lake, kicking her feet to create minuscule splashes. Rolling to her stomach, she dragged herself out from the liquid and threw her clothing on. Her hair dripped water down the back of her shirt, and she squeezed the locks before braiding them and tying the tip. The braid was the only physical part that still felt like her, besides for it being the color white instead of black.

Gathering her inner strength, she headed down the bumpy path to the garden where Anton had reassembled her. She was used to being alone and sleeping outdoors, so a cottage with four walls would feel too confining.

Her gaze fell to a bench she hadn't noticed when she'd woken in the garden. She'd been too focused on the fact that she was dead, and yet, somehow also alive. The bench looked like a distant relative of the cottages, made with fused bones, except for antlers protruding at the ends. Sinking down onto the remains, she peered out at the garden. Although not made of living plants, it was fascinating in its own way, decorated with bone flowers covered in long and thin clover-shaped petals, thorny bushes, and a mushroom in the dirt's center.

"Wait a second." She squinted her flames and took stock of the mushroom surrounded by flowers. "Why you're not a mushroom at all, are you?"

It was actually a rounded animal skull with two empty eye sockets. In fact, a petal-less flower stem next to it resembled a crooked tail, and the other protruding flowers were shaped like animal hands that were once paws.

Crouching to her knees, Nahli crawled to the animal bones. She plucked the skull from the ground, the base appearing to be a tiny rib cage. Hurriedly, she picked the other small bone flowers and laid them before her. They mirrored the fish in the pond, where parts, but not all, were connected. It would be simple for her to build if she tried, and what better entertainment did she have than this?

The spine curved in a delicate direction, and the arms hung before it in a graceful way as soon as she snapped them on. When she aligned the tail, it looked similar to one of a rat. The skeletal frame wasn't a rat, though—at least she didn't think so—as it stood on its haunches. She continued to piece the attachments together, amazed when each one fused to the skeleton.

After she completed her build, she scanned it over,

expecting it to move. The creature stood still, no flames alighting in the sockets. With the tip of her finger, she nudged the tiny hand. "Come on, move around."

She poked the other paw. "Don't you want to awake, so we can fill up this deserted valley with life?"

White flames matching hers lit and flickered within the eye sockets. Bones shaking, she scooted back, waiting for the creature to move. It thumped to all fours, shook its head, then stood on its haunches again.

As her nerves subsided, she stuck out her hand and crawled forward to let it sniff her palm. She couldn't smell anything here, but perhaps the tiny skeleton could.

Its head cocked near its shoulder and the skeleton stared at her hand. "What would you like me to do with that?"

Nahli's flames grew in size. The calm inside her relinquished, and she scurried backward on all four of her appendages. "Y-you can talk."

"Of course I can." His hands clasped together—like a human—and the sight could only be considered perplexing.

"But you're an … animal?" Or was it? She didn't know anymore.

"To be precise, a male meerkat, and my name is Roka." The newly-awakened creature bowed to her as though she were royalty.

She was a walking skeleton, so it shouldn't have been worrisome that a meerkat could talk *and* bow, but it was a little distracting.

"Hello, Roka. My name is Nahli." She extended a hand, and he grasped it.

Scratching the side of his skull, he said, "Forgive me, but I cannot recall much."

"Do you remember anything from before or how you came here?" If she remembered her past life in Kedaf and Huadu, then she was sure he should remember something. Although, she wasn't certain if it was different with animals, since they couldn't talk in her past life.

"I must apologize, but no. There seems to be a gap in my memory."

"You knew your name and that you're a meerkat," she pointed out.

"Yes, it is a quite unique thing, isn't it?"

She stared at Roka, not knowing whether to trust the little thing. But from building him, it gave her an idea.

"Follow me." She waved Roka on, explaining to him where he was and how she'd arrived to the Bone Valley as they headed toward Anton's cottage.

Once at the entrance, where several curving horns peeked out, she thrust open the door and threw herself inside. "Anton, wake up!"

Startled, he jerked awake and reached for the carving knife on the table. "What is it? Are you all right?"

He'd been slumped on the settee, flames closed. She almost felt bad for disturbing him, but this was too important.

"I'm fine, but I have something to show you." She glanced over her shoulder to find Roka already crouched there.

"Couldn't you have knocked on the door?" he muttered. "Perhaps appeared less like a wild creature, scaring me out of my mind?"

Nahli ignored him as Roka slid past her leg and entered the cottage. "I think the lady here has an idea she felt was important."

Anton's jaw dropped open. "What in all of Kedaf is that?"

"You mean the Bone Valley," Roka corrected him, maneuvering forward.

Anton's spine flexed against the back of the settee, the knife clenched in his fist.

Nahli hurried forward. "It's fine, Anton. I brought him back to life."

"You? You did this?" His tone sounded confused as he massaged his hair at his temple.

"Yes, I went to the garden and discovered his skeleton pieces!" She rapidly pointed out the door. "Then I built him."

Anton stayed quiet, not appearing at all as enthusiastic as Nahli felt. However, his spine appeared less rigid.

The meerkat dropped to all fours and proceeded forward, then sat back on his hind legs. "Anton, my name is Roka."

"Why can you talk?" Anton pressed, rubbing his temple again.

"Why can *you* talk?" Roka asked with clasped hands.

Anton's flames narrowed at the skeletal creature. "Do you know Maryska?"

Nahli hadn't even thought to question Roka about her. What if he belonged to her? But she waved off the thought. It would have been a strong coincidence for Maryska to guess that Nahli would find him mostly buried.

"Possibly. Possibly not. I only know what I know and what I know is that I am a meerkat named Roka who has awoken in the Bone Valley. Nahli provided me with the last part."

Perhaps it was possible that Roka had never even been alive before, and had never lived anywhere except for the garden. He could have been born of the Bone Valley and that was how he came about—a decoration of bones that she put together to give life to. She shook her head. To think about questions without answers didn't do anyone good.

"After I built Roka, an idea came to me." She sat on the settee, leaving a wide space between her and Anton.

"What's your idea?" Anton's tone didn't seem impressed.

"I think we should rebuild the city. We could start with the smaller piles that would be easier to find pieces in, and then move on from there."

"Hmm. Then what?"

"We can figure a way to break out of here with an army and perhaps retrieve our bodies."

The idea of having an army to possibly find a way out through the door would be beneficial if they came across

Maryska.

Anton tapped his jaw with his index finger. The clicking sound his digit produced was the only noise in the room. Nahli and Roka sat watching, waiting.

Finally, Anton said, "I like the idea. Now may I go back to sleep, and we can start on the task in the morning?"

Nahli was anxious to begin now, yet a small yawn escaped her, and she thought it better to begin when the fog cleared.

"Fine."

She left Anton's cottage and entered the thick fog, with Roka's padding feet behind her. After glancing back at the row of homes, she turned to the meerkat. "I'm not sure if you want to stay in a cottage or outdoors. They're all empty besides Anton's, though."

"I may venture around for a while and see if I can try to remember anything," Roka replied.

It was a reasonable idea, and one she hoped would work because, perhaps, then they could have more answers. "Don't go into the bone woods, though. There are three ghastly beasts with too many eyes and too many teeth skulking around in that area."

With a quick nod, he scurried off.

She trampled down the pebbled path that curved into the garden toward the bone bench. Curling up on the lonely piece of furniture, she closed her flames to fall asleep and wondered if she would dream. But did the dead even dream?

"Are you ready to build?"

A deep male voice pulled Nahli out of sleep. The answer to her question so far was that the dead do not in fact dream, or at least the first time she hadn't.

When she stretched to a sitting position, she straightened

her spine and extended her fists upward. She angled her head to gaze up at Anton, his white hair hanging loosely at his shoulders. He looked better with his hair down instead of tied back like it had been at the market. *Freer.*

"Yes, I'm ready."

Taking a moment, she studied him. His square jaw was one of his best features, she decided. Zikri had a weak chin that she was fond of, but those chins she would forever stay away from.

Nahli dragged herself to stand and hunched over the edge of the garden. "Do you want to begin with this one?"

"Wherever you want to start is fine with me."

She knelt to the dusty ground and reached for the skull.

Anton lightly touched her elbow. "No, the head should come last. It's easier to build from the feet up."

"The one time you built a skeleton?" She smiled.

"Yes. And she turned out all right, didn't she?" His voice came out playful.

Still smiling, she shrugged. "Perhaps."

Nahli started on one foot as Anton began on the other. He was already at the pelvis by the time she'd finished the toes. This was more complicated than she'd thought as she listened to the light sizzle of her piece connecting.

Roka appeared beside the pile of bones. "Would you like any help?" Nudging with the tip of his skull where his nose should be, he pointed at the pieces that might be next.

"How can you tell?" she asked.

"By examining the both of you, I am finding a similar bone," Roka said, puffing up his rib cage.

Why hadn't she thought of that? She could have been studying Anton's skeleton the entire time.

When she attached the last piece, the skeleton was almost as tall as Anton with chin-length, curly hair.

"Awake," she said.

Nothing happened. Grinding her jaw back and forth, she yelled the word again. It had been used in the sentence when she'd awoken Roka. She didn't understand why the word wasn't working.

Her flames fell to Roka who shrugged his tiny shoulders, then to Anton, who was scratching the side of his cheekbone.

"How did you awaken me?" she asked.

Anton stared up at the crackling sky. "I said *awake, my queen.*"

"All right. Awake, my king." The skeleton remained still, not even the slightest twitch.

"You awoke the meerkat, right?" Anton asked. "It could be possible we may only be able to rouse one thing."

That sounded possible... Her flames shifted to Roka. "Would you like to try?"

"I would be happy to try, my lady." Roka bowed and placed a hand against the skeleton. "Awake," he said. No movement. "Awake, my king." No flames. "Awake, my queen." Frozen. His gaze drifted up to Nahli. "I am sorry, I do not think it will work for me."

Frustration pulsed through Nahli's bones. She stared at the unmoving skeleton and kicked at his legs. He toppled to the ground with a loud thud.

"There's no need for that," Anton whispered. "We did all we could."

Whirling around, she scoffed, "You know, this is all your fault, Anton. If you wouldn't have shown up at the booth that day, I could have gotten the herbs Daryna needed, then I wouldn't be dead right now."

"Don't blame me for your actions!" Anton fumed. "You could have found a trade and made coin the right way."

"What? Like you? Go perform tricks for coin and hate myself for it?"

She knew she shouldn't have gone that far because he sucked in a sharp breath, clacking his front teeth against his lower ones without a word.

"Well, you're a *queen* now, aren't you?" he spat.

111

Instead of apologizing, she couldn't stop herself. "I am no one's queen, least of all *yours*. I would rather be deader than I already am."

"If I could go back and leave you in pieces on the ground, I would."

He whirled around and stormed off, leaving her with a hollow feeling inside her already empty rib cage.

FOURTEEN

PAV

Pav and his two sisters had laid Anton's body to rest in the back of Ionna's property. The burial of sorts took place in front of a large Sequoia tree, while Pav's sixteenth birthday had come and gone. He'd known Anton wouldn't have wanted to be buried at the family home where the memory of their parents had been. He would want to be with them, now that Pav and his sisters were going to stay at Ionna's home permanently.

It had been two weeks since his brother's death, and Pav only wanted to be alone. He'd shut everyone out, including Polina. However, there was one person who wouldn't escape his thoughts—Maryska. He *needed* to find her.

After he'd shown Yeva the teacup, she said there was nothing they could do. Maryska was gone, and the Enforcers never cared about a dead whore, much less a dead whore who had been the son of a criminal. Yeva knew going on a blind hunt would get them nowhere. In the end, she said they must trust that someday Maryska would get what was coming to her.

Pav didn't buy into that.

The four new walls—of his new bedroom, in his new

home, with his new feathered mattress that was his and his only—felt as if they would close in on him. He should have been pleased about having a room to himself for the first time in his life, but he wasn't. Sharing a bed with his older brother didn't seem like such a terrible thing anymore.

He brought the bottle of wine, that he'd taken from the cellar, to his lips and took another slow sip. It was intended for him to celebrate the glorious turn of events of their family leaving their rickety cottage and arriving at a new paradise.

Leaning his head back on the foot of the bed, he clacked the glass bottle against the wood floor and ran a hand through his hair. He wanted to rip out his curls and feel more of a physical pain than an emotional one. The walls surrounding him seemed to whisper Maryska's name over and over and over again.

"Pav, it's time for dinner," Yeva called from the dining room.

He didn't feel like eating dinner—he felt like hunting down a murderess. Food used to be his favorite aspect about life. Now, he wanted to stay in his room and drink his thoughts away, until they became nothing. Until *he* became nothing.

When Papa had passed, he hadn't been as destroyed as he was now. He knew he should take charge the way Anton and Yeva had when Papa died. But he wasn't Anton, and he wasn't Yeva. He was Pav. The person who could make people laugh. Now, it seemed even that ability was fading.

"Pavla!" Yeva's voice grew nearer.

She swung open the door without knocking and found Pav hunched on the floor. Her eyes were red-rimmed and her hair mussed, as though she'd just been crying as well.

"I'm not hungry." He lifted his head to look at her, and the world tipped sideways.

"Are you drinking?" Yeva marched over to him and picked up the glass bottle from the floor. "The whole thing is practically empty."

"So?" Frowning, he brought his knees to his chest and curled his arms around them.

"So? This isn't like you."

"I don't know who I am." The wine was making him act overly dramatic.

She let out a sigh and flattened a hand against her chest. "You're Pav. You're my brother. And you're Tasha's brother."

Moisture beaded his lashes. "I'm not Anton's brother anymore?"

Yeva sank down to the floor beside Pav and wrapped her arm around his shoulders, tightening her grip. "You will always be Anton's brother, but we have to keep living. Anton wouldn't want you to sit here and wither away."

She was right, and Pav understood that she could still accomplish things through her sadness, but he wasn't built like her. Death changed things, especially when it took the one person in the world he was closest to.

"What about Tasha?" she asked, stroking his hair like when he was a child. "You're the closest to her along with Anton, and you don't want to make it seem as though she has lost two brothers. Do you?"

"No." He loved his little sister, and he didn't want the way he felt to rub off on her.

"She hasn't read a book since he died."

Pav pulled out from Yeva's grasp to look at her. "Perhaps because Anton always read to her at night."

"I'm not asking you to take his place." She paused and sniffed. "But why don't you try reading to her?"

It was the least he could do. Something he should have already been doing.

"I will."

His little sister needed him, and he shouldn't be selfish about that, but his thoughts were jumbled.

"How about I bring dinner in here for you this once, so you

can come back to yourself? I don't want you stumbling and falling on the way to the table."

A pitiful chuckle escaped Pav, and Yeva wrapped her arms around him again. "That sounds more like my little brother. Next time you sneak a wine bottle, don't drink so much, all right?"

"All right."

Yeva went out of the room and moments later returned with a plate of food—steaming turkey seasoned with garlic, lush strawberries, grapes, and buttered rolls—before leaving to eat her own meal.

Pav wasn't completely drunk, but his head was a bit fuzzy as he popped a plump grape into his mouth. After three more pieces of fruit, his stomach released a nauseated rumble. He ran to the window, hung his head over the edge, and let his stomach empty. It wasn't only the wine that had made him feel sick but also everything else going on.

Even though Pav wanted to finish his meal for his sister, he couldn't, not that night. He scraped the helpings from his plate over the ledge to the grass below.

Pav set the plate on the floor beside his bed and decided to lay down on the mattress until his head grew clearer.

His eyes pressed shut, and he remained half in between sleep and consciousness, constant images of his dead brother floating through his mind. Alive Anton, dead Anton, Anton's rotten corpse decaying beneath the ground in front of the Sequoia tree. There was even one with him pleading below the ground to dig him back out, because he wasn't really dead. He had never been dead.

Pav's eyes flicked open. "All right, that's enough resting for now." He shook the images away and sat up in bed.

A small whimpering reverberated through the wall from the room beside his—Tasha. His head wasn't as dizzy, and he hated himself for having ignored his younger sister during their grief. He headed toward her bedroom, finding the door already cracked open.

"Tasha?" Pav asked in a low voice.

She kept silent and held back her sobs, yet a soft squeak slipped out.

"Tasha, may I come in?"

"I suppose." Her meek voice sounded unsure.

Pav opened the door the remainder of the way and stepped into her room. "Where are Yeva and Ionna?"

The candle beside Tasha's bed displayed her tear-streaked face. "They're playing chess in the sitting room."

"You didn't want to join in or read?"

She rolled to her side, tucking a hand behind her head. "No."

As if he was approaching a frightened animal, he slowly took a seat on the bed and lay down beside her. "I know Anton used to read you stories before bed, but what if I tell you some? Brand new and amazing tales told by yours truly—me."

Tasha giggled and a light cluck came from the other side of the bed.

"What was that?" Pav asked and dove to the edge of the mattress, leaning his head over to find black and white feathers. Juju was nestled in a nest of hay. He turned his head to his sister. "You brought the chicken inside?"

"Only at night." She smiled in a way that made him think she probably had the hen in there more often than that.

"Yeva is going to be mad if she goes on the floor." He'd like to see her reaction, actually.

"I don't know, she likes that Juju lays eggs quite often."

"I'll act as though Juju was never here." He pretended to lock his lips together as he smiled and lay back down beside her, straightening the rough pillow. "Are you ready for the story?"

Quietly, she nodded and rolled to face him.

He cleared his throat—twice—before beginning his original piece. "There once was a little girl with wild curly hair the color of tree bark, with hidden gold streaks that shone underneath the sun."

"This is about me, isn't it?" she asked.

"Shh. You aren't the only girl who has curly hair." He took a dark lock, pulling the curl and watching it spring back. "Now, no interruptions." Pav continued, "The one thing that always brightened this girl's day was to read."

Tasha gave him a knowing look and smiled.

"But more than anything, she wanted to live in the stars. She would reach as far as she could, never able to find her way to them. So, she climbed to the roof of her cottage and reached as high as she could, but the stars only twinkled in reply.

"Next, she went to the center of her village, deep into the woods, carrying her favorite book along the way." He paused to glance at her and winked. "One with dragons.

"There, in the middle of the forest, stood a tree like no other that led to the clouds. The little girl traveled up each branch without looking down, for fear she would give up. When she reached the top, she still couldn't touch the beams of lights.

"But then she remembered her book and opened it to read to them because everyone loves a story, even the stars. They answered her with a rapid twinkle, and out of the book flew a dragon with scales so blue they were almost as black as the night. A soft sheen slicked its skin that sparkled under the moonlight, as if its scales were made of the stars themselves.

"The dragon circled the top of the tree and hovered in front of the girl, flapping its wings, waiting for her to hop aboard its back. She was not afraid of the flying creature as she climbed onto its back without hesitation. The dragon then flew her all the way up to the shimmering stars. And you know what she did next?"

"What?" Tasha asked, her eyelids starting to drift closed.

"She wrote Tasha in the stars." He grinned, swiping his hand across the pretend sky.

Smiling in return, his sister closed her eyes, then. "Thank you, Pav. That's the best story you've ever told me."

"It's the *only* story I've ever told you," he whispered and kissed the top of her curls.

"Goodnight."

"Goodnight, baby bean." To call her by her nickname reminded him of Anton, and perhaps that wasn't such a terrible thing.

When Tasha had been born, she'd been so small. Anton had said she reminded him of a tiny bean because he could hold her with one hand.

He shut Tasha's door behind him and padded into the sitting room. Yeva lay wrapped in Ionna's arms while they rested in front of the hearth, watching as the flames crackled. Ionna kissed Yeva's cheek, and the moment seemed a little too intimate for Pav.

By softening his footsteps, he attempted to sneak past them toward the front door. Yeva must have heard him anyway.

"Pav? Where are you going?"

"I'm going to visit Polina before I go to bed. It won't take long for me to walk there and back." Polina's home was only down the hill from Ionna's.

"Pav..." Judgment tinged her voice.

"It's not *that* kind of visit, Yeva. I only want to apologize to her for my behavior."

She nodded in understanding. "All right, but be careful."

"Take a lantern with you," Ionna called.

He did as she said, taking one from the doorway as he stumbled out of the house. Outside, the dark sky hugged the village, and the light guided him, all the way to Polina's cottage.

The air was stagnant, but the smell of citrus fruit invaded his nostrils. Pav angled his head to his old cottage, his chest tightening at the sight. It felt unusual that Anton wouldn't be there if he walked through the door. Shaking the thoughts away before they led to an endless path of depressing images, he made his way to the back of Polina's cottage.

Lowering the lantern toward the dirt, he lifted several small gray pebbles into his palm. He tossed one at Polina's window, and a soft clinking answered back. No other response came. He threw another one a little harder.

The curtains drew to the side. A candle with a bright flickering flame highlighted the window, along with the silhouette of a person.

Polina opened the window, her red hair knitted with heaps of shredded white cloth.

"What's in your hair?" he asked, taking a step closer to her.

"Is that the first question you ask when you haven't spoken to me in two weeks?" Polina's full lips were pursed into a thin line, her gaze settling on his hand. "And why are you throwing pebbles at my window when you could have easily tapped it with your finger?"

"Can I not be a romantic? Prove to you the error of my ways, my beauty." He reached out and touched one of the strips of fabric in her hair.

She rolled her eyes and huffed. "Not everyone can have natural curls like you, Pav." She stuck out a hand and pulled on one of his strawberry blond locks.

"Ow, you wound me." He moved her hand from his hair and slipped his palm into hers, intertwining their fingers.

"I did *not* pull hard." She tried to hide a smile.

"Does that mean you forgive me?"

"Of course, I forgive you," Polina said, watching him with a sad expression. "You know you can talk to me anytime, and if you need to be alone, all you have to do is say so."

"Now I can ease myself into slumber." He gently squeezed her fingers. "Otherwise, I would have been thinking about you all night."

"Goodnight, Pav." She laughed, pulling her hand out of his

grasp to close the window.

"A kiss?" His body hit the wall of the cottage.

She didn't hesitate as she pressed her lips against his.

After leaving Polina's house, the citrus odor in the air seemed to follow Pav, reminding him of the mixture of oranges and something else he'd inhaled at Maryska's. An idea struck him as the thirst to find her grew once more. He may not be able to find her on his own, but what if he could find someone who could lead him to her? What if there was a way to question Anton, even though he was dead?

FIFTEEN

ANTON

Over the past few days, Anton had remained inside the cottage. Nahli's words had been a blow, and he believed it would be in his best interest if he didn't see her again.

A light knock tapped at the door. His flames lifted to the ceiling, then back toward the beast carving he was working on. He'd already completed the other two, but perfecting all the minuscule eyes took time and precision.

The knock came again.

It could only be one of two people—one woman and one animal, to be precise. He ignored it, but the door cracked open. He should have locked it.

"May I come in?" Nahli asked, her voice hesitant as she peeped half her skull around the door.

"You're already in the doorway, aren't you?" He continued staring at his carving.

"I wanted to apologize," she murmured.

With the sharp point of his tool, he dug out small shavings from the wood piece. "It took you long enough."

"I was mad and frustrated, but I promise I didn't mean it." Her tone came out pleading.

His gaze met hers then, and he set the knife and carving

beside him. "By the way, I never meant for you to be my queen literally when I brought you back to life. Being alone here—in this place—it was doing things to my mind. I never expected you to be able to move and talk, let alone that you would be the thief from the market."

Without being asked, Nahli closed the door behind her and sank down on the settee, all the way at the opposite end. He almost chuckled, seeing her so tense and nervous.

"Look, I tried to find a proper trade," she started. "Most of the vendors and shops didn't need anyone, or I wasn't qualified, or they didn't want someone from Huadu, or it didn't make as much coin as I needed. I was living under a bridge, for the love of bones!"

His head twisted to hers, his flames expanding. "Love of bones?"

"I was bored out there, desperate even, and came up with new terminology to occupy my time."

"Please don't ever use that sentence again. I think you can come up with something better."

"I was only trying to add a little humor."

He shrugged, amused. "Then, *for the love of bones*, continue using it."

"You can have a sense of humor if you try." Nahli laughed. "Anyway, the thing is, what you did for a living takes bravery. I'm not that brave. It's impossible for me to hold back emotions when being that close to another."

He ground his teeth in contemplation. "I'm not very brave either. I loathed it, especially during this last year."

Silence lengthened between them until she reached for the carving beside him, bringing it up to her face. Her jaw hung slightly open as she rotated the beast several times between her pale fingertips.

"It's eerie how closely it resembles the things out in the woods." She carefully set it back down.

"Its twins are on the table." He pointed at the other two

completed beast carvings. "Or should I say triplets?"

Her gaze followed his. "Will you make me something, possibly a ship?"

"I don't know." His jaw dropped into a smile. "I think you still owe me for stealing my clothing."

"But you stole my satchel." She nudged his leg with her hand.

"Was it your satchel to begin with?"

She crossed her arms over her ribs. "That isn't the point."

"Ah, my queen, but it is," he taunted.

"Don't start."

Thinking they were finished when they both stayed quiet, he reached for the knife to begin carving again.

"I want to show you something." She stood from the settee, motioning him forward. "Possibly a good secret."

"I'm intrigued," Anton said, stretching before moving for the door. "Where's Roka?" He was surprised the little meerkat hadn't followed her inside like the last time.

"He's right outside." As soon as she pulled open the door, Roka was there.

He stood on his haunches, hands curved downward in front of him. "I didn't want to bother you until you were ready to come back out."

"I don't think he would have shown up if I hadn't retrieved him," Nahli teased as she entered the fogless afternoon.

What she didn't know was that eventually he would have left the cottage. It would have taken a few more days for him to cool off, but he would have gone to the lake, then to find her. Being truly alone wasn't as easy as he'd always thought.

"How's your leg?" Nahli reached for his trousers.

Despite his injury, it hadn't bothered him enough to inspect the wound. Anton rolled up his pant leg to expose the punctured holes, still there, like a scar.

"The wound is still on my arm, too." She placed the scar near his flames, the hairline crack looking the same as it did the day she fell.

Anton wondered what would happen if one of them broke a bone. Would it heal, or forever be split into two? He would have to make sure they didn't do anything too reckless.

"Now what did you want to show me? A palm reading?" He chuckled, holding up his hand and wiggling his fingers.

"I will never attempt that again," she promised. "No, I went ahead and built more skeletons with Roka's help."

Anton entered the garden behind her, and focused on a long row of at least twenty dusty skeletons. "I'm impressed."

"I also learned how to do this without you standing beside me." She held up her hand. "Light." A white orb with a black flame center, that matched Anton's, appeared in her palm.

Anton's skull angled to Roka. "Can you do this, too?"

The meerkat held up his empty hand, dejection in his voice. "Afraid not."

"That's a shame. It appears right when we need it, yet the orb doesn't do much good besides give off light." He thought about when he'd changed the orb into a ball of fire and threw it at the beast in the woods. All it did was create smoke.

"Off," Nahli commanded, and the orb disappeared. "So I was thinking we could keep on building the skeletons, and perhaps, eventually we could find a way to bring them back to life. Most of all, it would be better than leaving them as broken remains on the ground."

Anton would do what he could to pass the time, but it wasn't just that. By the way she squared her shoulders, she seemed so determined, focused. And because of that, he wanted to help her.

Before they started, there was something he needed to tell her. "Outside ... when I mentioned that I wish I would have left you how you were? I didn't mean it. It was something I shouldn't have said, because that would mean you would still be dead. That is something I would never wish for you, no matter what else happened between us in the past."

125

Nahli bowed her head, avoiding his flames. "No, it's understandable. You had a right to voice your anger after what I said."

"Let's agree to disagree on that."

"Fine, but I'm right." She held up a finger to prevent him from arguing, then gazed out into the distance of the bone mountains. "Where do you want to start?"

"Hmm."

He tapped his chin and walked to the end of the row, passing by skeletons with curly hair to their waist, short hair, straight hair, yet all the same pale shade. From the sky, a sizzle and boom sounded as skeletons rained down, reminding him that no matter how many they built, the task would never be complete.

"We can begin here."

Anton rifled through a tiny hill of what would perhaps add up to ten skeletons. Through the remains, he searched for all the parts that would belong to the people's feet, so they could build upward like before. It would be trial and error to discover whose pieces would fuse together.

As they assembled the skeletal parts of each person, Anton wondered if his parents were somewhere in the Bone Valley. He'd been angered by them both for so long, but he didn't think they should end up this way. They weren't terrible people—his mother couldn't handle life anymore, and his father chose thieving when he couldn't provide for four kids by himself.

He watched Nahli as she shifted her jaw to the side and clenched it, not willing to give up. Something struck him right then, as he studied her. Perhaps they could have been friends before all this had happened. If the circumstances had presented one more run-in with each other, then they could have had a discussion. If only…

Day in and day out, Anton and Nahli slept and breathed building skeletons together. He'd been tired at times. She'd been the same. But they continued on because that was all they'd had, to wake and construct bones. Sometimes she was quiet, but mostly she wasn't. He had to admit that he didn't mind the words spilling out from her, and he found himself wanting to learn more about her.

Anton's thoughts were interrupted by Roka's shouting. "Anton! Nahli!" He scampered toward them on all fours, propping back on his hind legs. "I must show you something."

Nahli finished placing a clavicle bone on the skeletal frame that she was working on. Then her hands fell to her own pelvic bone. "What do you need to show us?"

Roka waved them on as he jutted forward, not waiting for them to follow. Anton started behind Nahli and caught up to Roka as he led them to the garden, where there were holes dug everywhere throughout the dirt.

"Is this what you wanted to show us?" Anton asked, incredulous, folding his arms over his chest. "A bunch of holes you've dug?"

Roka gestured repeatedly toward the gaping opening in front of him. Anton pushed forward to glance inside, his flames locking on a crystallized flower hidden in the dirt's depths. Vibrant. Sparkly. *Blue*, the color of sapphires. Startled, he swiftly yanked it out from the shallow hole as if it would vanish. And that was precisely what happened as the flower withered in his hand, losing its color and changing into alabaster bone.

Nahli's teeth parted as she stepped to another hole, peering inside. He moved behind her and followed her gaze. She shot him a glance over her shoulder, and Anton realized his hands were cradling her upper arms, so he hastily dropped them.

Inside the open space, covered in dirt granules, lay a blood-red rose with glistening ivy-colored leaves, resembling the sheen of glass. Nahli pressed her hand into the pocket and withdrew the flower. As before, when it hit the light fog, the flower turned to pale bone.

"This must have been what the flowers looked like before," she said, stepping to another spot.

"Good job, Roka," Anton muttered, tightening his jaw. "What did this prove, exactly? That we can pull up colored flowers, only to let them die?"

Instead of seeing this as a miracle, all it did was make Anton feel worse about himself and this place. He wished he could do more, for Nahli, for Roka, for these nameless people who were no more.

Roka didn't seem the least bit bothered by Anton's reaction. "It proves that perhaps, somehow, life can be restored. If these exist underground, color has not dissipated entirely."

"What do you suggest, then?" Anton asked, pointing to the skeletons they'd built and then toward the dirt. "To bury everyone underground? The rest of their bodies are still in Maryska's lake."

"No, but eventually it may be possible we can find a way," Nahli piped in. "Let me try something." She placed the bone flower back inside its grave and waited. No change. "We'll still find a way."

Anton pinched the edges of his eye sockets where his nose had been, then looked up at Roka. "The only way I see us accomplishing anything would be to go out the door of the tree, but it's locked."

"Have you even attempted to open it?" Roka asked, his tone sounding like he didn't believe Anton.

"I tried it the first day I was here, and so did Nahli."

"And I've tried every morning," Nahli said, inching closer to Anton like *she* was protecting his story.

Roka lifted his hands to his head, appearing more human than animal. It was an outlandish sight.

"There isn't a keyhole either"—Nahli stared off into the direction of the gnarled tree—"so it's strange that it would be locked."

"No stranger than anything else here." Anton exhaled. "It's obviously Maryska's magic holding the door. She said she'd come back for me, eventually."

He wasn't sure what he would do when she did make an appearance, or if she never did at all. Perhaps she'd forgotten about him and had found a new lover for herself. It wouldn't be that difficult. But something nudged at him, and he knew she wouldn't fail to remember him. She was a woman who went for what she wanted, and if it wasn't possible, she managed to get it anyway.

And if Maryska did take him out of there, what would happen to Nahli? Would she leave her there? His skeletal frame stiffened at the thought, and he hurried to face Nahli.

"If Maryska comes through that door, I want you to hide. You'll know it's her by the protruding antlers." Anton tapped his forehead and attempted to create a visual for how long they were.

Nahli tilted her head and clasped her hands in front of her. "All right, but I'll remain close and have your back."

His flames drifted to the crack on her arm. They'd been out there building and building skeletons who didn't come back to life. What kind of life was this for her? She needed something better. He *needed* to do something better.

"You said you've never been to one of the market dances, correct?"

Nahli's flames lifted to the sky. "Well, not to dance. Only to steal things and leave. It's easier to take items from someone when they've had too much to drink. Some are even willing to hand things right over."

Unable to stop himself, he let out a rumble of laughter. It

wasn't funny, yet somehow it was.

"Is that a real laugh, Anton? Did I just make you laugh?" Something akin to a smile formed in her words.

Since he was unable to see her facial expression, it was much easier knowing how she felt through words and movements. But still, oh, how at that moment he wished for those dimples of hers to appear with a real smile.

Anton wasn't sure why, but he planned to do something nice for her. Perhaps because she, too, was stuck in this endless purgatory with only him and a meerkat who could talk.

"We're going to take a break for now," he murmured. "When the fog grows the thickest, I want you to come search for me. Wear the nicest dress you can find." His gaze trained on her slacks. "Or nicest trousers, I don't care. But just come. Tonight, we are going to dance, and tonight, we are going to remember what it's like to live."

Nahli didn't answer for a long beat, making it seem as though he should have reeled back his suggestion, until she finally did.

"I'll come, but it won't only be for one night, Anton. We will have plenty of other nights to try new things," she said softly.

She was right. For now, they may not be able to leave the Bone Valley, but that was no reason to do nothing. Anton would build with her as many skeletons as she desired, because he wanted to do something for someone else.

And she was the one.

SIXTEEN

DARYNA

Since she had found out about Maryska poisoning Anton, Daryna had been warring with herself. How could she not have sensed her deception? If only there was a way for her to concoct a truth serum to feed anyone who came to her cottage. Perhaps there could be, and she would have to try and brew one.

Daryna's life had already become too much to bear as it was. She didn't know exactly how old she was, although her estimate was somewhere in her twenties. She didn't even know her real damn name.

All she knew was that the only memories she had were over the span of the past eight years. Another spell she should have been able to remedy was a remembering tonic. But she didn't know how to do that, either. Perhaps she wasn't even a true witch.

Because of Boda, Daryna knew where Maryska had lived, but she hadn't wanted to venture into the more populated section of the village just yet. Even though she'd been jittery to go into Verolc to deliver things, it didn't drive her nerves up as much as it did with the thought of seeing people in her own territory. Dealing one on one with a villager who came to her door was enough, and Boda had never been much for conversation.

Outside the window, the sun was settling into its resting place, and most of the vendors and shopkeepers would already be retired for the evening. Tonight would be the perfect time for Daryna to leave.

Uncrossing her good leg from her other knee in front of the table, she leaned over to grab her wooden appendage and strapped it on. She stuffed two candles in her satchel, along with a dagger, and headed out into the night. An owl hooted as she plodded through the woods, twigs snapping, and leaves crunching beneath her feet. She begged for silence, though it didn't come.

Should she have ridden Lilac? It was too late to turn back and draw the horse out of the barn. And Lilac's presence would be too noticeable when she reached Maryska's cottage.

When she arrived at the fork in the road, she followed the dirt path underneath the light of the moon, until she made it near the market. Flaming torches lit the spot, and smoke from cooking meat caressed her nose. It was supposed to have been quiet and dark on her way to Maryska's, not bustling in preparation for a market celebration that would soon be alive and filling the night. She'd never been invited to one, nor would she have gone if she had been.

Drawing up the hood of her cloak, she abandoned the area and hurried to Maryska's before someone caught sight of her.

Row upon row of cottages followed, each one separated by wide gaps. Maryska's was the nicest one of all with fresher paint and a high archway. As Daryna approached the door, a clacking noise sounded above her. She looked up, and underneath the silvery moonlight, bones clinked from a wind chime.

Lips tugged downward, Daryna pressed her fingers to the bones and her body stirred with warmth. Unnatural. Otherworldly. She yanked her hand away, still staring at the skeletal piece while opening the already-unlocked door.

She fished out a candle and stepped into the darkened shadows of Maryska's home. Her heartbeat stayed steady as she closed the door behind her. Placing her index finger and thumb together against the candlewick, she rubbed until a small flame crackled to life. With the flame out in front of her, and no signs of occupancy, she lit several of the candles around the sitting room.

Daryna lifted a silver candelabra from the center of a square table and searched through cabinets in the dining area. It seemed as though Maryska may have abandoned the place in its entirety. Fruit, now rotten, and dried meats had been left behind. Most people would have taken whatever food they could with them, unless she had enough money to start over, which was a possibility.

Nestled in the corner, beside two dusty brooms and next to the stove, was a medium-size black cauldron. She set the candelabra on top of the stove and lifted the rounded metal. Hoisting it to right under her nose, she inhaled the barren space deeply. She blinked, recognizing the scent, an attempt at a love spell—basil, catnip, cinnamon, with a tinge of daisy and dandelion.

Why would Maryska have come to Daryna if she practiced spells on her own? The deceiving little witch was going to do more than die. Daryna threw the cauldron down in the corner, and it struck the wall with a loud bang.

Snatching up the candelabra, she walked with desperate steps into a bedroom. For more light, she lit a few of the wicks around the area and set the candle holder on a nightstand. She sifted through a closet filled with clothing, taking in a familiar scent—oranges mixed with jasmine, and something else...

She pressed the sleeve of a golden dress to her nose and drank in the scent. She couldn't recall the smell, but it was familiar—more than from the day that Maryska had stopped by. Daryna hadn't paid much attention to scents then, but now she could remember a hint of something. Inhaling one more time, she faltered backward, and discovered what she should have known all along. Life and death combined.

"What are you doing?" a male voice asked from directly behind her.

Squaring her shoulders, she spun around and grasped the person by the throat, then slammed him against the wall.

When she caught a good glimpse of the stranger, he was tall and broad like a man but still had the face of a young boy. He had to be no older than sixteen with strawberry blond curls and freckled cheeks.

"What are you doing, boy?" she snarled.

He held up his hands, wincing. "I'm more of a man, in truth." With her free hand, she took no time grabbing the dagger and placing it at his stomach as he prattled on, "A lover as well, not a fighter, except if you give me a sword, but I wouldn't fight you, of course. Unless you wanted to practice, that is. I only came here to search through Maryska's things."

Not taking her eyes off him, Daryna lowered the dagger and released her hand from the boy's throat. "Try anything funny, and I'll remove an eye and four fingers." She thrust the blade to the side to show her words rang true.

Breathing heavily, he dropped his hands to his sides, not appearing as shaken as she would have liked.

"Now tell me," Daryna continued, "why did you want to search through Maryska's belongings?"

"Because Maryska murdered my brother," the boy spat.

Her hands quivered, the room closing around her. Backing up to the edge of the bed, she plopped down. "Anton's brother?"

"Yes, Pavla. But mostly, Pav. Unless people are angry, so it may be Pavla at this moment."

Was Artem coming back from the grave to haunt her with his children because she hadn't given him more coin from his stolen goods?

134

Her eyes met his. "I remember your father."

"I know you do, *Daryna*." The edges of his lips quirked up.

"How do you know who I am?" she snapped, dagger back at his stomach.

"Everyone has heard tales of your beauty and your magical existence," he rambled an obvious lie, still smiling, even with the tip of the dagger right under his ribs. "I was going to come visit you next."

Why would he want to come and see her? There could only be one reason. "I'm not going to give you coin for any of the goods you steal from here."

"That's not why. May I speak to you without your blade digging into my flesh? Battle wounds should be saved for … battle."

She loosened the blade a fraction. "Go on, then."

"I was hoping you could help me locate her. And it just so happens that fate brought us together on this night."

"Because you believe me to be a witch?"

"There are better words for it. Don't you think?"

"No, I think witch will do just fine." She removed the dagger from his stomach.

"You're the key to helping me find Maryksa."

"I know she's responsible for killing your brother." She didn't mean for it to come out harshly, only stating the truth. "There's nothing I can do for you."

But there was. The otherworldly odor. She knew how to find Maryska. Daryna spun on her heel to walk away and go home to make a concoction for herself.

"Wait!" he pleaded. "You're the one who sold the poison in the tea to Maryska, aren't you?"

She stopped in her tracks and turned back to face him. "How do you know that?" There wasn't time to waste denying it, when she had things she needed to prepare for.

"It had a scent I couldn't detect," he said.

135

"Maryska *lied* to me"—Daryna lowered her voice—"told me a story of an ex-lover."

"I'm not understanding why she had to use you for poison." Pav rubbed his chin. "I believe it wasn't intentional on your part, and I would like your help to get to where Anton is, so I can question him first before locating her."

Shoulders tensing, she asked, "You want me to *murder* you?"

"No, I want you to perform something temporary. If you can."

She took in a deep breath and smelled the citrusy scent of the room—Maryska. Not only her, but somewhere farther away—Torlarah. But how did she know that? It was as though a primal instinct had flung itself forward, familiar, yet she still couldn't recall why.

Daryna stared at Pav's soft features. This wasn't only her vengeance—it was his, too.

"On two conditions," she demanded, keeping quiet on where Maryska was from, for now. "You work for me as long as I require it, and I come with you."

"Easy enough," he replied.

Underneath his smile, a misery lay hidden that he was trying to hold back. And how gullible he was because he didn't even ask any questions about what he would have to do. She wouldn't make him do anything too difficult, mostly errand runs to Verolc, but he still should have thought to inquire. He must really love his brother. The thought of loving someone that fiercely could only be considered a weakness.

"You have access to herbs?" she asked.

"I do. My sister runs a booth at the market, and her fiancée has a large plantation."

Daryna shoved the dagger back into the side of her satchel, figuring he wouldn't try anything funny, but she had good reflexes if she needed it again. "I'm going to require you to bring me sage, thyme, and two eyeballs of a goat. One eye for you and one for me."

Pav's brows shot up, his hand shifting to scratch the back of his head. "Goat eyes?"

"Yes, two of them. I have the other essentials we'll need."

His nose wrinkled in repulsion, and the edges of his lips tilted downward.

"If you can't handle it, you don't have to do it. Yet if you want to cross over, this is your only option." She wasn't even fully confident if she could perform the task, as she'd never tried it before. But she would find out if her spell book was right.

"I'll do it."

"Tomorrow afternoon, then." Swishing past him, she stopped and turned to him one more time. "And do *not* tell anyone of this. Blow the candles out before you leave, otherwise, the cottage might burn down." She wouldn't mind it turning to ashes if Maryska were still here, but it would be a loss now that she was gone.

As Daryna passed the market, she came to an abrupt halt when the music of banjos, flutes, and tambourines playing drifted through the air. Laughter sounded, and the scent of pastries mixed with the meat from earlier caressed her nose.

A part of her yearned to join the celebration, but she loathed the idea of being around such a crowd. The thought of holding a conversation with multiple villagers twisted her stomach into endless knots. Before she'd awoken with her leg hacked off, Daryna didn't know if she'd ever danced.

The tambourines grew louder, and she wanted to follow that sound. *Just go and take a look*, she told herself. *It can't be that bad.*

From what Boda had said, most people believed her to be an elderly woman covered in wrinkles with a long, pointed nose. Apparently, one had to be an old hag to be a witch.

She drew up the hood of her cloak and walked away, but then spun back around and strolled into the market. As she passed a gangly boy around the age of ten, he held out a steaming turkey leg for her to take. Hastily, she flicked her stare from his and moved on.

People of all ages stood in the center of the market dancing, touching hands as they passed from one partner to the next. Daryna pushed her hands inside her cloak at the horrendous thought of touching so many sweaty fingertips, her own palms beading with perspiration. Dragging them back out of her cloak, she rubbed her hands against the velvety fabric.

She focused her attention on three girls with tambourines, and a part of her yearned to cradle the instrument in between one hand and tap it with the other. But then the noises of the market all clashed together, tearing her gaze away from the girls.

Clapping, stringed instruments, flutes, laughing, talking. Her eyes darted around the market to each sound, her head filling with dizziness.

An elbow nudged her in the side, and she yelped while jumping back, her hip striking the edge of an empty table.

"I thought you were going home." Pav's voice hit Daryna's ears, yanking her out of her uneasiness.

She scowled at him. "Did you follow me here, Pavla?"

"Sort of. I was passing through here anyway, since I have a girl to meet." He waggled his brows.

Frolicking. She should have known.

He held out a cup of ale toward her as he drank from his own. "I think you might need this."

Narrowing her eyes on him, she ripped the cup from his hand and took a long swig. She did need it.

He held up his cup. "So how about a *thank you, Pav*, for bringing me this benevolent drink?"

"That would be too polite of a response," she answered in a terse manner.

Pav set down his ale on the edge of a booth counter and held out his hand. "Dance?"

"I only do sacrificial dances."

He chuckled. "With goat eyes?"

"And chicken heads," she said dryly.

"I better hide my younger sister's chicken, then."

She didn't reply, only stared out at the crowd. He reached out a hand in front of her face again.

"Look," she said, "I'm not going out there. You're also a little young for me to dance with."

He kept his hand out for her to take. "I dance with my sister. You can be like my older sister for the duration of a dance."

For a short moment, Daryna was tempted, but she didn't think her dancing would be on par with the others. She may be able to walk well with a wooden leg, but dancing involved quicker shifting.

"Perhaps another time." She glanced up to see a curvy girl with sections of her red hair curled, a halo of flowers encircling her head, staring at Pav. "There's a girl over there who seems to be waiting for you."

Pav lifted his chin to look in her direction. "Ah, yes, there's my little red flower."

"Go dance and live the night away, because tomorrow you'll be leaving Kedaf." It didn't come out as daunting as she would have liked.

"I'll save you a dance when we return, then." Pav nodded, walking backward with a broad smile before turning around and sauntering toward the redheaded girl. When he took a flower from her halo and placed it in his own hair, the girl giggled.

Young love, Daryna thought. A waste of time, as was love in itself.

She shuffled through the crowd, until she ran into a man a little older than herself. He held out his palm.

"Care to dance, my lady?"

Heart pounding in her chest, she stared from the man's

hand to his mossy-green eyes, and back at his hand. She ran away from it like it would bite her in the neck. How could she not be afraid to stab someone in the chest like Boda, but the thought of holding someone's hand frightened the life out of her?

She wanted to stay hidden in the dark, away from everyone. Leaving the other candle in her pocket unlit, Daryna hurried back home to her sanctuary.

Breaths ragged, she stumbled into her cottage and calmed herself. She then gathered the supplies she needed for the next day, removed her wooden leg, and sat in front of a fire—alone—just the way she liked.

As the fluid sound of tambourines came to her once more, a nagging thought slipped into her mind. Perhaps living with loneliness was no longer a blessing.

SEVENTEEN

NAHLI

Nahli finished perusing the closet and hesitantly moved to stare at herself. An oval mirror hung on the wall, reflecting her anxious skeleton. Why was she feeling nervous? It was only Anton, but the idea of dancing with him, touching him, felt extremely intimate.

Unless he didn't mean slow dancing. He could mean the kind that involves laughing and clapping, while being happily inebriated. Except she wouldn't be tipsy, and there would be no one around to clap, unless he meant for Roka to do the clapping for them. She shook her head at her mirror image, urging herself to stop overthinking everything.

Her skeletal reflection didn't frighten her, yet she missed the rest of herself. But the thought of Anton possibly looking at her as if she were something more than bones tickled straight to her marrow. If only there was color in the Bone Valley, then she could try and highlight her cheekbones with rouge to take away from him staring at her teeth. The chipped tooth of her lower canine stood out now, more prominent than ever.

Enough with the mirror. Prying herself away, she turned to face the clothing lying on top of the mattress. One was similar to the dress she'd worn when she had first woken in the Bone Valley. The other was the pair of trousers she'd had on earlier.

Nahli decided to go bold. When she was with Zikri, there had been no friendly dances. Even growing up together as close friends, it was always composed of her following him everywhere and doing what he wanted to do. Whether it was watching his swordplay, drinking with his friends, or running his bow across his fiddle. Never did he ask her to practice swords with him when his friends were around or to drink some of his wine, nor had he taught her to create music on the fiddle. The realization had struck her after he left that she should have known how selfish he'd always been.

Anton hadn't told her what to wear tonight—as Zikri would have—he'd left it up to her. And tonight, she wanted the dress. Nahli peered down at the white silk, embroidered with black roses along the bottom. Taking the smooth material in her arms, she slid it over her head. The sleeves fell right below her elbows, dark lace peeking out along the edges. Black thorns with vines were stitched across the waist, and the neckline displayed part of her upper rib cage.

As tedious as it was, she managed to clasp the buttons lining the back and tie the sash at the sides into a bow behind her.

Nahli peered down at her toes and wiggled them in delight before pulling the strap from her hair to loosen it. She hadn't worn her hair down in so long, usually only when bathing. The white hair was strikingly different compared to her naturally dark strands, but the texture felt the same—straight and thick, though slight waves remained from the braid.

She secured a black ribbon with a silver pendant tightly at her neck and gazed into the mirror one last time. Feeling as satisfied as she could, she went into the other room where she found Roka lounged in a rocking chair, knitting.

His two skeletal hands were tiny in comparison to the large

needles, but he worked the dull yarn fluidly.

"You know how to knit?" she asked, surprised.

"Apparently so," he said, holding up a needle. "This scarf was already started, and I examined the material to see how it was done. It is quite relaxing, if you want to try."

"Perhaps later, though I'm much better with a needle and thread." When she lived with her parents, there was a lot of sewing to do around the house. Mainly Nahli's or her mother's clothing would get ripped during swordplay, and she would have to mend them.

Before leaving, she gave Roka another glance. He was still rocking in the chair. "Are you coming?"

He shooed her away. "Possibly later. I think Anton meant for you two lovers to be alone tonight. No meerkats allowed."

"Don't say that!" she exclaimed. There was no "L" word between them. Nahli had started to enjoy his company—that was all.

"One male skeleton and one female skeleton. Your options are not aplenty here in the Bone Valley," Roka teased, waving a needle in her direction.

She ignored him and strolled out into the dense fog.

Its thickness enveloped her until she thought she could feel the precipitation entwined around her bones. With how much the fog had draped down upon the Bone Valley, the distance was difficult to see.

Flipping her palm up in front of her, she whispered, "Light."

The bright white orb appeared in the middle of her hand, and Nahli let it guide her way. As the light bathed her surroundings, it cast everything in a beautifully eerie glow while she stepped along the stone toward the garden.

That was the first place she guessed Anton would be. It was the spot where they'd spent most of their time together, besides for the day in the lake after escaping the beasts.

The only sounds surrounding her were the usual clanking

of bones falling from the sky. She was growing used to it, and sometimes she didn't even notice or hear them anymore. Up ahead, a bright light, that matched the one in her hand, caused what felt like a heart to speed up in her chest, even though she no longer had one. She thought, perhaps, the shadow of a heart could have been left behind.

Nahli took a measured step into the garden, spotting the exposed holes from where Roka had dug. Roka had decided to leave them open in case Nahli or Anton wanted to latch onto a glimpse of the color that was almost forgotten, a reminder not to lose hope.

She wanted to believe in that word, and she chose to do just that.

A silhouette of Anton arose, his hair neatly tied back. He wore a dark jacket, with a coattail in the back, over an ash-colored vest. Gray trousers covered his long legs and stopped just above his bare feet. Handsome. That was how she chose to describe him. She wouldn't say he looked better than before, because whatever he wore suited him, but the clothing made him seem like a different version of himself.

Displaying his orb in front of him, he tossed it into the air, like a trick, so it floated above the two of them.

The brightness of it shone above them as the blackness inside glittered. Nahli glanced down at her orb, before laughing and tossing it in the air beside his.

The orbs seemed to watch each other as the darkness inside shifted to the edges. They then circled each other, round and around, in a slow spinning waltz.

"Are you doing that?" Nahli asked in awe, teeth parted.

"No." Anton's flames dropped from the spectacle to meet hers. He stared at her for a long moment before mumbling, "You look—you look lovely."

"Are you sure?" She smiled. "You sounded unsure."

He nodded and reached a hand toward a lock of her hair. Then he seemed to think better of it as he squeezed the air, slowly pulling his fingers away. "You don't have your hair in a braid."

"Thought I'd try something different."

"Both styles suit you," he said.

The flutters in her chest appeared again, the butterfly wings expanding in size. Slightly on edge, Nahli combed her nervous fingers through her hair and studied the rock path under her feet. "Do you prefer it black, though?"

"I like it either way."

Remembering to be bold for the night, Nahli reached out and stroked the collar of his jacket. "I think you look dazzling yourself."

His jaw fell slightly open, in what she knew would be a wolfish smile if he had his lips to form around his teeth. It should have been haunting, grotesque, and bizarre standing in a dead garden in front of this skeletal man, but it wasn't. It felt positively splendid.

"Shall we?" Anton asked, stretching his hand out to her.

Angling her flames up to the orbs before making contact once more, Nahli placed her hand in his. There was no perspiration, and if this had taken place in Kedaf, her palm would have been clammy as soon as their fingertips brushed.

His touch released tingles in her digits that spread up to her skull, all the way down to her toes. Her flames couldn't quite meet his. Anton drew her in, and she placed her arms around his neck, still avoiding gazing into his blazing eye sockets.

When he placed his hands on her lower spine, she held back a shiver. They moved in sync with a steady step forward, sidestep, backward, sidestep, forward—over and over and over, until she took initiative and spun him around.

He chuckled out of surprise, seeming not to have expected that from her. But then he twisted her around three times before lifting her feet from the ground. A small squeak escaped her teeth, her flames finally meeting his, and holding, until he lowered her.

145

Above them, the dancing orbs highlighted Anton and Nahli in the fog, and something made her want to reach up to stroke his strong jaw. But she didn't. What was it about this night that was different than the other times she'd spent with him? Was she moving too fast? Either way, she didn't care.

They danced, and they danced, not once tiring.

Nahli and Anton fell back to a steady pace, and she felt this was the right moment to tell him about her past. Because she wanted to, not because she had to.

She studied his chiseled features as she spoke, "I came to Kedaf because my parents wanted to marry me off and send me away for a profit."

His rhythmic movements stalled, and his lightness faded. "And that's why you started thieving, because you had to run away?"

The next part was harder for her to admit, because she'd been a thief from the beginning. "I had a childhood friend named Zikri, and he wanted to take me away, save me from my family. More than anything, I wanted to save myself.

"I stole from my parents to get us away. Not a little, but a lot of coin." She hurried on, "But I was going to pay them back. I just needed us to get away first, and we would each find work, and send back as much as we could at a time."

Their dancing had stopped, but Anton still held her hand in his. For some reason, it made Nahli feel braver, rather than wanting to run away. If this had happened in Kedaf, she didn't know if she could have revealed the rest to him. She wasn't used to this vulnerability.

"When we came to Kedaf, we were starting to figure things out. He confessed his love, and I felt that I loved him, too." She stared at Anton's face, forcing herself to not look away from him. "So, I—I gave myself to him. The next day, he took with him everything I had and fled, leaving only me behind."

"You had absolutely nothing, then?" Anton whispered, no judgment in his voice.

She took her hand away from his. "It was my fault, though. None of this would have happened if I hadn't left Huadu."

"And then what? You would have been sold off." Anger etched through his voice, but not at Nahli, as he stepped closer toward her. "It's almost as unfortunate as me having to do what I did, except you wouldn't have been getting paid for it—your parents would have."

"I tried, Anton. I was serious when I told you before that I looked for work everywhere I could." If she had tears, they would be falling down her cheekbones. "I'm sorry I tried to steal from your family that day. I only wanted to get home to pay mine back. But if I had returned, I would have still been forced to marry. And I mean beaten, bound, gagged and sold off, so I started to think about going somewhere else."

"I wish you'd told me this that day in the market, then I wouldn't have stolen your satchel."

"Then I wouldn't have taken your clothing, but I still would have had the chicken and bread with me."

He chuckled, rubbing his bony thumb against her forearm.

"It resulted in pocketing jewelry that wasn't worth anything," Nahli said. "Daryna was so frustrated. She said some pretty nasty things, and so I ran out of her house with the chicken and the bread. I probably shouldn't have done that."

"She could have cast a spell on you, correct?"

She gave him a soft shove. "Come on, Anton, you know that's all gossip. I've worked with her on many occasions."

"Then why would she need herbs?" he asked, tilting his skull to the side.

"She does tinker in healing remedies, I believe." As to whether or not those worked, she couldn't have said.

The sound of hands clapping echoed through the fog behind her. Nahli whirled around and Anton brought her closer to him, only to find Roka making the noise.

"I thought you two were going to dance." Roka ended his clapping charade as he hopped on all fours toward them. "It looks like there is only talking occurring out here."

Annoyance radiated through Anton's posture, but Nahli knelt to let Roka scurry up to her shoulder. "Did you tire from knitting already?" she asked with a laugh.

"Yes, I did. Anton, you now have a new scarf." He pointed a finger toward Anton.

Rolling his flames, Anton clapped his hands with cadence. Nahli felt shy at first, but she began to slowly spin while Roka held onto her neck and shoulder.

After five spins, the meerkat said, "Enough. I must get down—my head feels nauseated."

She came to a sudden halt, and Roka scurried down her spine, hopping to the ground.

"Do you want to dance again or sit for a moment?" Anton asked.

Nahli wasn't feeling tired at all, and she was having the most fun she'd ever had in her life.

"Dance for a little longer," she murmured, extending her hand out to his.

With an open-jaw smile, Anton threaded his fingers with hers. He pulled her close, his hand resting on the lower edge of her spine, and she pressed the side of her skull against his shoulder. They swayed side to side, her thumb rubbing the vertebrae of his neck. A low sound escaped through his teeth, and she shifted forward as close as she could get.

A speedy clap came from behind her, and she turned her head to Roka. "No fast dancing right now." She grinned, then her jaw shut tight when she discovered that it wasn't Roka clapping, but a woman.

Nahli stared at her harder. No, not a woman, but someone otherworldly—beautiful and deadly. Two long deer antlers protruded at the female's forehead, dark curled hair tumbled down her waist, and she wore a sheer black dress, revealing everything underneath. Obsidian eyes stuck out against her silvery skin, boring into her.

Maryska.

Gripping Nahli's hand tighter, Anton hauled her behind him and shielded her. His skeletal frame shook with fury and Nahli peeked around him at the intruder.

Maryska's clapping ended abruptly, and she inched nearer. Anton stepped backward, causing Nahli to do the same.

"How sweet," Maryska purred. "My king has built himself a queen, one you can't hide. Too bad bones can easily become broken."

An intense, fiery pain ran across Nahli's thigh bone, followed by a loud, deafening snap. She would never forget what it sounded and felt like, as her body slumped to the ground. Anton tried to catch her but came a moment too late. Nahli's hand hit a rock beside the garden, saving her skull from cracking against it. She motioned him away, letting him know she was all right.

"What do you want?" Anton gritted his teeth, making himself a barrier between Nahli and Maryska.

With how badly her femur throbbed, she wanted to scream. But instead, she held it in, not wanting to show any weakness to this cruel creature.

Maryska tapped her cheek with a dark, pointed fingernail. "Since you seem to have taken a liking to the skeletal female, try piecing her back together again." She slammed her hands against one another, clasping them tightly before her.

A heavy ache enveloped Nahli before she fell away into a cloaking darkness.

She couldn't feel any part of herself, unable to move her arms, legs, or even the flames that were in her eye sockets. Were the flames even there anymore? Before her, there was nothing except for emptiness.

Nahli tried to scream, prayed to her gods to listen to her, and let her at least make this one sound. But she knew they wouldn't hear her, because they didn't really exist in the afterlife. Only this creature with antlers did.

149

She wished she could have at least curled to her side, holding herself, but she couldn't even do that.

Thoughts swam through her head. Her parents were there. Mother, with her hair shaved to the scalp and her disappointed face. Father, with his belt in hand, and his head cocked.

A rope was in one of her mother's grips and chains in the other. "How could you steal from us?" she asked, edging closer.

"All you had to do was get yourself wed, then we all could have lived happily," Father said, slapping the belt against his palm.

I'm sorry, she tried to say, but no sound emerged.

The image shook from her head, and Zikri was there, kneeling before her, cheeks flustered. "You knew how this would always end. Sweet, innocent, and gullible Nahli. Did you think I really cared for you?"

Yes, she wanted to whisper.

"You did, didn't you? You should have seen how many other girls I'd tumbled with. In the moment, I feel like I'm in love, but then after I seize what I want, it's not going to keep me around." He dangled the bag with all her parents' coin before her. "This will help me on my journey, and maybe I'll find someone I truly want."

Daryna came before her next. "All I asked was for you to do simple tasks. Was it that difficult to bring me what I requested?" She lifted her hand to slap Nahli across the face. "Boda will have to do the rest of the jobs for me."

Muscular Boda appeared behind Daryna's back and ran for Nahli with the same dagger that had brought her to this wretched place.

Anton now stood with his siblings, Tasha holding onto the hen Nahli had stolen from Daryna. "You think giving a chicken that you stole from someone else makes up for anything you've done?" He lazily walked toward her and spat, "You are nothing but a filthy thief, a lowly life not worth living. And that's why you're dead. Dead—dead—*dead!*"

Villagers with faces she recognized, and others she couldn't see clearly, came one by one to her.

"I could have used the money to purchase medicine for my sick child."

"The engagement ring was for my love."

"My family didn't have food on the table that night."

On repeat, images and accusations played in her head. Nahli wanted to yell at them all to stop, and shut her eyes to avoid seeing those things anymore. She yearned more than anything to go back in time, to before Anton had built her, when she remembered nothing—*was* nothing.

EIGHTEEN

PAV

Pav stood holding a sword beneath the blazing sun. Two wide eyes stared up at him. Perhaps they weren't wide, but they were studying him with some hint of emotion.

"Listen, it will all be over quickly if you turn around and gaze at the trees," he whispered, making a circular motion with his sword behind Ionna's home.

Retrieve two goat eyes, Daryna had said. Oh, how easy *that* would be. Daryna didn't have to help him search in another realm for his dead brother, but she'd chosen to. Pav had killed plenty of animals for meat but not a goat, and it wouldn't stop *watching* him.

"What are you doing?" Ionna asked from close behind.

He jumped at her voice and twisted his head over his shoulder to see her tight curls bouncing as she came up beside him.

"I'm starting a meal today," he said. "I thought a goat stew would be a spectacular meal." It would be, too, if this goat would just turn around.

"Tired of pig already?" She laughed.

Pig was delicious. If this had been a pig, he would have had an easier time preparing one.

"No, I wanted to try something different, and I thought it would be a nice gesture to get this goat ready." He grinned on the outside, but inside he felt he might lose everything in his stomach. How could he hope to become a soldier, if he couldn't even handle killing one goat?

Ionna's copper skin glowed under the sun as she took the sword from his hand. With one swift motion, the goat's head plopped on the ground, spilling crimson.

"Next time, don't think about it, Pav. If you over analyze the situation, we would never eat." Producing a yellow cloth from the pocket of her trousers, she wiped the red specks from the blade and handed the weapon back to Pav.

Wonder filled Pav at how fluid her movements had been. "I didn't know you were good with a sword, too."

"I'm good with *all* weapons."

"Perhaps you can spar with me sometime. Anton isn't … wasn't that good at it."

In their younger years, it was entertaining when he and his brother would clack their wooden swords together. Even though Anton was older than Pav, he hadn't ever outlasted his younger brother. Their father had made them swords from his spare wood and had shown them the basics. Only Pav was a natural at it.

Ionna patted his shoulder. "It may be hard to talk to Yeva and Tasha about Anton since they loved him as much as you. But if you ever need someone to confide in, I'm here. You're about to be my brother too."

She was kind yet had a protective side to her. He was grateful Yeva had found someone like her.

"You want to help me skin the goat?" Pav asked.

Blinking, Ionna stared at the animal. "You know, it would have been better if I had stabbed it, skinned it, then removed the head. But this will work, too."

Pav casually picked up the head to hide, searching for a place to cut out its eyes in private. As he started to the side of the house, Ionna called out to him, "Where are you going?"

Letting out a deep breath, he whirled to face her while holding the goat head. "I'm going to bury this later. Some religions say it helps the animals cross over to the other side with ease."

"What religion is that?" Her dark brows slid up her forehead.

The only thing he could think to say was the first thought that came to him. "Something my father used to tell me. I can't recall the religion, though."

"All … right."

He didn't know if she believed him or not, but she dropped the subject.

Setting the head beside the house, he hurried back to Ionna who had already grabbed a smaller knife to cut into the goat.

After they finished and went inside with the meat, Pav found Tasha on her stomach reading a book by the fire in the sitting room, Juju cozy beside her. *I suppose Juju doesn't have to be snuck in anymore.*

"Do you want to help make goat stew?" Pav asked his younger sister.

"Yes. But Juju is coming." Closing her book, she made clucking sounds to get the chicken to follow her.

They headed into the kitchen and he grabbed a glass jar and a knife from the drawer. "Can you start on the carrots and potatoes? I'll meet you back in here in a little while."

She nodded and reached for a carrot as Juju pecked at scraps on the floor. Pav hurried out the backdoor, not spotting Yeva yet. His sister must have been collecting herbs out in the field still.

Pav picked up the goat head, squinting his eyes as he widened the animal's lids. Sliding in the knife with a squishy crunch, he detached one eyeball and placed it in the open jar. He then worked on the other one, sealing the jar shut after plopping the second eye inside.

He strode out by the trees and buried the head before returning to meet Tasha. His stomach dropped, knowing he wouldn't be able to tell her a story tonight.

Not wanting to vanish into thin air and have his sisters worry too much, Pav picked up the quill and wrote a note to Yeva, then one to Tasha.

Pav let Tasha know he was going on an adventure and would tell her as many stories as she would like when he returned. And to Yeva, he let her know he was going to find Maryska and avenge Anton. He didn't mention he was going to look for Anton first because she would think him mad. Quietly, he placed the letters on the pillows of their beds.

When he came out of Yeva's room, he found Tasha still reading her book.

"Your eyes are going to turn into words, you know that?" he said, trying to sound serious.

"That's impossible."

"I'm going out." He held his arms open for him to wrap around her. "Can I have a hug?"

She stood from the floor and threw her thin arms around his waist. "See you tonight."

"I love you, baby bean." That was the only response he could give her for now.

Before walking out the front door, Pav stuffed the herbs and the jar with the goat eyes into his satchel.

Outside, Yeva and Ionna were sifting through different herbs and binding them with cords. His heart thumped with regret since he wouldn't be able to help his sister at the market tomorrow, but this was important to him.

"I'll be back later," Pav said. "The stew is already cooking."

"Did you get that goat head buried?" Ionna gave him a half smile.

That was one thing he didn't have to lie about. "I did."

Yeva glanced up, crinkling her nose while winding a cord around the lavender. "Why would you bury a goat head?"

"Papa told me once about a religion that buried the heads of animals to help them cross over to the other side."

She pulled her wheat-colored braid over her shoulder. "He never told me that story."

"Perhaps because you never asked about animal heads?" Pav shrugged.

Yeva stared at him like she could read straight through his fabrications. She probably knew he was lying, but she didn't say anything.

With a final goodbye, he crossed through the tall grass until he hit the dirt path. He wished he could have seen Polina before he left, but he'd already run into her the previous night at the market and had told her it would be a few days until he would see her again. Hopefully, he lived up to his promise.

The night before invaded his thoughts. The dancing and the kissing, mainly the kissing, put a smile on his face until he came to the fork in the road. He continued through the woods toward Daryna's cottage.

Pav had never met Daryna in person before the previous night, but he had known what she looked like. Without Papa's knowledge, Pav used to sneak out and follow him into the woods, believing that his father was dallying with the woman who lived there. Until he'd found out Papa was stealing things to sell to her.

Daryna was younger than he'd originally thought, somewhere in her twenties with brown skin and a lovely, crooked nose. He didn't know what to think of her, but he found her interesting.

A speckled chicken clucked when he opened the white-painted gate, leading to Daryna's cottage. The hen then pecked his boot.

He brushed past it and made his way to Daryna's bare porch. She yanked open the door while his fist was in midair, preparing to knock. "I said afternoon."

"It is afternoon." He pointed to the sun.

"I meant later in the afternoon."

"Well, you didn't say that."

"Come on." She huffed and pulled him by his collar inside.

A stench, like rotting mushrooms, overpowered the delicious scent of baking bread, turning Pav's hungry stomach and making the thought of food revolting. The sitting room appeared cozy with a fireplace in the corner, fur rugs, and a satin settee. He couldn't remember if the inside of Daryna's cottage had been the same the time he'd peered in when his father had come to visit. But he did remember the circular kitchen table that was still there. He moved toward the settee to sit down.

"Not there." She pointed toward the table. "Here."

Taking the satchel from across his chest, Pav tugged a chair out and unbuckled his bag. He placed the herbs on the table, along with the clear jar.

Without a word, Daryna took out a sharp knife and cut the sage and thyme into smaller pieces on a cutting board, before dumping them into a large cauldron.

"What did you put in there already?" he asked, his gaze not leaving the dark liquid.

"Ten human fingers, five human teeth, and a human heart." Her hazel eyes fell to his chest.

"Really?" He took a hard swallow.

"No." She stirred the pot without looking back at him.

"So, what *is* really in there?" He stood from his chair and moved closer to get a better look.

She released a heavy breath. "A chicken beak, owl's heart, bird feathers, grass root, dirt, water, my hair"—she plucked a strand from his head and tossed it into the pot—"and your hair."

He rubbed the sore spot on the side of his scalp. "Next time let me know beforehand, and I'll gladly pull out a strand for you."

Ignoring him, Daryna took the jar from the table and unscrewed the lid. She let the eyeballs drop into the cauldron with a small splash. He wrinkled his nose as the eyes floated to the top and swirled around.

"What do we do now?" he asked.

"We wait for it to finish."

"Do you want me to come back later?"

"No, sit down," she demanded.

He took a seat and tapped his fingers on the table while watching as Daryna grabbed a tea kettle to pour in water. She placed it on the stove to heat, then pulled out a large loaf of bread that had finished baking. His stomach awakened again at the yeasty scent.

Daryna cut the sweet bread in two and placed half in front of him, along with several slices of dried meat.

"Thank you," he said, tearing off a large piece of bread and savoring the taste.

"I can't let you go to the afterlife hungry. I'm not sure how much food they have over there." The edges of her lips twitched as if she was trying to fight a smile.

Daryna stood by the cauldron, chewing her bread while stirring the liquid.

"What made you come here?" he asked.

"Hmm?"

"You didn't always live in Kedaf, so why did you come here?"

Frowning, she stopped stirring and met his gaze. "I don't know. My former life doesn't matter."

"Ah, so you wanted to build a new life somewhere else. I can understand that."

"Yes, something like that." A line between her brows

remained, as if she was thinking deeply about something.

"But a secluded cottage in the woods seems more like hiding than building a new life, doesn't it?"

"Not if I like it," she spat.

Pav avoided her sharp stare and started on the dried meat.

Daryna poured the tea into two cups and slammed his on the table. "*Tea?*" she snapped.

He tried to hide a smile and keep a serious expression as he drank the tea. It burned his tongue, and he let out a curse.

"You should have let it cool first before drinking it." She finally smiled as she blew into her cup.

After finishing her drink, Daryna studied the liquid in the cauldron for what had to be the hundredth time. With the ladle, she lifted the concoction and poured it back in after inhaling. "It's ready."

Pav rubbed his hands together in anticipation. He should have been nervous about what was to come, but his focus and determination held strong.

She poured the liquid into two new cups, giving him one. "We have two days to find Anton."

"Only two?"

"Yes. Now, let's go to the settee. Otherwise, when your body drifts off, you could fall over and crack something, and then you might never wake again."

Pav followed her into the sitting room and lowered himself beside her. Two swords rested on the table in front of the settee, and she handed him one to attach to his hip, while taking the other.

"By the way, I believe Maryska is from Torlarah, which is the afterlife where we're going. And I'm thinking Anton will be able to lead us straight to her. Cheers," she said, taking a long swig of the tonic.

NINETEEN

ANTON

"Try piecing her back together again." Maryska's words repeated in Anton's head as he stared at the empty spot behind him for several long seconds. Nahli had been there one moment and gone the next.

"I doubt you will ever find her." Maryska's defiant voice pulled Anton away from his trance.

"Where is she?" he growled.

Frantic, he scanned the garden, then toward the trees and hills of the Bone Valley. Everything appeared the same, bones piled high, more bones descending from the sky. Bones, bones, *bones*, and no Nahli.

"She's scattered in pieces across the valley," Maryska mused, her tone scathing.

Anton's gaze drifted up to the floating orbs above him. There weren't two moving around each other any longer. Only one—his—was left, spinning in a lonely circle. Frustration and anger pulsed through him. He held up his hand and let the orb drop into his palm, then seethed, "Flame."

The ball turned to a giant black flame, burning with an intensity that spoke of the way he felt. Without one more thought, he threw the dark fire at Maryska, hoping she would burn to ash.

She blew out a puff of air from her pouty lips, and the flame changed into a cloudy smoke. Anton's shoulders slumped with defeat. If he could do the things she could, he would turn her into bones and scatter them across the land.

Swiping her tongue across her charcoal-colored lips, she sauntered toward him. "My sweetest Anton, have you not learned that it is better to do what I want?"

"I refused you before, and I'll do the same a thousand times over," he ground out. "I will *not* be your king."

"Then stay here and look for your pathetic skeletal *queen*." She paused, rubbing the crown cuff bracelet on her wrist. "And when you decide you've had enough and are ready to be my king, then you will come and search for me. The door will be unlocked this time," she cooed, flicking her hand in the direction of the shriveled, twisted tree.

He would not go out that door to be hers—ever.

As she walked away, swaying her hips, she turned her head to look one more time over her shoulder. "Oh, and by the way, your female is not asleep like she was before. There might be some demons in her head haunting her." Her high-pitched laughter rumbled throughout the Bone Valley.

With that, Maryska vanished into the fog, a loud shutting of a door reminding him of what he must do.

He stood still, frozen, panicked. His skeleton trembled as he spun around, seeing nothing but the bones he and Nahli had put together, now scattered across the ground.

It was only him once more, as though Nahli had never been there. Everything was back to how it had been when Maryska had first thrown him into the Bone Valley. As if Nahli had never built the row of skeletons by herself, and then with him, nor brought Roka to life.

Roka.

"Roka," Anton roared, growing anxious. "Roka!" Maryska must have broken him into scattered remains, too.

"Anton?" Roka asked, protruding from the fog so Anton could see him better.

Relieved, his stiffened shoulders dropped a little at the sight of the bone meerkat. Anton knelt toward him. "What happened to you? Where did you go?"

Roka's head drooped, his chin nearly touching his ribs. "I ran inside like a coward. When the female with antlers came, I ... I felt something. I'm not sure what it was, but I remember her here in the Bone Valley, stripping the flesh away from the humans. Some instinct told me to hide, so I went back to the cottage until I heard you shout my name."

Anton should have been angry with Roka for fleeing, but his decision to run had saved his life, leaving Anton someone to keep him sane while he figured out how to find Nahli. He'd told Nahli to run and hide if Maryska ever came, but they'd both been taken by surprise, unprepared.

"Maryska... She broke Nahli into pieces and scattered her all over the Bone Valley. How am I going to find her?" he whispered, looking out at the thousands upon thousands of bones.

"It seems you have all the time in the world, Anton. You cannot have these negative thoughts." Roka patted Anton's leg. "Search for her, then rebuild her."

Anton let Roka's words sink in. The thought of Nahli not being able to move, and knowing that she couldn't, ate at him even more. He needed to find her as soon as possible.

"All right, I'm going to begin now." Anton didn't care how thick the fog was this time of day—he didn't dare think about anything except uncovering her.

He rushed to the bones before him that he'd built with Nahli, and sifted through them on the ground, confirming that there was no sign of her there. But did he really know? All these bones looked the same now that he could barely focus with his trembling fingers.

A crumbling hill piled with remains lay before him.

"Light," he demanded, holding out his hand for the orb to appear. The lighted orb illuminated all the ivory-colored bones. As he dug in and tossed skeletal parts aside, Anton apologized silently—to whom, he didn't know—but he was desperate. Each time he made a larger hole, bones collapsed, and he'd have to dig again. The search was an endless, impossible quest.

Anton thought about the way he and Nahli had danced together earlier. He remembered the times that she'd infuriated him—both in life, and in death—but he had discovered that she had been worth knowing more about. That she was a person he was lucky to know, no matter that she'd been the only other person alive in this tragic land of bones.

She'd opened up to him with what he hoped and believed to be trust. Learning what a childhood friend had done to her riled him. He would never have done that to anyone, and he would never falsely claim love to someone, either. With his customers, he never once told them that strong word which could lead to so many things. He stayed truthful with them, no matter the price.

Nahli might have been in the wrong for attempting to steal from his sister's booth, but he understood her now. Her parents had been trying to sell her off like an unwanted mare.

While dancing, his mind had shifted to different things, possibly pulling down the sleeve of her dress to study her exposed shoulder. He knew what her skeleton had looked like from when he'd built her, but with her dancing under the lit orbs, and moving and being alive, how he'd yearned for a moment to brush his fingers along her bare shoulder and down to her hip bone.

Anton shook his head from the thoughts because he wouldn't even know what to do with her in that way if he found her. But he would figure it out, with or without skin. He had started to feel something, and he thought that maybe she had too.

With more precision, he examined each bone he came across to make sure they weren't hers. Then he would second guess himself and have to inspect the bones again.

Raking his hands through his hair, he yanked his locks free from the low ponytail. Searching and searching, he continued to come up empty. The one thought he desperately wanted to push away, refused to leave his skull. He might never find Nahli.

TWENTY

MARYSKA

Maryska made her way back to the throne room, livid, her heart bubbling with blistering fury, destroying what little satisfaction pulsed through her veins at knowing she'd destroyed Anton's false Queen of Bones. The girl was nothing, and he could be nothing, too—if she chose such a fate for him. Yet she didn't want to break him down into a pile of bones the way she had the others.

Eventually, Anton would come to her, crawling. After he begged for mercy, she would return his flesh, and he could crawl to her some more, naked.

Peering down at the crown cuff at her wrist, Maryska squeezed the metal as if she were removing a life from it. She should have waited to choose him as her king, until he'd officially agreed to be hers. Then he wouldn't have been able to bring the female to life.

Around her, the dark walls quivered and swayed, accelerating in strength as her anger grew. She took a seat on her throne of bones and massaged speckles of old blood away from its arm.

From the round bone table to her right, she whisked an ornate silver goblet to her mouth. The liquid contained a mixture of blood from different animals. Licking her lips, she found it to be horse, sheep, and squirrel—it calmed her a fraction.

Maryska had gone to the surface on several occasions to find lovers, but none of them were deemed worthy to be her king. Until she'd come across him. Anton with his honesty. Anton with the loathing in his eyes as he gave her pleasure— she relished that feeling.

At first, he felt sorrow for her. She'd told him lies of her last lover, that he'd beaten her. But even those couldn't make him bow down to her. Each time he came to her, Maryska became a little more insulting, and the more he hated her, the more she wanted him.

Puckering her lips, Maryska let out a low whistle. The heavy sound of paws grew near as two beasts entered the room. Perched on one's neck was the head of a horse. The rest was a body of an ape, stripped of skin, its bloody muscles rippling as the beast hobbled toward her. On the other, the head resembled that of a ram and the body of a large dog with saggy, tan skin surrounding it. Two curled horns protruded from its head.

"Callie, Neru, now!" she yelled.

The beast with the head of a horse, Callie, quickened her pace as Neru darted to the right side of Maryska. She stroked Neru's fleshy head and cooed to him how beautiful he was. Callie appeared on the opposite side, and Maryska slammed a hand against the beast's head, scarlet staining her palm.

"Human!" she screamed, disgusted with Callie for dallying like she shouldn't have.

The male human entered the room, too pale and thin, red muscle throbbing beneath his skin. He held his chin high, so he could see Maryska. Out of boredom, she'd rearranged his face and placed his eyes below his jaw, so he would have to work harder than initially. His nose sat on his forehead, his ears at his cheeks, and his mouth in the back of his head.

166

He wobbled as he halted, then dropped to one knee. "Yes, my queen?"

"I cannot hear you." She grinned, baring all her teeth, and staring at the bone collar around his throat.

The human stood and turned around so his mouth now faced her. "Yes, my queen?"

"Why aren't you bowing?" she seethed, more than exasperated.

"Sorry, my queen." The lips moved slowly, his rotting teeth clenching as the male lowered to one knee. He leaned his back toward her at an awkward angle, mouth facing the floor, body trembling as he held the position.

"Now, rise and turn." She should have made him lean back until his mouth kissed the floor. When he whirled to face her, chin lifted and eyes meeting hers, she demanded, "Clean my hand."

The male servant moved at a quick pace to the back of the room, lifting a satin cloth and a pitcher of water, before placing them in front of Neru. The beast curled back his lips and growled.

"There's no need for that, Neru." Maryska petted his head, observing the human with disdain. "Unless I say so." Her smile widened wickedly.

The servant brought the cloth to her hand and wiped away the crimson. With a dry satin one, he absorbed the dampness as he patted her skin several times. Maryska admired the flex of his muscles against his thin skin as he stroked her hand. She could take him to her bed and sew his lips shut so he'd be unable to form a single squeak as she rode him to bliss. But alas, he was not Anton, no matter how quiet he could stay for her to pretend he was.

These heathens outside the Bone Valley deserved their punishment.

"I wish to bathe now," she told the servant, reaching out a gray hand toward him. Exchanging a glance from Callie to

Neru, she motioned them forward. "Bow down to my throne until I return."

The servant helped Maryska rise from her chair of bones and led her down the dimly lit hall. Floating golden orbs guided their way until they reached her Lake of Flesh.

"Retrieve grapes for me and fill my goblet," she commanded, waving him away.

The human nodded and left to fulfill his duty.

Sliding the straps of her sheer dress down from her shoulders, Maryska watched it glide to the stone floor. The Lake of Flesh stood still before her as the shades of liquid skin alternated colors. Slowly, she stepped one foot into the milky texture.

As she trudged through bits of muscle and pieces of organs, the liquid thickened when she moved deeper to its center. She lowered herself so that the lake covered her entire head and antlers.

Needing pleasure from somewhere, she brought a hand to her breast and lowered it down her body to the spot in between her legs, her body heating from the touch, the circular movements.

Maryska thought about one of the greatest things she'd ever done as Torlarah's ruler—create the Bone Valley. It hadn't always been that way, though. No, it had once been the Divine Valley, serene and tranquil, the most dazzling of places one could step foot into after their life had ended.

The first time she'd seen the Divine Valley, she watched it with hunger, tasting all the colors. There was the knowledge that in Torlarah she could gain even more control than what she'd already been gifted. That thought consumed her.

After a night she longed to forget, she gathered the strength she could from the two crowns and took away all the flesh of the people, leaving them as walking and talking bones.

She thought she'd done a good deed by allowing them to survive, but they wanted back what was rightfully theirs—the skin to let them truly feel, a heart to beat against their cage of bones, and all the other missing pieces to make them whole.

Maryska would not be undermined any longer. Sliding her arms down to her sides, she brought her hands together in a furious clap that echoed throughout the entire valley. After the clatter of bones fell to pieces against the dirt, silence was all that could be heard.

The cottages still standing were all made of bones—trees were bones, flowers were bones, and bones were scattered across the once glorious fields.

She looked at what she'd created. The Bone Valley.

Maryska swallowed the lovely memory as her body spasmed from her touch and the power it absorbed from the Lake of Flesh. She gasped in satisfaction while rising to the surface.

At the lake's edge, the bowl of grapes and silver goblet awaited her. She moved toward the things and picked up the goblet, bringing the warm metallic taste to her lips, reminding her of the poison Anton drank to end his life.

She'd heard rumors that Daryna was a witch, and she had gone to see her. And what a surprise it was when Maryska had met her. The entirety of the visit, Maryska wanted to smile and taunt Daryna, but she'd proven she could make anything believable.

Since Maryska had come to Kedaf from Torlarah, she couldn't simply stab Anton with a dagger herself. Besides, she wanted something less messy.

But a poison remedied by someone else and poured into a cup by that person would be the answer. All she had to do was heat up the offerings and give it to him as if it were a gift from another. And drank it, he did.

Now, she figured she had all the time in the world to wait for Anton. With that thought in mind, she shifted to her animal form, hooves shaping and fur sprouting, until she closely resembled a stag.

As she retired to her bedroom, she envisioned all the ways Anton would please her once he belonged to her—as her king.

TWENTY-ONE

ANTON

With a heavy and disheartened sigh, Anton peered up to the glowing orb in the sky. He leaned his back against the mass of bones, tapping his fingers rhythmically along the ground below him, dirt gathering at the tips.

Not one bone. To be clearer, not one single bone he'd touched had belonged to Nahli. He let out a roaring scream that spilled throughout the Bone Valley, and it felt good, but it still wasn't enough.

From Anton's left, soft skeletal feet padded through the loose gravel of the dirt.

"Rip me apart, Roka. Just tear me apart, and throw my scraps anywhere you please," Anton groaned, meaning every word. What good was he to anyone?

His entire body had grown exhausted, and his flames had started to close numerous times, but he forced himself to remain awake. The thought had crossed his mind that he could walk through the door, find Maryska, and let her do her worst to him. He deserved it. He knew she would come back at some point, and it was his fault for parading Nahli out in the open.

"Have you really tried to look, Anton?" Roka pulled up beside him on his hind legs, head bobbing.

Of course he had! Narrowing his flames, Anton hitched his thumb over his shoulder. "Have you seen this newly formed hill of remains? That's all my doing."

"Hmm."

Anton slapped the dirt below, causing several bones to rattle. "Hmm, what?"

Roka pawed at something on the ground to his left, and Anton edged forward to see a skeletal piece that appeared to be an ulna. "Another bone to add to the pile, I suppose."

"Look closer," Roka murmured, twisting out of the way so Anton could crawl nearer.

On the ivory bone rested a fissure that had never healed completely. He snatched up the skeletal piece, feeling as though his bones had their own lightning-fast heartbeat. "It's hers!" He held the ulna under the orb in the sky's light. "It's a piece of Nahli." A look of astonishment crossed Anton's features as his jaw widened, and his flames brightened.

"And you believed it to be impossible." Roka's delicate jaw fell slightly open in a grin.

"This is just one part of her, though." He gazed out and scanned the entire valley of bones. "How will we ever find the rest?"

Roka patted the side of Anton's leg. "Time, Anton. Time."

"We do have plenty of time—I know this, but if we can't find her..."

Anton couldn't let that happen. Determination filled him, greater than when he'd started. One piece was more than he had to begin with, and he would find another and then another.

Something about the gnarled tree seemed to call to him as his gaze drifted that way. He dashed in that direction, the door on its trunk silently taunting him, waiting for him to walk through it. But as he stared up to the branches, he noticed something that hadn't been there before. Three large bones dangled from the claw-like limbs. One broken—a reminder of what Maryska had done, and could do again. Maryska must have left them behind as a gift, or perhaps more of a torment to give him hope, only to find the realization of failure.

Reaching up toward the branches, Anton plucked the two femurs and tibia like precious fruit. He clutched them to his chest and hurried to his cottage. Once inside, he set them gently on the floor next to the table where he'd carved his trinkets.

Roka appeared beside him, waiting eagerly. "Remember how your orb danced with Nahli's above the two of you?"

"Yes." He didn't know where Roka was going with this, and he tried not to grow impatient or agitated with having to stand there and waste crucial moments.

"Perhaps the orb can find the remainder of her bones," Roka suggested.

"Her orb is *gone*." Did he not realize that when Nahli had vanished, so had her orb? *He didn't, because he'd run off and hid inside a cottage.*

"It is not gone, only dimmed inside of her. Same as yours is when not lighted. It's inside of you, awaiting its moment to shine."

"How do you know this?" Anton crept closer, growing skeptical, and partially suspicious.

Roka's shoulders slumped, and he eased forward. "I do not know how I know. It is only something I *feel*, the same as how I knew something was not right when Maryska arrived."

"Well, it's something at least."

Cradling the top of his skull in both hands, Anton tried to think. While he searched for Nahli's bones in the fog, he had lit the orb, and nothing had happened besides it hovering above him and giving off light.

Closing his flames, he wished for and spoke the word, "light," before opening them to look at the familiar orb.

"Try talking to it," Roka murmured, scooting backward as if he was giving Anton and the orb space to connect.

Anton felt ridiculous staring at the sphere while

determining what to say. "Do you remember Nahli?"

The flickering black flame inside stilled. Perhaps it *was* listening. "You danced with her orb in the garden … or orbited her light. It's a part of her, the way you're a part of me, correct?" He chose to believe what he was saying, because he had nothing else in that moment to believe in.

The dark flame blazed again, forming its own lullaby, but this time it expanded.

"I think you may have seen her orb disappear in front of you, just as Nahli's body vanished from me." Then Anton pleaded, "Will you help me find her bones, so I can piece her back together? Then perhaps you and her orb can dance together once more?"

Inside the orb, the flame pulsated, darkening the white layers, consuming it until only the shadows existed. Anton's flames widened and shifted to Roka, who only cocked his head at the sphere.

After several moments, the orb elevated from Anton's hand. He watched it abruptly pass out the door, leaving Anton to rush after the orb, following its flight. Through the garden, toward a meager hill, where the sphere flashed a brief pearly white. Anton dug where the orb floated, the ball of flame pulsing continuously with flashes when his hand wrapped around a small phalange.

It must be Nahli's. He prayed it was hers, and for this place to have mercy on him.

Anton placed the bone in his trouser pocket as the orb looped around to the other side, where yet more bones lay, protruding from the dirt. A burst of white came again, before fading away. He sifted through smooth remains until his hand latched onto a radius, and the orb drummed a quickening beat of ivory.

"Let me help," Roka said, jutting forward.

Anton handed him the piece of Nahli's arm, and fished from his pocket what would be her pinky toe, placing it gently in Roka's free palm.

The meerkat darted off to take the bones inside the cottage, adding them to the growing collection. Turning around to continue the task, Anton found his orb floating next to a broader and taller hill, flickering with a soft pale light, calling to him.

This happened over and over with the sphere. After two bones were retrieved, Anton would pass them to Roka, who would bring them into the cottage. Then he and the orb would move on to endure more.

Two hundred and six bones made up Nahli's skeleton. Breathing heavily, his palm on his sternum, he'd found two hundred and five with the orb's help. There was only one left to uncover—the most important—her skull. The one piece that could tell him she was all right.

A buzz and sizzle came from the orb as it flew and dipped, back and forth, side to side, then circled the dusty remains around the Bone Valley. They hadn't come this far not to find her.

Hovering on all fours, Roka patted Anton's foot. "Do not fret, Anton."

If the meerkat was taller, he assumed Roka would have been patting Anton's shoulder to comfort him. He didn't feel comforted, though—he was restless, as if he needed to keep moving.

When the orb zoomed off in the direction where he and Nahli had first entered the woods with the beast, Anton chased after the light. The orb glimmered once as it stalled in front of the most massive mountain of bones in the valley.

The mountain climbed high into the sky, filled with a generous collection of human remains. Anton worried he wouldn't be able to sift through them all, and it was just his luck that this was the place where her skull would be.

"I don't know how I'll find her," he whispered, lowering his chin in defeat. The impossibility became overpowering.

"The pity must end," Roka said with finality. "You will find her."

Something in his words put Anton back into action, gathered strength, and helped to clear the rest of his doubts. With a firm pressure of his hands against the remains, Anton started to climb toward the top where the orb dangled in midair, waiting for him.

His hands trembled as he went skyward, then slid, climbed, then slid again. Bones clanked and clattered to the bottom of the mountain, spilling on top of him, beside him, and below him as they tumbled downward. For a moment, he thought he could feel whatever life was in her calling to him, but it was only his wishful thinking.

Tasha, Pav, and Yeva passed through his thoughts, and he pretended his siblings were there with him, cheering him on in the way they always used to do for each other. Tasha with her book in hand, Pav with a smirk on his face, and Yeva with her palms clasped together.

Anton's feet slipped when he reached the section he needed to unbury, but he held his grip, constantly shifting his footing as he stripped bone after bone away. A hole formed for him to push his way through and crawl inside.

He combed and dug in a depth that seemed to be never-ending—tibia, fibula, sternum, phalanges, skull, skull, skull— not her skull. *Is she even here?*

When he was about to turn away and explore a hole in another part of the bone mountain, he spotted another skull. Did he dare to hope? Tension from his shoulders lessened when his gaze landed on the left chipped tooth set in her lower jaw. The orb blinked and illuminated. Shooting his hand forward, he gripped the skull tightly in his palm, not wanting to release it.

"Nahli?" he asked.

A mixture of his heavy breathing, and the clatter of bones beneath his feet were the only sounds that could be heard. But it was undeniably her.

"Roka!" he yelled. "Roka!"

Shuffling upward, he crawled out from the hole he was buried in. Roka came running. "Did you find her?"

Despite her still not being put together, Anton smiled and held up the last piece of Nahli as he scaled his way back to the ground. "I have her." He exhaled.

"Let us rebuild her then," Roka said.

As Anton's feet struck the pebbles, he sighed in relief, but he wasn't done. The orb followed them as they headed for the cottage. Anton stretched out his hand, and the sphere spiraled downward into his palm.

"Thank you." The orb was a part of him that never gave up.

"Off," he murmured. At that, the orb turned back to white as the dark flame grew smaller, before the sphere disappeared.

"I still wonder why you don't have an orb," Anton said.

Roka angled his head over his shoulder. "I do not know. Perhaps I do, but I cannot summon one. Nahli had tried to let me hold hers, but it failed as well."

Anton quickened his pace while Roka barreled ahead. He reached the cottage, the door already partially open from Roka's to and fro delivery sprints. Nahli's pile of bones rested on the floor, the way she'd been the day in the garden. Shifting his arm forward to her skeletal fragments, Anton planned to start at her toes—like déjà vu.

With his tiny hand, Roka bent forward to help, and Anton reached to clasp his wrist. "I have this, dear friend." Anton murmured. "I'd like to be the one to rebuild her."

Before all this happened with Nahli, Anton wasn't sure how he felt about Roka, but that's what he had become—a friend. He'd helped him not only physically by bringing Nahli's bones to the cottage, but he was there in support with the words that helped Anton not give up.

Nodding his small skull in understanding, Roka sat back on his hind legs to watch. The first thing Anton grabbed was the broken femur, and he hoped Nahli wouldn't feel this, but he had to set it. With one swift movement from the strength of his hands, a loud pop reverberated through the cottage.

Once again Roka nodded, as if telling Anton it had to be done. Otherwise, Nahli would have suffered more greatly.

After placing the femur on the floor, he started to build her. It took him much longer than he would have liked to piece her together. Secretly, he was afraid at first that when he connected her bones, they wouldn't fuse. But they did, like magic.

Time seemed to stand still when he picked up her skull and cradled it in between his hands. He placed it on top of her cervical vertebrae, making her now complete. Only, she needed something before he awoke her.

Anton quickened his movements toward the bedroom. "We need to find her clothing." He grasped the first thing he could find, a gray dress with a black rose. The head of the flower took up the entirety of the back as a large stem with thorns hit the hem, pearl buttons lining the front.

Using hurried motions, he undid the buttons and placed the dress on Nahli's body, then clasped the front.

"Awake, my queen." He whispered the same words he had the first time she'd awoken, except this time, he meant them. But she didn't stir.

"Kiss her awake," Roka suggested.

Anton shot him a glare, because he knew it was idiocy and lunacy to think a kiss could awaken her. That only worked in the stories Tasha read. And he didn't even have lips. But still, he leaned forward to press his teeth against hers in the only way he would be able to kiss.

Before his teeth touched Nahli's, a loud inhale came from her, and two bright flames lit inside her eye sockets.

Then she collapsed.

This time, Anton caught her in his arms before she hit the floor and became broken pieces once more. He'd been impatient at waiting for his words to work, but they'd only come late, was all.

Holding Nahli tight, he murmured against the side of her skull, "Welcome back."

TWENTY-TWO

DARYNA

Daryna opened her eyes, finding herself in complete darkness, reminding her of the day she'd awoken without a leg. The air was stagnant and heavy with a citrus scent. She should have been panicked, but being alone never fazed her. But she wasn't alone.

"Pavla?"

"You can call me Pav, you know," he answered, nearer than she would have liked. "We need light around here."

After he said the word "light," a white spherical shape appeared on his palm, illuminating the room as he floundered backward. Across the roof of what had to be the inside of a cave, dark shadows slid and swirled.

"Light," Daryna commanded.

An alabaster orb with a blackened flame burst to life in the center of her palm. She couldn't make out what the shadows across the ceiling were. Some held the form of a human with long thick horns attached to their head, while others crawled on all fours with a beastly shape.

Pav didn't appear frightened, more in awe than anything as he scanned the walls with his head tilted all the way back and his mouth partially open.

"Are you ready to move on, *Pav*?" Daryna asked. "Or do you only want to keep watching shadows with the two days we have?"

Tearing his gaze from the moving shapes, he focused on her and lowered his brows. "Why didn't you tell me about Maryska beforehand?"

"I did." She shrugged.

"Yes, right before you drank the tonic." His facial features relaxed as he seemed to go deep into thought. If she could guess, he was probably overjoyed that he didn't have to search outside of Kedaf to find Maryska, when the woman could very well be here somewhere in Torlarah.

"Because it's more of an instinct," Daryna said. "That odor permeating her cottage is one of life and death. And I would bet all ten of your pretty fingers that she's down here."

"I need all my pretty fingers." He flashed the hand holding the orb in front of her, surveying the wall again. "The shadows truly are interesting, though."

Daryna arched a brow. "You'll have plenty of time to visit the afterlife once you die."

"Not anytime soon, I hope." He formed a tight-lipped smile. "Let's try to find Anton first."

Daryna wasn't a fortune teller, so she wouldn't be able to read what Pav's future would behold. But if he continued to watch shadows all day, it might take place sooner than he expected.

As Daryna breathed in the scent of Torlarah, something about the place felt familiar to her, as if she'd been here before or seen aspects of it in her dreams. Perhaps she'd once been inside a cave similar to this one, in the parts of her life she couldn't recall.

Daryna touched the sword at her hip, confirming it was still there. She was relieved that by attaching swords at their hips, the weapons came with them. Pav's blade hung at his side, slapping his thigh as he moved forward.

As they trailed deeper into what she still believed to be some sort of cave, the room lightened with orange orbs near the roof. Sharp and rough edges created the ceiling, but along the dark walls, a lazy movement caught her attention.

"Are those hands?" Pav asked, sneaking closer to the wall.

Daryna snatched him back by the collar. "What are you doing? Trying to get taken?"

Pav's green irises slid to hers, his freckles appearing dusky under the light. "I was only going to confirm my suspicions that those are indeed hands."

Squinting, Daryna held the orb up to the wall, and her heart lodged in her throat. Hands—hundreds upon hundreds of them—crawled along the wall, covering the rough surface, the sight of them sinister somehow.

Daryna blinked, shaking off the fear that threatened to overwhelm her. But Pav stood in awe again.

"If you die here, you're going to awake before you ever get a chance to talk to Anton. And that means missing out on Maryska with me," she seethed. "As one of your tasks, you'll watch me put a blade through her heart."

"All right, as you wish." The edges of his lips tilted upward, even though his eyes remained heavy with burden.

Before she could feel sorry for him, Daryna stomped away. When they came face to face with Maryska, she was certain there wouldn't be any sign of a smirk from him unless the woman was dead.

"Don't go too far ahead, because you might die and wake up, remember?" Pav called.

"If we do die, I don't have a way to get us back here again either," Daryna replied. "That particular remedy only works once, the body can't handle it, and I don't know any other similar spells." She hadn't even known if she could really get them here in the first place. Most of it had all been wild hope on her part, but it had worked.

Under the flame-colored light, Pav's skin paled. "You

didn't say that. I assumed if we woke back in Kedaf, then we could return here."

She frowned and pursed her lips. "That's what you get for assuming and not asking beforehand."

He stayed silent for a while after that, but not as long as she would have liked. As they moved on past stony walls, her wooden leg dug into her skin, the recognizable throb of pain there. While they were in Torlarah, she thought perhaps it could be possible to have two legs for once, but that pesky attachment was still there. Forever a reminder of something she couldn't remember. One day, she would burn the godforsaken thing, not caring if she'd have nothing there to support her leg.

"Have you ever been in love?" Pav interrupted her thoughts, reminding her once again that he couldn't keep quiet.

"Only with myself."

His familiar smirk formed. "Really?"

"Pav." She sighed. "Not all of us have lovely redheaded girls vying for our attention."

"Ah, so you prefer women over men."

Daryna wanted to go back to her cottage in Kedaf, away from this conversation. "No, I prefer neither."

In their own ways, women and men both looked fine, but she would never know if she was being deceived or not. She could only ever trust her own mind. However, there were times she'd dreamt of a man with braids and dark skin, running his hand up her naked body, then down between her thighs. She shoved him to the back of her mind, where she always kept him hidden, because he didn't exist.

"That's interesting," he said, bouncing his orb up and down.

Her gaze stayed snared on his single juggle as she turned their chat back on him. "We both know how you feel about a certain girl."

His eyes seemed to sparkle under the light with bright red hearts. "That could one day be a strong possibility." Judging by his expression, the day had already arrived.

Daryna chose not to tell him young love typically doesn't end well. For some reason, she didn't want to let that light shining in his eyes flicker out.

"You know, Pav—"

He stuck his arm out, causing her to cease moving forward. "What. Is. That?" He spoke softly, so only she could hear the alarm in his voice.

Straight ahead, through the poorly-lit cave, she couldn't see anything except for gray stone speckled with brown.

"Not ahead," he whispered. "The hideous things against the walls."

Daryna stepped closer to examine where he pointed, and gasped, stumbling back. The walls were not walls at all. Human bodies, blended together, made up the structure surrounding them. Legs. Arms. Torsos. Naked skin of all colors and ages intertwined together, a massive wave of flesh, ready to come crashing down on them.

And not a single head.

She shivered, thankful no eyes were there to stare at her from amongst the horrible sight.

Who would create something like this? And why?

"Retrieve your sword," Daryna said, coming back to herself, then turned to the orb. "Off."

She dropped the orb to the ground, watching it vanish while Pav did the same. As several gangly bodies, with thin skin, stumbled from the wall, she tightened her grip on the sword. Three headless bodies jerked and swayed, as they moved toward her and Pav.

The orbs running along the ceiling gave Daryna and Pav enough illumination to see that two were male, and the other a female, their flesh a murky color matching the walls. She would have expected some sort of rotting smell, but there was still only that citrusy scent combined with something not from the world of the living.

Daryna held her sword high, prepared to fight. Except Pav leapt in front of her before she could perform the duty, his blade easily slicing the male in half.

"That was mine," she said with a dry tone, scanning the other direction. "You need to focus on the one coming at you."

Lunging forward with precision, Daryna thrust her sword into the chest of the female, striking her heart. The body slumped to the ground with a soft thump.

As she turned to the side, she found Pav already beside her, holding up his blade with dark thick sludge running down it. Daryna was not only surprised by Pav's skills, but impressed. She'd assumed he would have stood there the entire time smirking at the headless creatures. But he could perform a task when needed.

A similar thick consistency coated the edge of her sword, and she rubbed the tip of her blade against the leg of her trousers, wiping it clean.

Pav focused on the walls, watching for any sign of more bodies that chose to come forth. "Anyone else?" he called.

Daryna scowled at him, nearly jumping out of her skin when a light scrape on the ground came. It took her a moment before discovering the first body Pav had torn into was attempting to claw its top half back to the wall.

"Let's move," she said.

Not waiting for Pav's answer, she hurried past the wall of bodies and his steps stayed in sync with hers. The shade of the walls faded into a clear color, closer to murky water. More movement, as though something was swimming inside.

A hand slammed against the surface, the sound recoiling through the cave. Pav darted in front of Daryna to try and protect her. She shoved him away. He needed to stop doing that and watch his own back, otherwise he would end up dead. Although not truly dead, but back at her cottage.

Silhouettes of heads pressed against what appeared like glass, but was more of a clear stone. As the things crept closer to the wall, Daryna noticed they were without eyes, ears, noses and mouths, their entire facial structure a smooth skin surface. The skin along where their mouths should be was stretched and pulled back, as though calling out for help. There was no way for her or her magic to help them.

"What if one of those is Anton?" Pav asked, a look of horror crossing his face.

"I think if Anton was in this part of Torlarah, he probably deserved it." She paused, her gaze locking with Pav's. "He wasn't a terrible person, was he?"

"No." His voice quavered. "My brother was the best."

"Then he won't be here." Daryna wondered what would happen once she died, since she'd done some pretty awful things in her life. Never with malice. But did that make a difference? "We'll eventually make it to a more *flowery* territory for you." Or, at least, she hoped so.

"If we don't die first," he pointed out.

"I think you have it handled. You're quite good with a sword. I'm amazed, actually."

"I am, aren't I?" He gave her a half smile. In return, she frowned at him.

When they approached a wide opening, the cave walls stretched to a heavy shade of gold. It could possibly be a way out, and guide them to Anton or Maryska.

Ignoring the bite in her leg, Daryna quickened her pace and came to a halt when she reached the mouth of the cave. Before her, a thick blue-black liquid swirled around, continuing on for a good span, leading to what looked to be trees and hard ground on the other side.

Pav placed his sword back inside its sheath, then held out his hands toward her, preparing to be a hero. "Let me carry you across."

Squeezing the bridge of her nose, she shook her head. "I'll

186

be fine. I don't know how deep it is, though. Can you swim?"

"Yes, can you?"

She could, even though it would be a challenge with the wooden leg. "Yes."

With resignation, she pushed the tip of her boot into the liquid. It easily broke through, so she slid into the blackness, holding a consistency which felt like softened mud combined with too much water. Pav pressed in next to her.

Despite trying to seem nonchalant, Daryna's heart sped up with each step they took, sinking deeper and deeper down into the mud. At the halfway point, the black sludge now rose up to her waist. Her insides quivered as the mud neared her breasts, and she no longer found herself confident as her breaths increased, coming out unsteady. She needed to get out. She wanted to cry. She yearned to break something to distract her.

"We're almost there," Pav panted, taking hold of her upper arm with a concerned expression.

Daryna wanted to rip her arm away, but she tried to relax and let him guide her until they reached the other side. She inhaled and exhaled when she realized they were indeed almost there. The thickness of the mud had increased and brushed all the way up to her neck. The force of moving through the slosh was drinking in all of her energy.

A stinging sensation struck her right ankle, and Daryna flinched. Before she could say something to Pav, a strong hand wrapped around her leg and yanked her beneath the surface. She tried to scream, but the mud filled her mouth. She couldn't breathe, couldn't see, couldn't even hear anything but the squishing motions, and perhaps the heavy beating of her heart.

The hand crushed her ankle harder. The panic within her boomed and boomed again at the possibility that she could potentially lose her good leg. Gathering a storm full of fury, she kicked and tried to reach for her sword but couldn't.

Two arms wrapped around her waist, squeezing hard. They

tugged her upward, until she felt the release at her ankle. She continued her rise toward the surface until she met the shocked and worried look on Pav's face. Splotches of wet dirt covered him too. She couldn't get the words out to thank him for helping her, not because she hated saying those words but because she was still struggling to catch her breath.

"Swim, run, whatever you have to do!" he shouted, dragging her forward.

He didn't have to tell her twice. She thrashed her arms across the black pit, splashes hitting against her eyes and mouth, until her hand met dry ground. Hauling herself up, she leaned over and clasped Pav's hand to help pull him up before something took him down.

Heavy, relieved breaths escaped her mouth as she shuffled backward, staring out at the black sludge and pressing her hands to her lips. As if a demon had cast a spell, heads and more heads bobbed up from the slosh, same as the featureless ones that were inside the cave walls. If the mud connected to the cave, which had to be the answer, perhaps they'd followed them.

Daryna unsheathed her sword, but the featureless people didn't draw forward, only seemed to study them from beneath their thin skin.

"You frightened me back there." Pav stepped in front of her, worry lines creasing his forehead.

"You, frightened? What about me?" she asked, incredulous. Not wanting to think about the touch of the thing's hand that had been on her ankle.

"The both of us then."

"Thank you," she muttered the words late, but they were there.

Smiling and biting his lower lip, Pav curled a hand around his ear. "I didn't quite catch that."

Daryna wouldn't repeat the words a second time, but she was thankful he'd pulled her out and not left her behind. She didn't know how long it would have taken her to die down there and return to Kedaf, but it would have destroyed her chance at getting vengeance against Maryska.

"What's this?" Pav asked.

Daryna turned to find Pav standing in front of a forest covered in bright oranges, yellows, and browns, specifically a tall tree with a wooden door in its center. The forest was like autumn, and that season always reminded her of dying, the slow death before a chilly winter wiped the world clean, allowing a rebirth to come in springtime.

Squaring his shoulders, Pav inched toward the trunk and rapidly tapped the door twice. To her astonishment, he did it again, and then one last time.

Daryna shot forward, tugged his hand away, and whisper-shouted, "Why did you do that?" She didn't want him to draw in unwanted attention from any more creatures.

"To see if anyone's home?"

Why did I bother asking? "You're like the brother I never had *and* never really wanted."

A shuffling sound came from the other side and Daryna swung up her sword, prepared for who—or what—would answer.

TWENTY-THREE

NAHLI

Nahli's eyelids dropped, opened, and dropped again before she pried them up. No, not eyelids, but flames. Her body slumped to the floor with delirium. Two arms caught her around her rib cage, with two soft words coming out from between his teeth.

"Welcome back."

Memories swarmed around her skull, trapping her in darkness. She let out a scream of terror, jolting forward in an attempt to escape the arms capturing her. They only tightened as she screamed louder. "Let me go. Let me go. Let. Me. *Go!*"

The arms loosened, releasing her, and she drooped like a wilting flower to the floor, her skeletal hands propping her up. She breathed heavily, catching a scent of nothing. That was all there was. All *she* was.

A small body appeared before her, an animal of bones, holding his hands up for her to not be frightened. "It is only me."

It took her a moment. Only one to recognize him. Roka.

Turning her body around, she came face to face with the skeletal man who had been holding her. "Anton," she whispered, ashamed. "I—I'm sorry I reacted that way."

Coming down to a crouch beside her, Anton placed her hand in between his. "If you need to scream more, let it out, as long and as many times as you wish. I'll cover the sides of my skull since my ears aren't attached at the moment," he teased, but she could have sworn she heard a sniffle as well.

She wanted to smile, but she just ... couldn't. It was as though she was still trapped back in that place, that darkness where others came and haunted her, never once leaving her alone.

Anton must have sensed that she wasn't all right because he pulled her into his lap, cradling her as he rested his chin on top of her head. And she let him.

Roka maneuvered himself forward and wrapped his hand around her thumb. "Anton went through the entire Bone Valley searching through all the remains to find your pieces and rebuild you."

Nahli gasped, realizing how many bones he would have had to search for. She looked up at Anton. "You did that? How was that possible? What even happened?"

She didn't know what Maryska had done exactly. One moment she was there with Anton, and the next she was gone in a nightmarish place, unable to move.

"To answer your third question first," Anton started, "Maryska separated your bones like they were before, but hid them around the entire valley. While you were absent, did you feel anything?"

She took a deep breath and lowered her head. "It's hard to explain. I was in a place where I couldn't feel any parts of my body. My eyes couldn't shut, no matter how badly I wanted them to." She didn't want to think about that—she wanted Anton to keep talking. "And my other two questions?"

"For the first question, yes, I would do that, or at least keep trying. Maryska told me she left you conscious." His grip on her tightened. "Of course I would scale every bone mountain until I found you. What kind of person would I be otherwise?"

191

Something about that answer made her non-existent stomach drop. If she'd been unconscious, would he have still sought out to find her? She wouldn't have blamed him for that, though—the task had been near impossible.

"And my second question?" she asked.

"Do you remember how our orbs circled each other in the air, in what resembled a dance?" he murmured.

How could she forget? It had been one of the most miraculous sights she'd ever seen. "Yes."

"Roka suggested asking the orb to search for you, since they're made from us. I'd hoped it would work, and that the light would still be hidden inside your bones. It must have been true, because the orb found all of you. All I had to do was dig and retrieve, so perhaps it was a bit of cheating at such a foul game." He let out a low chuckle, his bones rattling against hers.

And Nahli smiled.

Roka released her thumb and came closer. "Do not even ask how I knew that. As I told Anton, it was more of an instinct."

"I could believe anything at this moment," she said, forcing herself to stay smiling as she thought again about Maryska's torture.

"How's your leg?" Anton asked, concern filling his words.

"My leg?" she asked, but couldn't see anything under the dress.

Then she remembered Maryska breaking her leg, and she lifted the skirt of the dress up to expose it. Across the bone rested a thin jagged line—a new scar to add to the one on her arm.

With a gentle brush, Anton ran a finger over the line. "It doesn't hurt, does it?"

"No, it's fine." If she had eyelashes, they would have fluttered right then at his touch.

As her thoughts turned to Maryska again, something more

192

than hatred crackled through her bones. Maryska was beautiful on the outside, but on the inside, there was only cruelty. In the world, she'd encountered people like that. But this was worse because Maryska caused the ruination of *everyone's* afterlife.

At some point Roka had died, and what should he have been doing in the afterlife? Basking in a garden of real flowers, perhaps while stuffing his belly with bugs and fruit. Instead, Roka had been broken into bones, buried in a garden, and he couldn't even remember anything of his past.

"She'll be back, won't she?" The question wasn't directed at Anton or Roka, it was almost as if she was talking to herself.

Roka's head tilted toward Anton, waiting for him to answer.

Anton took a few moments to speak, his voice resigned. "Maryska left the door unlocked for me. When I gave up my search for you, she expected me to come and find her."

Peeling herself out of the comfort of Anton's lap, Nahli stood to full height. She stretched her spine and for the first time since being back in her bones, anticipation and a bit of eagerness were there to drive her forward. "The door is unlocked?"

Anton rose from the floor and gritted his teeth. "Yes, but I'm not going through it."

"Why not?" Roka chirped.

"It's none of your business, Roka," Anton scolded. "We aren't going through the damn door."

"Then what will happen when Maryska grows bored," Nahli started, "and decides to come back here because you never went to her? What happens if she breaks *you* apart this time? Trust me, you won't want to be conscious with the visions." Nahli held her hands up, then yanked at the hair near the edge of her scalp. If there was an option to try and leave, she would take it.

"Visions?" Anton asked.

"My own personal purgatory, Anton. I can't stay here—I

won't stay here." She tightened her fists and took heavy breaths.

"You won't let me go alone either, will you?" He ran his hands through his messy ponytail and jerked the strap out that was holding his hair back.

In response, she narrowed her flames at him.

"We will all go together," Roka answered.

Anton folded his arms across his ribs. "No."

"Yes." Nahli placed her hands on her hip bones, and they both stared each other down.

Neither one budged, until finally, one did.

"All right," Anton grumbled, holding up a finger, "but I need to get one night of sleep before we leave."

Did Anton not take any breaks while searching for her? She assumed he had, and it made something selfishly flutter inside her chest knowing he hadn't.

She could do that. Besides, she could use the sleep, too.

Nahli nodded and as she started for the front door, Anton caught her hand before her fingertips touched the handle. "Please, don't leave."

"I was only going to rest in the other cottage." She didn't want to sleep out in the garden any time soon, for fear of being caught off guard again by Maryska.

"Will you stay here for the night?"

The ghostly flutters beneath her rib cage accelerated because he was worried about her. Wouldn't she feel the same way if she'd traded places with him? Now that she thought about it, she really didn't want Anton to stay alone, either.

"Yes, I'll stay here."

"You can take the bed. I'm used to sleeping on the settee anyway."

"I'm going to another cottage for a while," Roka said.

"Are you sure?" Nahli asked.

"Yes, I have to keep myself busy. I can't stay in one place."

Anton opened the door for Roka, and the meerkat darted

194

out into the fog. He stayed silent and turned to Nahli.

She didn't know what to say or why she was feeling strange, different. No, she knew. She'd felt the same with Zikri. Worse, she'd known Zikri for almost all her life, and he had still turned his back on her. Yet this man who she hadn't known for that long had done more for her than anyone ever had. And she knew Anton wasn't the kind of person to act as Zikri had.

"I'll see you in the morning," she finally said, breaking the silence.

Quietly, Anton headed for the settee, scooping up his knife and part of a carving from the table. "Let me know if you need anything."

Nahli thought he was tired, but perhaps his head spun with too many thoughts. Like hers.

Once inside the bedroom, she drew the covers back and slid underneath them. Her bones sank into the cushions, comforting her into possible sleep.

Only, she couldn't sleep. Tossing and turning. Tossing and turning. Closing her flames, opening her flames. Every time she shut them, she could see everyone she'd stolen something from. Frustrated, she released a small grunt, trying to squash the memories.

A knock on the half-opened door jolted her from her struggling.

"Are you all right?" Anton asked, cracking open the door all the way.

She clutched the blanket to her chest. "No, not really."

"May I come in?"

"Why aren't you asleep?" She bet he'd been carving this entire time.

He entered the room but remained several paces away. "I'm … trying."

"By carving?" She smiled.

"Generally, carving helps me drift off, but it hasn't yet."

Dragging herself up to a sitting position, Nahli leaned her back against the headboard and watched as he settled at the edge of the bed, his glowing flames studying her.

"Why can't you sleep?" she asked.

His teeth ground back and forth. "Maryska."

"Why are you so afraid of her? I fear what she can do too. But you weren't even worried about the beasts in the forest."

Deep laughter escaped him, and she had never heard such a beautiful sound. It felt like a rarity, or maybe there wasn't much to laugh about in the Bone Valley. His laughs were something she wanted to grasp in the palm of her hand and keep for when she needed to feel better.

Anton clasped the back of his neck and looked up at the ceiling. "I'm not afraid of her, per se. I just don't like encountering her and remembering how she used to make me feel. Then there is what she has done to you, to me, to *everyone*."

"But you should want to destroy her." Even if Maryska could break Nahli apart again, she couldn't sit there and wait for the woman to return to do it.

"Oh, I want to do more than that. I want to slowly rip her head off with my bare hands and feed it to the beasts with all those eyes along their bodies, watching." Her jaw had opened, and she must have appeared disturbed because he hurried on, "You must think me horrid with these thoughts."

"I wasn't upset with what you said, more surprised that it came out of your mouth." She chuckled, stroking the edges of the blanket. "If we get to that point where anyone is going to be removing body parts, it's going to be me."

"Fine, but I'll be right there beside you."

"As for before, may I ask how she made you feel terrible?"

Anton cocked his head as if thinking how to word what he wanted to say. "I felt as though I was nothing, and that she owned me. Lessening my payments, prolonging my payments, threatening me all the time that she would destroy my reputation so no one else would want to use me. I wouldn't have cared, but the thing was, I relied on that money. Then, finally, the night before I came here, I was going to work for my sister's fiancée and try to do something with my carvings. No longer would I have to sell myself for coin—I had a goal that I could grasp and see it expanding. I could have been worth something."

Why would he ever think he was nothing? "You're worth more than you know," she whispered.

"Thank you," he said softly after a few moments had passed. "I'll let you try and get some rest."

"Please stay longer. At least for a while." She pulled the covers back, knowing he needed someone's company. "You look cold."

"I'm not cold." He smiled, but climbed in beside her. "What happened while you were gone?" His head turned to face her.

She already loathed thinking about the things she'd seen, but perhaps it was better to discuss what had happened aloud instead of bottling it up.

"When I was out there, I kept getting visited by people I'd hurt or those who'd hurt me. My parents, Zikri, a lot of villagers I'd stolen from ... you were there with your family."

Anton's flames flickered. "You know that wasn't really me, right? No matter what any of those people said to you, they weren't truly there."

"I know. I have a lot of guilt, and no one to apologize to." Her flames shifted to meet his. "I'm sorry, Anton. I'm sorry for that day in the market ... and your clothing."

"I'm sorry about your satchel." He paused as if in thought. "If I can find a way one day to return it to you, I will."

"It was stolen anyway ... but I loved it."

He chuckled and his white flames closed, turning into darkness behind his eye sockets. Nahli rolled onto her back and shut her flames, feeling Anton's hand clasp hers, gripping it tight. As she drifted to sleep, she held his hand firmly, hoping it would help to keep not only her nightmares away, but his too.

Anton swept Nahli's dark hair away from her face with a bright smile. She reached forward to touch the scar beside his right eye. Their bodies lay swaddled under the satin sheets, unclothed from the night before.

"You want to go to the market tonight?" Anton asked.

Nahli could hear the music now. "Only if you promise to dance with me the whole night."

"Tasha might have to disagree with that."

"Fine, I'll share the dances with Tasha and Yeva."

"Don't worry, most will be saved for you." He twisted his body, sliding her beneath him. He hovered over her, his naked skin pressing deliciously into hers.

"I like the sound of that." She smiled.

"Keep doing that."

"Doing what?"

"Smiling." He placed a kiss to each side of her cheeks. "Those dimples get me every time."

When his lips moved down to meet hers, Nahli's flames flicked open from the taunting dream.

She shifted, discovering her skull was pressed against Anton's ribs, her other arm draping across his spine where his stomach would have been. He painted his fingertip slowly across her upper arm, and she relaxed into the soothing motion. Then she jerked up when she again thought about her strange dream. Perhaps this kind of dream was worse than a nightmare, because it couldn't come true. Or could it?

"I was trying to wake you but didn't want to shake your skeleton," Anton said. "I'm going to take a quick rinse in the lake before we leave … if you want to go."

She didn't know if she should be bathing in any lakes with Anton at the moment. It wasn't as if she hadn't done it before, though.

"How about I meet you there? I'm going to gather some things," she said, needing to become unflustered.

"All right."

If she knew better, she could have sworn one of his brows was arched while looking at her, even though he didn't have them.

When Anton left the room and after hearing the front door shut, Nahli went to the closet and grabbed a tunic and a pair of trousers that tied at the front. She thought about what she'd said about gathering some things. What should she even bring? They didn't need food or water, or really anything.

However, there had been the beasts with the dozens and dozens of eyes. She most definitely needed a sword. After grabbing the blade and daggers, along with the clothes, she headed out to find Anton.

As she surveyed the area, there was no sign of Roka yet.

The thick fog had already lifted by the time she made her way down the pebbled path to the lake. When she rounded the corner, passing by a pile of bones and thorny weeds, there stood Anton, wearing no clothing. Water beaded on his pale bones as he pushed a leg into his trousers. Gasping when she realized she was just standing there watching him, she whirled around, and clutched the belongings to her chest.

"You can turn around, Nahli. Like I told you before, it's just bones."

No, no. It was more than bones. Spinning around, she marched up to him, her dress swishing as he slipped on his tunic. "If that's so, then why do I have a dress on every time I wake in this place?"

"Uh…"

"No answer?" she demanded.

"It's more for your benefit than mine."

Sure it is. Nahli smiled, unbuttoning the top clasp of her dress, while his flames lowered to her hand. She didn't know why she suddenly lacked embarrassment, growing braver. Perhaps because it was more of a challenge.

Anton leaned forward, his teeth brushing the side of her skull as he spoke. "Just know, if we do manage to retrieve our full bodies, we can do more in the lake besides swim. If you want to, that is." Then he walked away, throwing a glance over his shoulder one more time, chuckling. "See you at the tree."

Shaking from his bold words, what should have been her promise to him, Nahli's frozen hand moved once again to finish unbuttoning the rest of the dress. If only what he said was possible.

She'd been dead-set on finding their bodies right when she woke in the Bone Valley until they'd entered the circular forest of death that wrapped back around to the bone pit. Then she met Maryska, and uncovered that, perhaps, things wouldn't be as easy as she'd originally thought.

Letting the heavy dress cascade to the ground, she kicked it to the side and stepped into the lake. She rubbed off as much debris as she could, not bothering with the bottom of her feet since they would only get filthy again.

She pushed herself from the lake, not feeling a single breeze. There hadn't been any of that here, either. After throwing on her new clothing, she carried her sword and Anton's daggers. With all the distraction he'd caused, she'd forgotten to hand him his weapons.

Nahli still hadn't heard the pitter patter of Roka's feet. Hopefully, she wouldn't have to try and hunt him down. However, when she reached the tree, Roka was perched there on his hind legs, speaking with Anton.

Anton's gaze automatically drifted to her, and he seemed to smile.

"I come bearing gifts." She held out the two handles of the

daggers.

His flames flickered as he took them from her hand. "I don't know how good these will be, but hopefully that"—he looked down at the sword attached to her hip—"will do some damage."

If they didn't, she'd find a way to do something or die again trying.

And then Nahli froze, her flames meeting Anton's in alarm.

Someone—or *something*—was knocking on the tree's door.

TWENTY-FOUR

ANTON

Anton studied the door leading out of the Bone Valley. The knocks had startled him, and he almost expected the tree's gnarled limbs to move toward them.

He was a moment from asking Nahli and Roka to hide somewhere, when she said, "Answer it?" But it came out more of a question. She was unsure, the same way he was.

If it was Maryska behind the mystery door, he was certain she wouldn't have knocked. Yet that didn't make what was on the other side of the door any less deadly.

Whatever the threat was, Anton chose to face it. Clasping a dagger in his skeletal hand, he pulled open the door with the other, and revealed a forest of color, the world painted in warm shades of autumn. Not only that, but two figures covered in what looked like black mud. He raised his weapon higher.

The two guests leapt back and lifted their own swords high in the air.

Still gripping the dagger, Anton took a step onto the golden grass. It crunched beneath his feet. "Who are you?" His flames focused on a tall, shapely woman with pursed lips.

"You can talk?" the other person said. It was a male—a voice Anton immediately recognized.

His head angled to the boy, his brother, and he brought down his dagger. A sense of home washed over him. "Pav?"

The muddy texture cloaked his brother's curly blond hair, making it appear more brown than gold. Dark clumps splattered his entire face, but it was undoubtedly him.

Pav's sword lowered, his hand trembling. The woman shot his brother a dirty look, not yielding her weapon even an inch.

"Anton?" Pav asked in a shaky voice.

"Pav!" Anton yanked him in a fierce hug, overwhelmed, and not minding the dirt and grime in the least.

"I can't squeeze you as hard—you're all bones," Pav gasped, but gripped Anton tightly.

He'd heard the smile in his brother's playful tone. But a moment later, he released his brother and pushed back, as if he'd been bitten. If Pav was there, then that meant he was … dead.

"Daryna?" Nahli's shocked voice came from behind Anton.

As he started to turn, Nahli rushed out the door and knocked the sword from the woman's hand, before slapping her hard across the face.

Nahli stood there, inhaling and exhaling heavily. Anton had never met Daryna, but even covered in mud, she appeared younger than he'd thought she would be.

"You shouldn't have done that," Daryna gritted out, her lower lip quivering and eyes burning with fury.

"She has a right to do more than that," Anton started, shifting closer to Nahli while focusing on Daryna. "You're the one who had her killed."

"I must apologize, but I don't waste time in murdering skeletons. What purpose would that serve?" Daryna scowled.

"I wasn't always a skeleton," Nahli seethed. "It's me, Nahli."

Daryna's nose wrinkled in confusion for a moment. As recognition set in, her eyes widened in disbelief. "*Nahli?*"

"That's right. Look at me now." She gestured up and down at her skeletal body.

"I *didn't* send Boda to kill you," Daryna said. "If I had wanted you dead, I would have stabbed you through the heart myself. I told her to retrieve my chicken and a new loaf of bread." She paused, shaking her head. "And perhaps give you a couple slaps, one for each thing you stole from me."

"Sorry, Daryna, your henchwoman didn't hold up to your bargain," Nahli ground out. Anton had never seen her so angry.

"I know." Daryna sighed. "She's dead now."

"And I suppose that makes everything all right, then?" Nahli shrugged her thin shoulders.

Anton pulled away from the conversation and focused his attention on his brother. Pav was there, but should have been in Kedaf. He placed his hand on Pav's shoulder and asked, "What happened? How did you die?"

Pav straightened and waved his hand. "No, no, I'm not dead. Daryna brought us here to find you and Maryska. We drank a magical brew to allow us entry, but it's only temporary."

"Before you become hostile, too, Anton," Daryna said, "Maryska purchased the tea you drank from me, but she said it was for an abusive ex-lover."

Maryska had purchased poisoned tea from Daryna? He could be angry about that if he chose, but that dormant release of emotion needed to be for Maryska. Besides, if Daryna hadn't given the tea, Maryska would have gotten poison from elsewhere. However, she brought Pav to this horrid place, and he couldn't be happy about that.

"You should have kept my brother home."

"A bargain's a bargain. It was his decision." Daryna motioned to Pav. Strands of hair dangled from her bun, and she blew them away from her face.

"What bargain?" Anton demanded, glaring his flames at

his brother.

"I'm to be her newest helper," Pav said with a smile.

Anton rubbed the temple of his skull with the tip of the dagger handle, already finished with the conversation. He stared hard at Daryna. "Send him home."

Pav couldn't stay here. It was too unsafe.

"No can do." Daryna tapped the ground with her sword. "It has to be two days, or he has to die here to return."

Even if killing Pav would send his brother home, Anton couldn't harm him. And who knew if Daryna was telling the truth or not? He hardly knew anything about her besides his father stealing goods to sell to her, or the rumors of her being a witch, which he supposed were true after all.

Pav attempted to brush his way around Anton, as though he wasn't traipsing around a place where the dead come after death. "May we go inside and discuss things? Standing next to a lake filled with heads with no faces doesn't seem like the best of options."

Right before he set a foot inside the Bone Valley, Anton dragged Pav back by the collar. "Do. Not. Walk through that door. Unless you want to become a skeleton."

If Pav and Daryna went inside the Bone Valley, Anton wasn't sure if their skin would vanish or not since they weren't really dead. But he remembered the crystallized flowers buried underground and what had happened to their color once they touched the air above.

"What do you mean?" Daryna asked, peering over Anton's shoulder.

"There's a chance that if you walk into the Bone Valley," Nahli began, "both of you will end up like us. Walking skeletons."

"Also," Anton said, "the Bone Valley doesn't lead to anywhere, only loops in a circle. We're going to the Lake of Flesh."

"Lake of Flesh?" Pav appeared taken aback.

"It's the place where Maryska hid our bodies," Anton said.

"Then we're going to find her," Nahli added.

He didn't want Nahli to go near Maryska again after what had happened to her, not if what little life he had depended on it. But she was determined, and he would help her.

"So, Maryska *is* here." Daryna drawled.

Nahli nodded. "She's the ruler here."

A deadly calm surrounded Daryna at Nahli's answer, while Pav absorbed everything and caressed the handle of his sword.

Anton scanned the dead grass, the tree and its fall leaves, not seeing Roka anywhere. "Where's Roka?"

Nahli searched beside her feet until Roka finally answered, "I am still in here, waiting for you all to finish."

"What in all of Kedaf is that?" Daryna spat.

Pav's gaze fell to the meerkat skeleton. "It's sort of cute. It reminds me of old times. Remember when you brought us that chicken, Nahli?"

"What chicken?" Daryna blew out a harsh breath and stepped toward Nahli.

"I um … gave his family the chicken." Nahli cringed.

"You *what*!" Daryna growled, bringing her sword up.

"Enough of this!" Anton whisper-shouted, pressing a finger to his teeth. Everyone needed to keep their voices down.

Quiet enveloped them all.

"Yes, your chicken is with Pav, Daryna." Anton said. "Perhaps he can give it back to you later."

Pav held up a finger. "Except her name is now Juju and she belongs to Tasha." He spun to Daryna with his widest Pav smile. "My younger sister."

"Enough chicken talk," Anton said slowly. "Maryska wanted me as her king. I said no, so she stripped away my skin, muscles, and organs, adding them to the Lake of Flesh, which contains all the layers from other people too. Then she brought me here, to a place called the Bone Valley, where I built Nahli.

Somehow, I awoke her and then she awoke Roka, who yes, is a meerkat that talks. Now, let's go." Anton held open the door as Roka scampered out then closed it.

Roka perched on his haunches, tilting his head up to the four of them. "Well done. I could not have said..." He stopped talking as if under a spell and continued to stare at Daryna. "Kezia?" he murmured.

Daryna's brow furrowed. "No, as stated earlier, my name is Daryna."

Roka's head angled to Anton, motioning to the door. "Open it, I need to go inside and think. Now."

There wasn't time to pace around back in the Bone Valley. "Not now."

Nahli let go of the handle. "It's locked. What's going on? You look spooked."

Instead of holding his head high in his usual proud manner, it bowed to the ground. "I remember. I remember everything." Roka seemed to dig somewhere inside himself as he lifted his chin, and Anton thought Daryna looked on the verge of panic for a moment as her gaze drifted to the dark lake before coming back to them. "I'm the true king here. Maryska is my wife, my queen. She altered her appearance to pretend she was my betrothed, her sister, Kezia—you." Melancholy sewed through Roka's words as his gaze shifted to Daryna.

Anton couldn't bring himself to comprehend what Roka had confessed. How? Why?

Daryna curled her lip in disgust. "I'm sorry? What? I, in no way shape or form, would have been betrothed to an animal."

Nahli knelt and held out a bone hand, jabbing a finger at Roka. "I think we have time for this explanation. And you better know a way to defeat Maryska."

Anton studied the meerkat, unable to see him as a king, not when the first thing he'd done was hide from Maryska when he'd discovered her. Roka could be mistaken, but then he began his story.

TWENTY-FIVE

ROKA

Roka had to speak the words, desperately say the words, because there she was before him. And he had forgotten her, when he thought he never could.

Roka had been king in the afterlife—Torlarah—where he preferred to remain in his human-like form. He would venture up to the surface, usually to find maidens to take as lovers. Their bodies felt different, more fragile, and he liked that— because their existence was not immortal.

After growing tired of visiting women in Verolc, he decided to make way to Narwey, the territory directly adjacent to it. The first village he spotted appeared to be full of life, with fragrant spice markets, blossoming trees, crowded cobblestone streets, and a colorful variety of traveling caravans. All around him the humans laughed and drank, clapping their hands as the women danced provocatively, while the air filled with intoxicating music.

Roka breathed in the heavy scent of pine trees and edged closer to the crowd. One of the dancers watched him with flirtation as she clacked her metal finger cymbals together. But his gaze did not linger there, and would not drift back, after it had shifted to the young woman hidden in the corner on the tambourine. A light brown complexion made up her skin, her hair falling in thick dark waves down her back, and her eyes were the richest of hazels.

The woman clapped her instrument, then rattled it with pursed lips, as though she loved playing but loathed being there. In that instant, he knew she was the one he would bed that night.

As the show ended, he sauntered toward the woman in what he considered to be her corner. But another woman placed a hand to his chest, preventing him from moving. His eyes caught the dark brown irises of the dancer from earlier. He could not deny she was beautiful, with a curvy physique, and the swells of her endowed breasts and belly on display.

"You were watching me earlier," she said, leaning closer.

"Sorry, I need to talk to someone else." Roka brushed past the dancer to catch up to the woman in the corner, who was walking away.

He rushed forward and grabbed her arm. "Excuse me, what is your name?"

The woman's eyes snapped to where his hand was and lifted her gaze to his. "You best remove your hand from my arm before I cut it off," she said, ripping her arm from his grasp and turning to leave.

"You would do best if you don't attempt to woo Kezia." The dancer came up beside him. "My sister won't give the pleasure you're searching for." She arched her back, making her breasts push out farther.

It would have been so easy for him to have taken the dancer as a lover for the night, then leave to find someone else. But instead, he said, "Perhaps I will try tomorrow."

"If it doesn't work out, which I know it won't, you can search me out. I'm Maryska."

Roka didn't look at anyone else, only kept his gaze locked on Kezia as he continued, "It took well over a day for you to have a full sentence with me. And by being in your company,

I discovered I enjoyed something I had never had with the other women.

"I then discovered that you and Maryska were witches, and I admit I did lie at first by fabricating that I was a warlock of sorts so we could conjure things together. I remember the one spell you couldn't get quite right and, when you finally did with my help, I kissed you, only to receive a slap on the cheek in return.

"But that slap led to more new things. Eventually, I asked you to marry me and leave your home to come to my kingdom in Torlarah. When I told you what the missing piece was, that you would have to end your life, I received another slap in the face.

"Somehow, our love grew, and finally, miraculously, you chose me. But what I did not know, Kezia, was that your sister had grown envious. I do not know the entire story but when you appeared to me that night, the night I was to bring you home, it was in fact Maryska. She had conjured up a way to change her appearance to look exactly like you.

"In Torlarah after being married, I told you—Maryska— all my secrets. I wanted you to know *everything*. A few nights later after I made love to Maryska, she snatched my crown, leaving me to my natural meerkat form and taking all my essence. Then she revealed herself as Maryska.

"She then threw me into the Divine Valley, which she soon transformed into the Bone Valley. In skeletal form, the people tried to revolt and that was when Maryska broke everyone into pieces and hid me in the garden."

Roka's tale came to an end, and an eerie silence fell on the group. Neither Anton or Nahli backed away—they only pushed closer to him in camaraderie. But in that moment, that didn't matter, because he watched with hollow bones and a broken ghost of a heart as Kezia turned to him, her gaze darkening.

211

TWENTY-SIX

DARYNA

Daryna stared in disbelief at this skeletal liar. What he'd just spoken of could not possibly be. Roka was the king of Torlarah. Maryska was his queen. Daryna should have been his queen. Daryna's real name was Kezia. All false.

Daryna had felt it in her blood that Maryska was from Torlarah, but she never expected the bitch to be the ruler—or her sister.

False.

And yet, her body twitched with nervousness as she lifted her gaze from Roka to everyone in the room, studying her, waiting for her to speak. She didn't want attention like that drawn to her.

Daryna flushed crimson, whether from embarrassment or anger, she couldn't tell because she felt them both. She stepped forward, pointing the tip of her sword at Roka. "I don't know what kind of lies you are spouting, but it isn't true. I'm not her."

She wanted to believe it wasn't true, because the story was something she couldn't recall. Her instinct was to split him in two and flee to the safety of her home, away from all the prying eyes.

"It is true, Kezia, you have a birthmark on the left side of your lower back," Roka said, "and a scar above your belly button."

"How do you know that? And don't call me that!" she growled. But she did have those things, and no one should have known it but her and her alone.

"Because I love you." His voice was gentle.

Love? What did the little bastard know about that? His tale was horrendous.

"If the story you say is true," she continued, "then you're as good as dead to me, seeing as you couldn't tell me apart from Maryska." Daryna paused as though she'd been struck with a blade. The gap in her memory. "She's the reason I can't remember, isn't she?" She took a step closer to Roka, the sword wavering in her hand. "Did I have a missing leg before?"

"What? No," Roka sputtered. "I do not understand why you would ask that."

"Then let me tell you a story, *Roka*." She rolled up the leg of her trousers to reveal her wooden leg. "One eventful day, I woke up in an unfamiliar village with a bloody stump where my leg had been cut clean off, and not remembering anything of my past. The. End. So if this is all true, then thank you for being the cause of all this, for making Maryska your glorious queen and resulting in the deaths of Anton and Nahli."

Several sharp inhales took place, but she ignored them.

"If it weren't for you, I would never have lost my memory. I could have been back in a caravan playing a tambourine and never would have had to live in Kedaf, *you bastard*." She whisper-shouted the last two words because if she said them any louder, tears would have streamed down her cheeks. And she didn't want to cry in front of anyone.

It had been years since the last time Daryna cried, and once her tears had dried, she'd decided to let her heart harden. And that was how it had always been.

213

She thought about the tambourine girls playing at the market and how something inside her had yearned to place her hands against one of the instruments. If this was true, in her past, it sounded as though she could have loved it.

With a caring touch, Pav moved Daryna backward and said, "How about you put that anger to better use, like toward Maryska?"

Somehow this young boy, who'd annoyed her to no end, had become the smartest person in Torlarah.

She studied Nahli's and Anton's skeletal features, wondering if she could do something to bring them back to Kedaf. A part of her came forth, believing Roka had meant no harm, then the angry part of her chased it away. She had to hold herself back from kicking him.

Daryna and Pav had found Anton. Now, she needed to follow Pav's direction and focus on Maryska. "We're leaving." She turned on her heel, tugging Pav with her, and prepared to storm off.

"On to the Lake of Flesh then?" Nahli asked.

What a stupid name for a lake, Daryna thought.

"Yes, please, we've been here too long," Anton said.

Daryna was in full agreement.

"If you remember, Roka, show us the way," Nahli said.

Roka didn't say a single word as he skirted around Pav's leg. Daryna understood that Roka hadn't recalled his past events either, but he could recall them now. She wouldn't feel sorry for him remembering, when she still couldn't.

As they moved forward, Nahli had calmed for the time being, explaining to Daryna and Pav other things that had happened. The world around Daryna was causing her to feel heightened emotions, and one was more empathy for Nahli.

Daryna had helped with Pav's goal of finding Anton. Now about the flesh lake, she was finding herself curious as to how it would work. Would they just step into it? If it could get them clean, she may join them just to wash off the filth covering her.

To her left, the sludge swished like water, causing a slurping sound to bounce off the walls and autumn trees. Roka led them farther through more fall trees that turned into white and bluish ice, along with a thin layer of snow spread across the ground. Her fingertips brushed the frost on one of the trunks, and Daryna couldn't feel any coolness from it. No one else was shivering, so they must not have been cold either.

Up and down the length of the trees, something glowing appeared. Eyes. The trees were filled with them, from roots all the way up to branches. She didn't even flinch, but everything was too close to her.

Pav wrapped an arm around Daryna's shoulders, and she didn't have the strength to shove it off. "If it makes you feel better, when we make it back to Kedaf, I'll ask Tasha to return Juju."

What a ridiculous name for the hen. That chicken was half the reason she was here, and she didn't want to see it ever again. If she did, it would be headless.

"That chicken has done nothing but cause me problems. Your sister can keep her." She also wouldn't want to take something away from a child.

"I knew you had a heart, Daryna." Pav smirked, patting her back as he removed his hand from her shoulder.

As the group walked farther, the trees thinned out until there were none, and a narrow hallway appeared. It was so thin that Daryna didn't think she would be able to pass through it. Although, the pair of skeletons would be able to squeeze right in with no problem.

"We are almost there," Roka said.

The closer she got, the more she shouldn't have been aghast. Moisture slicked the walls where faces were embedded, their stone eyes shifting from side to side.

"Not as terrible as the headless men and women," Pav said, holding out his arm. "Ladies first."

Rolling her eyes, Daryna squeezed her body between the

open space and even though she could fit, panic swelled in her chest. She stepped back out, breathing hard. "I can't."

Roka must have heard her speak and somehow slithered his way past Anton and Nahli, until he was by her side. "It is all right, Kez. Close your eyes and I will be beside you, guiding your every step. It will not take long." His head lowered a fraction in defeat. "I would hold your hand and whirl you past this, if only I had my crown."

For a moment, only a minuscule one, she wondered what he looked like as a man. Had she really been attracted to him? For now, she would believe it untrue. Then she pushed that thought away, changing her focus to Maryska.

"I'll hold your hand if you want," Pav said.

No, that would only cause sweat and that would make her panic more. "I can't, but can you … hold onto the sleeve of my shirt?"

She loathed asking him for anything, but the thought of everything pressing in on her would be too much. Why did she have so many weaknesses? She could hurt people who deserved it—like Boda—but she couldn't walk through a tight area. *Pathetic.*

Pav clasped the tunic by her bicep. "Just tell me when you want me to let go."

Shutting her eyes, Daryna felt a small hand grab onto her trousers, but she didn't shove it away as she sucked air in, wiggled, and shuffled through the narrow space. The stone rubbed her breasts, belly, and backside as she pressed forward, and she knew the faces inside the wall watched every step she took.

Her stomach churned and she wanted to expel everything from it. Instead, she took a deep breath and pushed herself with the help of a boy she'd only met a few days ago and a meerkat who was really a man claiming to love her.

"You can open your eyes now," Roka murmured.

Not yet. Not until she felt herself being drawn out from the tight space did she open her eyes. As her sight adjusted to the light, Daryna should have felt accomplished, worthy, and capable of overcoming her fear, but she didn't.

When this is all over, I will go back to my cottage, stay inside, and never come out again.

TWENTY-SEVEN

NAHLI

Nahli stood next to Anton, watching in disbelief as Roka and Pav helped Daryna through the tight space. Or perhaps she should be calling her Kezia. Daryna always seemed like a woman who feared nothing, but right then Nahli realized that everyone had their hidden fears. Her. Anton. Daryna.

She nudged Anton's arm to distract herself from sinking back into that darkened nightmare Maryska had put her in. "You never told me Pav is such a caring soul."

On the day she'd met him, he'd been different, perhaps a bit flirtatious. But this sensitive side could be considered adorable. He didn't even complain once while fitting through the space by being the most muscular out of the group.

"Yes, Pav is an interesting sort." Anton chuckled, but there was pride there too.

"He reminds me of you."

His flames slid to the side to stare at her, his jaw unhinging into a smile. She bet it was a sly one.

Daryna dropped to her knees as soon as she entered the room with the glistening lake. When she'd exited the space, Nahli had only peered at the Lake of Flesh briefly, to make sure there wasn't anything dangerous lurking around.

Including Maryska.

The room stood clear.

Daryna moved her good leg away from Roka, who bowed his head in shame as he fell back a step.

Pav let go of Daryna's tunic and held out his hand to her. "My lady?"

"I've got it, Pav," Daryna said in the friendliest tone that Nahli had ever heard her muster.

Nahli turned her head to the side to survey the lake once again. The liquid skin wasn't one solid color. If she looked one way it appeared mahogany, another showed it olive, then something pale. As if it was alternating through different shades of flesh.

Bright orbs dangled above them in hues of green, blue, and yellow. On the walls, white specks twinkled like stars, their light strobing in sync with the beats of a human heart.

"Which one of you wants to go in first?" Roka asked, interrupting Nahli's staring spell. She'd seen so many horrific oddities, and the beauty hidden within them, but this was hypnotizing.

She regarded Anton who was observing her, allowing her to decide. "How about you go first, Roka? You've been here the longest." It only seemed appropriate to do it that way.

He nodded, resigned. "It will only gift me my fur and muscle until we retrieve my crown from Maryska."

With a scamper of his feet against the stony floor, he plummeted into the still liquid. It rippled but didn't splash the way water normally would.

Anton inched to the edge of the lake, peering in. "Is he going to come back up?"

"It's a good thing you two had him test it before going in," Daryna said.

There was no bitterness in her voice toward Nahli. In fact, it was almost strange that Daryna might feel concerned if something were to happen to her or Anton.

Tiny bubbles floated to the surface and started their sail across the top, before popping their voyage.

"No, I think he's all right," Pav said, squinting his eyes.

While watching in anticipation, Nahli's hands shook with worry for Roka. He was her friend, the rightful ruler here. Out from the side of her flames, she looked at Daryna and understood her for once. She would have been angered by the story as well, but Roka couldn't hold all the blame. How would he have known?

Although, he did know about Daryna's scar and birthmark. Did Maryska illusion those, too? Or perhaps he was too caught up in the moment. She didn't want to go there and imagine intimate moments between any of them. If they ever had a chance, she hoped Daryna and Roka could figure things out.

As they watched, the liquid began to change, turning a rusty brown as it spread apart, revealing a furry animal. A meerkat.

"Roka…" Nahli breathed.

Roka paddled his way through the fleshy liquid, then pulled himself up and onto the edge. He rolled onto his back, breathing—exhaling—with real organs, and stared at the ceiling. Not even a drop of moisture clung to his golden-brown fur.

"It worked," Anton uttered in disbelief.

"Did you really think it wouldn't?" Nahli nudged his shoulder.

"Perhaps. I don't know. It was hard to hope, but we haven't gone in yet."

"Anton," Roka said, "let us hurry because who knows how long Maryska will stay away. All the dead in Torlarah know I am back, and they will not let her know this. However, I am still without any power."

If Maryska could dislodge an entire city, perhaps they were in over their heads.

"Go ahead, Anton." Nahli motioned him forward to the

lake.

He set down his daggers before removing his pants and tunic. She swiveled her head to look at Daryna who was gazing down and inspecting the edge of her blade like she needed something to keep her occupied.

Pav knelt to the ground, quietly asking Roka question after question. "What is the difference between having fur and only bone? Why do the dead on the outside of the Bone Valley still have flesh?"

Her attention focused past them and onto Anton, who was near the center of the lake. His flames caught hers, and he shared a silent exchange with her before dipping down into the thickness.

The walls beat harder, the pace becoming wild and frantic, or perhaps that was only Nahli's shadow of a heart.

"Don't worry, he'll be fine," Daryna said.

Nahli didn't look away from the lake, too afraid if she did, she'd miss something. "I hope so."

"A man who gives himself to others for coin and a woman who takes things from others for profit. I can see why you two make a perfect pair. I mean that in the best way."

Nahli wasn't sure if she should thank Daryna or take what she said offensively, but she smiled anyway. Perhaps the two of them had found a truce.

The lake rippled, but no bubbles floated to the surface as they did with Roka. "Why is it taking so long?" Nahli asked Roka.

"He is a larger specimen. It takes more time to piece him together."

Nahli wished she'd gone in first to make certain it would work because if something had happened to her, then Anton would have known not to go in. As her thoughts swam with images of his bones disintegrated to flecks of dust, or worse, something finally started to happen.

The top of the liquid swished then separated, and Anton's

head emerged. From what she could see, he was whole, his blond hair dry, falling to his shoulders.

As more of him rose from the liquid, she couldn't help her thoughts from wandering to new places. If her bones could flush, that's what they would be doing in that moment, altering to a bright scarlet. She scooped up his clothing from the ground when he slid his strong arms through the tan-colored film, making his way to the edge.

Averting her gaze but not completely, she watched him roll over the ledge, breathing hard. She knelt beside him and handed him the tunic and pants. Like Roka, he was completely dry, his hair no longer white but back to the brownish-blond that fell to his muscular shoulders.

Perhaps anything would appear muscular to her now, compared to seeing bones.

While Anton slid on his trousers, Nahli turned to Daryna who was not averting her gaze, but she wasn't watching him with yearning, either. Her brows were furrowed like she didn't understand something.

"What is it?" Nahli asked.

"Nothing." Her expression turned grim as she peered down at her leg. "I can do so many things with what you would consider magic, but I can do nothing of this sort. I'm slightly envious."

Once they retrieved the crown, Daryna could talk to Roka about it. From his story, he'd already wanted her down here before. If Daryna never chose to come, perhaps Roka could still help her.

"It is miraculous, isn't it?" Nahli said instead, not only referring to the magic of the lake, but also Anton.

After tugging on his shirt, Anton locked his gaze on Nahli and smiled at her. One she'd been waiting all this time to finally see. Softly, he placed a hand on her arm. "Your turn. It doesn't hurt, I promise."

Nahli set her clothing and sword on the ground. His words

echoed in her skull, and relief washed over her. She remembered what it was like to have her skin and insides ripped away when she'd died. But even if it would feel like flames burning away flesh, she wouldn't care. It would be worth it to truly feel again.

Anton held out his hand to hers. A few small pale scars etched his fingers, and they were wonderful to see. She clasped her skeletal palm with his as he guided her into the unmoving liquid.

His fleshy hand against her bones was one of the strangest and most beautiful things she'd ever experienced. While his bones lay hidden under his skin, they were still there, and she knew once hers were hidden as well, they would always remember his.

"See you when you come up," he whispered, his smile radiant.

Nahli grinned back, taking in his old, yet new, features. And she hoped he knew she was smiling at him. She shifted through the milky liquid until she reached its belly. Holding her breath and thinking hopeful thoughts, she let her body sink down until her skeletal frame was covered.

At first, she didn't feel anything, not even the laziest of movements to her bones. But then small objects brushed her rib cage, and it felt as if they were being guided into her by liquid hands. A beating heart thumped fiercely against her rib cage, a set of lungs ready to take breaths, her jaw being lowered, and a tongue inserted. One by one the organs came, finishing with two spherical balls being inserted into the hollow pits of her skull.

A warmth—one she didn't know she'd thoroughly been missing—wrapped around her bones, embracing them tightly as another layer came. She wanted to run a hand along every inch of herself to feel what she had missed, to watch what was happening, but she couldn't see through the thick liquid.

It was as though Nahli wasn't even submerged beneath the

223

surface as she could now breathe—*real* breaths. Inhale. Exhale. The bubbles rose to the surface.

Above her, the lake opened to the orb-lit ceiling and her body was pushed upward. The first person her dark eyes—not flames—connected to was Anton. In that moment, she didn't want to look away from him, but she had to in order to stroke her way to where the lake met stone.

"Pav, turn around," Anton whisper-shouted at his brother.

With a half-smile, Pav rolled his eyes but faced the other direction as Anton helped haul Nahli up. "You're ... you're perfect," he murmured. "Not that you weren't beautiful before."

He would see her flushing this time, now that she could. Before this happened, she would have never found bones to be so beautiful, but now she felt the same.

Anton lowered her down and turned around while Daryna handed Nahli her clothing. She hurried and slid them on and took in the citrusy scent of the room.

"Finished," she said.

The males, including Roka, spun around. She tapped and flexed her toes against the cool stone. Her feet were bare and she didn't even care that she would be walking around without boots, regardless of how uncomfortable it may be.

"Where do you think Maryska will be?" Anton asked.

"My guess is the throne room or the bedroom connected to it." Roka rubbed his chin, right under his whiskers. "Unless she's up on the surface."

Nahli dropped her shoulders, trying to hold back her fear. She may not have powers or a crown, but she had a sword and a group of people with her who wanted the same thing she did.

"Take us to the throne room to retrieve your crown, Roka."

Keeping their footing light around the lake, they followed Roka down a long passageway, its stone surface marred with deep cracks. Nahli covered her mouth from making a single sound when she noticed body after body pressed tightly against the walls and along the ground. She crossed over a frail person with protruding veins and facial features attached in all the wrong places.

Long gangly arms and legs were attached to another woman's back, her thinning hair matted in blood. She writhed on her stomach, like a turtle turned upside down on its shell, struggling to roll back over. A man glanced up, only his eyes had been replaced by ears. He held up a bloody hand, and in the center of his palm, a dark mouth screamed at them as they passed. Not a single sound escaped his dark lips.

Roka spoke softly, "These are ones who were horrible in their past lives. But even then, I'm generally not as cruel."

Nahli wondered what Roka usually did to them, and she quickly shook away the thoughts.

Up ahead, several hallways appeared, each lined with silvery orbs. Roka took a left, and they followed closely. She stepped over more bodies, trying not to peer down at the horrors before her. Eventually, they reached a large metal door without anyone guarding it.

Roka pressed an ear to the entrance. "Pav, you stay out here, and slice down anyone who attempts to enter." Then he held up a hand to Anton. "I'll intervene if I need to, but he'll be fine."

Before Anton could argue, Nahli reached for his hand and gave it a gentle squeeze. Daryna had crept her way to the front, silently prying open the door.

They entered the new room.

Out of her periphery, Nahli caught movement and held her sword higher. But she paused when she noticed the movement had come from the walls. Ripples drifted across their surface, swelling in size, like the waves of an ocean.

Closing her lips, she looked to the left and discovered two empty thrones constructed of bones, one with antlers attached at the top. As she moved forward, the floor dipped, making the room similar to a spherical globe.

When her gaze met two beastly animal forms and four humans bowing down with their arms, *or* paws, stretched toward the empty thrones, she stepped forward with her sword high. Did Maryska make them stay like that all the time? Again, she wondered what unspeakable crimes these people had committed.

Nahli tore her eyes from a muscular bloody animal, with broad shoulders and long arms, to find Roka pointing at another door across the hall, this one a wide, wooden circle. *That must lead to the master room.*

Daryna and Nahli raised their swords even higher. As Anton followed Roka to the door, his fists tightened around his daggers.

For the first time in a while, Nahli truly felt her heart thumping against her rib cage. Anton quietly opened the door, his hand slightly trembling. Her eyes drifted across the walls of deer after deer skulls, until they met a large bed. However, Maryska wasn't lying there sleeping.

A living, breathing, gray deer lay in her place.

TWENTY-EIGHT

ANTON

Anton stared at the gray, deer-like creature for a moment too long before it dawned on him that the animal was, in fact, Maryska. On her head rested the same silver crown he'd previously seen, along with the matching one around her front leg.

Daryna ground her jaw, a pulse throbbing along the vein at her neck. She didn't hesitate—she tacitly lunged for the creature.

Maryska's head darted out of the way right before Daryna's blade decapitated her. The sword hit the bed with a low thud, but Daryna skillfully brought it up again, thrusting the weapon with a powerful blow through the crowned leg, slicing it off.

The creature wailed with a deafening screech. Daryna came up again with her weapon, but Maryska was too quick, flicking her unhurt leg forward, flinging her supposed sister back. A loud crack sounded as Daryna's body struck the floor.

Anton lunged forward and scooped up the bleeding leg and tossed it to Nahli, who caught it with one hand. She ripped off the crown from the appendage and practically slammed it down on Roka's furry head.

The screeching wail from Maryska turned murderous, becoming more human. Anton held his breath when hands and feet formed where hooves had been, the head shrinking and flattening as it curved into Maryska's face. The fur vanished, replaced by a silken dress, but the obsidian antlers remained.

Anton's grip was so tight on the handle of his dagger, he feared he would crush it as he prepared to aim for her heart. The opportunity appeared, and he blew out his breath as he hurled the weapon as hard as he could, knowing it would aim true. But Maryska raised a hand and the blade flicked to the left, clattering when it landed on the stone floor.

The sides of Anton's head throbbed in agony, as though a cacophony of tiny fingers or bird beaks were poking and pecking inside his skull. He pressed his hands to his temples as images came to him one by one. His father howled in misery, holding up his handless arms, blood pouring from the stumps, and blaming Anton. Then his mother swung from a noose, the rope creaking, while she glared down at Anton, telling him it was all his fault for being born. Nahli ran at him and shoved his chest, spatting, "Whore. Whore. Whore. That's all you will ever be."

As though the images had never come, the torment ended. Anton drank deep breaths in, feeding his lungs as much as he could. He had ended up curled on his side with Nahli's hand resting on his back.

"Damn," he gasped, patting beside him for the dagger, his eyes seeking Roka.

For a moment, when his fingertips brushed the blade, he almost threw it at the man standing a few paces away. His skin was the color of mahogany, and dark, long braids cascaded down his back. He was wearing no shirt, and a pair of brown trousers. What stopped him from ending the man was the tail hanging behind him.

Roka.

Daryna still lay on the floor, clutching her head, tears

228

spilling down her cheeks. Anton wiped his own away. Roka's crown sat upon his head, larger than it was when Nahli had placed it there.

Roka's right hand was held high, firmly in place, same as Maryska was doing, neither of them moving. Maryska wasn't missing one of her arms as expected, both were there.

"How was your rest, my sweetest Roka?" Maryska purred. "I see you found your way out from the dirt grave I buried you in, you pathetic rodent."

Her gaze didn't waver once from Roka's, as if he was frozen ice that she yearned to chip away. Roka's jaw remained clenched so tightly, it was quite possible at least a few of his teeth would crack.

"I did," Roka seethed. "Not without your help, of course. By bringing Anton into the Bone Valley, a glorious ripple led from one thing to another, leading his queen, Nahli, to uncover me."

If the situation wasn't so dire, Anton would have chuckled from the blow.

Maryska's stare found Nahli, a hard line appearing in between her brows, her lips pulling downward. "It can't be possible that he found you after I broke you to pieces." She tightened her hand into a fist and flexed her fingers at Nahli. Nothing.

Anton wanted to toss his last dagger at her, but he needed to save it after what Maryska had done to his last one. He just needed to draw closer.

"I did." Anton took a step forward, his lips turning up at the corners. "Did you really think I couldn't?" He made it seem as if the task had been too easy, even though it was one of the greatest challenges he'd encountered.

"Maryska, we are done," Roka barked, reaching out his left hand while the other still held its place. "Give me back the crown, so we can be finished here. Otherwise, we can stand like this for an eternity, if you prefer."

Her smile menacing, Maryska twisted her arm in the air, then let out a cry of frustration.

"You are not going to whirl yourself away, either."

In the palm of his hand behind his back, a bright white glow appeared. He flung the sphere at Maryska, and she easily flicked it toward the ceiling. It burst into tiny sparks that rained down upon them, slowly becoming ashes, before vanishing.

With a roaring growl, Daryna was off the stone floor, running toward Maryska. Roka held up his other hand, freezing her into place.

"Not yet." His whisper was only meant for Daryna, but Anton was close enough to hear it, too.

Daryna glowered at the true king, not lifting her glare for a moment as her nostrils flared. That look, more than anything else, told Anton she wanted Maryska badly enough that she would split apart Roka if need be.

"Hello, baby sister." Maryska's gaze seemed to sing as it danced toward Daryna. "I suppose you must know that you're Kezia, yet you still don't remember your past, do you? I did leave a small, although permanent, mark on your leg to slow you down, wouldn't you say?"

Daryna appeared taken aback, but only for a moment. Her chest heaved as she focused on Maryska, growing more murderous with each passing breath.

Maryska let out a cackle, one of a true witch. "As for my disguise, that piece of you helped me hold onto your appearance when I needed it. Then I thought it was absolutely amusing how we found ourselves in the same village, where we met once again. When I stumbled upon a witch named Daryna to help me, what a coincidence it was to discover that she was my long-lost sister, Kezia. And when I told you a false story and showed you fake scars, you were oh so willing to sell me the tea that brought my sweetest Anton to his new home. I should be thanking you for what I've been given. Although Roka was an *exquisite* lover, he was no Anton. And

Anton *will* enjoy his stay here."

Nausea bubbled up in Anton's stomach and lodged into his throat. He swallowed past the lump, pushing it away. While luck hadn't always been on his side, there had been glimmers of fortune through the obstacles he'd faced. When looking at Maryska, he couldn't imagine having to be trapped with her for eternity.

Maryska released an ear-piercing whistle and then shouted, "Callie, Neru!"

From right outside the room, something stirred to life. Roka didn't bat an eyelash as his gaze remained trained on Maryska, but Anton did. Over his shoulder and out the door, the six creatures that were in a permanent bowing position slowly rose from the floor and hobbled toward the bedroom.

Four of the creatures were human, all their faces appearing similar with torn-out eyes, missing noses, and ripped off lips displaying teeth, making them all smiles. They reminded Anton of the skeleton he'd been.

The other two were more beastly. One was mostly ape attached to a horse's head, its bloody muscle leaking fluid onto the floor. The next was part ram and possibly dog with saggy skin that made a strange flapping sound as it took steps.

Anton couldn't just stand there, so he moved toward the door at the same time Nahli did.

"Do not go out there. Pav has it handled," Roka yelled. "Pav! Now!"

If Roka wasn't holding his hand up and keeping Maryska away, Anton would have punched the king in his face.

As soon as Roka called Pav's name, he burst through the throne room door, swinging his sword like a god. The creature with the ram head and saggy skin snapped its teeth viciously at Pav. In answer, his sword sliced through the neck before it could bare its teeth again.

Then Pav's blade thrust into the heart of another, cutting clean across two other necks and puncturing two more chests, until they were all slumped on the ground. Only Pav remained standing, sprayed with blood on top of the mud already caked onto his body.

As Anton peered down, the creatures weren't dead, but wriggling.

Roka's fiery gaze met Anton's. "Anton, Nahli, Kezia." He paused, chest rising, and whispered, "Now."

Anton had no idea what Roka meant by "now." There had been no chat about any kind of plan beforehand. But Maryska's hard glare was focused outside the door as she still held her hand up toward Roka.

She was too focused on trying to rouse the dead, so Anton sprung forward with everything he had, throwing the dagger right at the center of where her heart—if she even had one— would be. Again, she flicked his weapon to the side, but it still caught her off guard.

Anton didn't stop this time, he continued toward her and leapt forward to knock her to the floor. Inches from her, his body came to a stop, as if he'd hit a wall. His heart felt aflame when a sharp ache lit up inside his chest, as though she was squeezing the blood and essence out from the organ. Nahli dodged around him and swung her sword at Maryska's shoulder. It barely broke the flesh before Nahli's knees buckled and she collapsed to the floor, clenching her stomach.

The pressure on Anton's chest lifted, and the world around him spun.

Through his peripheral, Daryna took the opportunity to attack her sister. Maryska's palms pushed forward, ready to pulse out magic.

A crow-colored light shot out from Roka's hands and shoved Maryska's arms to the side. Daryna's blade moved through the air, and it slammed with perfect strength, decapitating Maryska.

The head made a sickening thump as it hit the stone floor, blood pooling around it. Her body didn't slump to the floor though, instead it was already twisting and moving to reunite the head with her neck. Anton couldn't let that happen. He'd never felt as brave before as he did right then. He rushed to the floor and held onto the antler of the head as he tore off the crown, not pausing as he threw the shining silver to Nahli.

Nahli released the headpiece in Roka's direction. He caught it, his eyes burning silver, and a cold wind stirred around the room. Anton recognized it, the same one that had followed him around in Kedaf. It had always been Maryska, even with the wind.

Jaw clenched, protectively holding the crown, Roka snapped his head to the side. Maryska's skin and everything beneath disappeared, except for her bones. He didn't stop there—he cocked his head again, and her remains were no longer in the room.

Anton's breath came out deep and heavy, his heart palpitating against his sternum. Everyone was in the room except for his brother. He raced to the door, just as Pav came toward him, sword dripping blood.

Anton pulled his little brother in for a tight hug, relief spreading through him. "You scared me out there."

"You know I'm one of the best." Pav grinned. "Could you really doubt my skill?"

Even as Pav boasted, more creatures lunged forward to attack from the shadows, but Roka brushed past them, dark light shooting from his fingertips, and the skin vanished from the creatures before their bones themselves disappeared.

The crown that had been on Maryska's head was clenched in Roka's left hand. Anton noticed the king's fingers fumbling as his gaze found Daryna.

She hadn't moved from the spot where she'd sliced off her sister's head. The only reason Anton knew Daryna was still alive was because of the rise and fall of her chest. Her gaze finally swept across the room, landing on the crown in Roka's hand. The piece that should have belonged to Daryna, if

Maryska hadn't done all of this.

When Daryna's eyes lifted to Roka's face, Anton could see something in her gaze for a moment that didn't resemble hate, but relief, love. But then her face hardened, and she jerked her head away from him.

"What do we do now?" Nahli asked.

Her fingers brushed Anton's, catching him by surprise. He interlaced them and gave her hand a gentle squeeze, filled with hope.

Roka's gaze fell to their joined hands, then to Daryna, and back to their interwoven fingers. "I am ... sorry." His tone was sullen.

"What did you do now, Roka?" Daryna marched toward him, anger radiating off her.

Pav stood watching with wide eyes.

"Anton." Roka ignored Daryna. "I will be sending you back."

"To the Bone Valley?" Nahli's voice rose an octave.

"No, back to Kedaf."

Anton's brows lowered. "I don't understand." He remembered the poison, his body dying.

"You're not dead. We can't kill mortals and bring them here." Roka's eyes shifted to Daryna. "She knows this. You would have had to end your life of your own accord."

"But I gave and sold Maryska the tea," Daryna said, taken aback.

Roka's gaze latched onto hers, not releasing. "You did, but it was still under Maryska's order. She was the one who gave him the tea, which he unknowingly drank with the poison inside. He would have had to be aware of the poison in there and choose to drink it."

"You couldn't have told me this earlier?" Anton could barely grasp what was happening. So he wasn't dead?

"I didn't know the entirety of her memories until her crown was in my hand."

Anton didn't miss Daryna's jaw grinding back and forth when he'd said the words "her crown." Confusion and relief bloomed inside his chest until Nahli removed her hand from his.

"And Nahli?" Anton asked, believing she would be able to come home, too.

Roka's head drooped, the way it had as a meerkat. "I really am sorry to you both, but Nahli must remain here. She was killed by another human who was not Maryska."

Daryna moved forward, shaking her head, cheeks growing crimson. "No, it was a ripple effect because of the things Maryska had done. You can send her home too."

Roka ran his hands over his thick braids, chewing on his lip. "I'm sorry, Kezia. Maryska as a *human* cut off your leg and sent you away, before she came to Torlarah."

Anton's chest tightened. He wanted to see his siblings again, but he couldn't leave Nahli down here alone. Pav nodded in understanding as Anton searched his brother's face.

"What if I stay here with her?" Anton asked.

"You would have to still return. And if you want to come back, you will have to die up there," Roka said.

The thought was already crossing his mind, but words died in his throat as Roka turned to Pav and asked, "Where is Anton's body?"

"Buried."

"Make sure you dig it up, or he *will* suffocate."

"No, Roka," Daryna interrupted, lips in a tight line. "You claim to have all this power, but you can't give Nahli her life back? If you can't do this, then you really are a bastard."

"If I could reverse time, believe me, that is the first thing I would do." Roka reached for Daryna's hand, and she yanked it away before he could grasp it.

She spat on the floor by her feet. "I want nothing to do with you. If you so much as try to touch me, I'll cut off your hand."

Daryna turned to Nahli. "I really am sorry for what

235

happened to you, and I wish there was more that I could do."
She looked back to Roka, tears springing to her eyes. "From
the moment I sliced off Maryska's head, I-I remembered
everything. And I can't be around you any longer."

Snatching Anton's dagger from the floor, she pressed the
blade against her throat, creating a red incision. Anton
watched in horror as her body wilted to the floor. Roka lunged
forward and would have caught her, but her body was no
longer in the room.

Pav trembled, jaw set, fists clenched, angrier than Anton
had ever seen him. His brother pushed Roka away from the
floor. "Where is she?"

Roka shook his head in frustration. "Back at her cottage."

As quickly as Pav's emotions came, they left, his shoulders
relaxing. He must have believed she had really died. "I think
you have a lot more than apologizing to do, but perhaps there
is a way."

Anton didn't believe that Daryna would be forgiving Roka
anytime soon. She wasn't like Pav.

"I do. The first thing I am going to do is start here." Anton
noticed Roka's tail swishing side to side like a ticking clock.
It was so very different seeing him this way. "You will all need
to hold on to me. I am going to make it so we do not have to
walk."

Nahli, Pav, and Anton placed their palms to Roka's back.
Before Anton could even blink, they were all standing back
inside the Bone Valley.

TWENTY-NINE

NAHLI

It was like a dream and a nightmare at the same time. Nahli stood back in the Bone Valley with Anton, Roka, and Pav. She stared out across bone mountains, wide hills, leafless trees, all while listening to remains pour from the sky. Nothing had changed. A horrible thought crossed her mind and she swung her hand up in front of her face, but skin still covered her bones.

Nahli relaxed and turned to look at the hand resting on her arm. It was only Anton attempting to calm her, while Pav examined the scenery in wonder. She couldn't help thinking about Daryna, the blade going across her throat. But she was alive—back in Kedaf.

Roka gnawed on his lower lip, his brows knitting together. "It's not finished yet. I must focus on undoing what Maryska has done."

At that, he closed his eyes, and the ground beneath their feet quaked. Bones rattled and clacked against one another, the sound growing stronger, as though the world itself was moments from destruction. Nahli noticed Roka still gripping the queen's crown, but there wasn't anyone now to wear it.

Her eardrums throbbed as the noise grew to a roar. Bones

lifted from the ground, mountains of remains separating. All throughout the valley, countless bones floated off the ground, frozen in levitation. Pure magic.

Nahli's lips parted as the hovering remains began to piece themselves together, shifting in different directions, finding all of their companions. Full skeletons formed from the bones and once complete, they slowly descended to the rocky ground, not yet awoken.

Under Nahli's feet, the pebbles vibrated as the ground made a thump-thump, thump-thump noise. Her chest tightened at what was to come, and she couldn't even blink, for fear she would miss something. A flutter of emerald green spread across the dirt as tiny blades of grass sprouted, twisting and molding together to form luscious fields.

Grassy hills now stood where mountains of bones had been, some small, others stretching far into the sky. The fog cleared completely as a sapphire sky came out of hiding, producing a golden orb that shone down on the Bone Valley. But it could only be the Divine Valley once again.

Trees, flowers, bushes—all of it—came alive with color. The cottages rid themselves of their boned outer walls, revealing new shells of vibrant blues, yellows, browns, greens. *Color.* More than she could have ever imagined. In Kedaf, there was color, but not like this.

The place was beginning to look like spring and summer, while outside the door had been autumn and winter. She didn't have the words to describe how brilliant it all was.

Nahli waited with impatience for the skeletons standing in the grass to come alive, but they didn't stir. Instead, in front of her very eyes, the ground shifted and separated. She tugged Anton to the side to prevent him from falling into what had opened to a milky liquid—familiar.

Peering over the edge, Nahli watched as the Lake of Flesh swished in gentle motions. Not still, as it had been before.

It was then that the skeletons rose from the earth, and their flames came to life. Some rubbed their eye sockets, waking from their deep slumber. If it was anything like when she'd died, it would have been a dreamless sleep.

Roka cupped his hands and called out to the people in the Divine Valley, his voice spreading throughout. "One at a time in the lake, and all will be well."

At first there was silence, until skeletons chattered with one another across the fields, repeating the words Roka had spoken. A dusty skeleton walked to the edge of the lake and sank into the liquid.

Roka turned to Nahli, Anton, and Pav. "This will take a while, but once it finishes, I will close it back."

"Where did you send Maryska?" Nahli asked.

Because Maryska had been left as bones, Nahli thought she'd been sent here. And if that were the case, would she be one of the skeletons now alive and moving?

Roka brought the tips of his fingers together and didn't look at anyone in particular. He gazed out at the Divine Valley, deep in thought. "Maryska's flesh is in the lake, and her bones are in the walls of the narrow hall we squeezed through earlier. The liquid is deep underground here and runs to the room, connecting to the Lake of Flesh.

"I will have to re-arrange the work she has done with the humans outside of the Divine Valley. But do know, there are reasons why they have to stay outside the door and face their punishments for now."

Nahli didn't feel the need to question further. Secretly, she hoped Boda was out there in the wall for murdering her.

Nahli scanned the area, her new home. When she found out that she wouldn't be leaving, it hadn't surprised her. She had never expected to go back. The first time she discovered she'd died, she never thought there'd be a way for her to return to Kedaf.

Nahli hated to admit that she was a little disappointed about Anton returning. She loathed herself for having that tiny

239

flame of misery, trying to burn down all the relief and happiness she felt that he'd be reuniting with his siblings. She would eventually blow it out.

"They all seem to be adjusting rather well," Anton said, observing the lake.

The people could now return to their homes to begin anew. Nahli attempted to not look too terribly hard since each one coming out was naked.

"Yes," Roka said, "but so much time has passed, and new bones have fallen in, that everyone will have to adjust, and the recent ones will have to find homes."

They would figure it out, the way she'd have to, as well.

Roka inched toward Pav. "I am going to have to send you to Kedaf now."

"Anything you want me to tell Kezia?" Pav asked, rubbing the back of his neck.

Eyes wide, Roka looked taken aback, nervous. "No, but please check on her for me."

"I was going to anyway." Pav turned to Anton who hauled him into a hug, squeezing tight.

After pulling away from Anton, Pav surprised Nahli by dragging her into a fierce hug, too. "You would have been good for Anton. But when I meet up with you again one day, we'll have to practice with our swords, since Anton is shit at it."

Nahli laughed. "I'll be waiting."

When Pav shifted back, he pressed his sword at his own throat.

"Wait," Roka said. "You do not have to be so dramatic." He pushed Pav's hand back down, placing his palm on the boy's shoulder. "Ready?"

"I hope so."

"From when you wake, make sure you uncover Anton before the following morning."

"I will," Pav answered softly.

Roka closed his eyes. Pav was there one moment and gone the next. A weight lifted from Nahli because Pav was now in Kedaf, and could start unearthing Anton's body before it was too late.

"You're sure he'll be okay?" Anton pressed.

"Yes." Roka nodded. "Anton, I'm allowing you to wake in the morning so that you and Nahli can have a little time to say goodbye. If this is not what you wish, you will at least have the opportunity to change your mind." His lips formed a sad smile.

Nahli took a deep swallow and bit the inside of her cheek to keep from crying. She wouldn't want Anton to feel like he was doing something wrong by returning home, because he wasn't.

"The cottage where Anton has been staying will be yours for the night." Roka paused for a moment, then met her gaze. "It is yours now, Nahli."

She'd already slept there once, and the fact that it was Anton's for a bit made it seem not so terrible. But she'd still need to get used to sleeping indoors again.

"I have something I need to take care of later," Roka continued, "so I will be indisposed. It is too important to leave unsorted."

Nahli and Anton said their goodbyes to Roka.

After Roka left, Nahli and Anton strolled together down the path, blooming with flowering trees and a litter of different-colored crystalized daisies. It felt like a whole new world, even the brown path was vivid. As Nahli passed skeletons waiting in line to go into the lake, several gave a "hello." Even after the hellishness they'd gone through, the people here were friendly.

Anton stayed silent as they approached the cottage. The merged bones were gone, and in its place stood a beige home, with a blue thatched roof and matching door. It was simple but cute.

241

When they crossed through the door together, it felt like home. The inside of the cottage was the same as before, only it now had color. Even Anton's carvings were still sprawled out on the table.

Nahli dropped down on the settee, and Anton sat beside her, leaving a narrow gap.

"Sometimes," he said, "I don't always have the right things to say, but getting to know you was unexpected. And I wanted you to have something." Anton reached deep into his pocket and pulled out a carving, placing it into her palm.

She brought it closer to her face, her eyes brightening as she let out a laugh. "It's a chicken!"

He smiled, cheeks flushed, while rubbing his jaw. "That day when you were running with the chicken in your arm is something I won't ever forget. I wanted you to have a reminder that I'll always be thinking of you."

"Are you telling me that you carried this in your pocket the whole time we were outside of the Bone Valley?"

His eyes shifted to the side. "Yes. I made this one before you came. I know you wanted a ship carving, but I didn't have time to complete one yet."

"It's perfect. I don't need a ship to sail away anymore." Nahli set the chicken on the table, letting her fingertips feel the texture.

As her chest expanded at the emotion consuming her, she leaned over and wrapped her arms around Anton and pecked him on the cheek. His eyes connected with hers, his expression appearing stunned by her affection.

She'd closed her heart off after leaving her parents, then even more so after Zikri abandoned her. And she should really continue to leave it closed, especially since Anton was going back to Kedaf. He would be gone in the morning. But how could she shut off something that needed a pulse to live?

Slowly, she leaned forward again, so close that their lips were only in a shadowed touch, then closer, as if a feather was

242

running its tip across. Then finally their lips completely embraced, and she moved hers against his. His mouth was as warm and soft as she'd imagined it to be. She drifted her finger to the scar on the side of his eye, feeling the uneven dip in his skin.

Anton's hand scaled her back, the tips of his fingers running the entire length of her spine until they were tangled in her hair. The kisses, sweet and innocent, felt like butterfly wings fluttering against skin.

She ached to appear valiant, like the kind of girl who went for what she wanted, but her hand quivered as she reached for the edge of his tunic.

His hand fell to her wrist. "I know what I said to you at the lake about doing things together if we succeeded, but I don't want to leave you feeling like I was only looking for a quick tumble. We don't have to do anything. For the rest of the night, we could spend our time talking, and I'd be perfectly fine with that."

"You would?"

"Yes. But I'm not going to lie, I'd keep thinking about it." He chuckled, rubbing his thumb along her wrist.

"Good, because I'd be thinking about it, too."

She yanked at his tunic again, and he let her remove it over his head. His body wasn't overly muscular, more of a lean and fit build. He was perfect.

Anton lifted her into his lap, kissing her as her hand traveled up from the curves of his abs to his chest. He ran the tip of his tongue along the center of her lower and upper lip, causing her to part her mouth. She then moved her lips with his, caressing them, tasting all of him that she could. He slid his tongue into her mouth, slowly flicking his against hers, making her release a low moan.

She knew he was much better at this than her, but it didn't matter. Nothing mattered but for him and her and this moment.

His hand dropped to her lower back as the other one shifted

again into her hair, and she wanted more, pressing against him even as he pulled her close.

She grabbed the hem of her tunic and dragged it up and over her head, exposing her breasts, waiting for his touch. He trailed a finger down the center of her chest, and warmth spread through her, straight to her center.

Anton hugged her close, lowering Nahli to her back on the settee. She kept her arms around his neck, the weight of his hips between her legs.

"At any time, you can ask me to stop," he whispered.

"At any time, *you* can ask me to stop." She grinned.

Anton's eyes caressed her skin as he looked at her shyly. "This is a first for me, because *I* want to."

Her heart sank knowing he'd only done this before because he'd been getting coin. When she'd been with Zikri, it was because she'd wanted to, even though it wasn't a choice she should have made.

This time, it was different.

She cupped his face in between her hands and kissed him deeply, praying he felt how much she yearned to be with him, too. If only for stolen moments.

The rest of their clothing came off until all that was between them was warm skin—something she would never take for granted. She could feel with bones, but the nerve endings that were associated with the human body were a glorious thing. It was proof of that as Anton cradled her breast, pressed his mouth to her nipple, and stroked between her legs, making her body arch.

When she reached for his manhood and tightened her grip, he groaned into the crook of her neck. She then guided him to the spot that desperately yearned for him while nipping at his bare shoulder.

As he pushed inside her, they both gasped in pleasure, gazing at one another. And when his body started to move, she wrapped her legs around his waist, urging him on.

Inside their bodies, their skeletal bones still reached for one another, as a beautiful feeling built and built with each roll of Anton's hips, until an array of colors blasted through her, and all her nerve endings ignited at the same time his did.

Neither moved, just held onto each other, chests heaving, hair damp, and smiling.

Through the remainder of the night, there were plenty more kisses and touches. But most of the time was spent talking, and the words they spoke to each other intertwined in the same way their bodies had.

Before she drifted to sleep, Nahli reached for the chicken that Anton had made, and she nestled it in her palm as she nodded off. In the morning, she wanted to wake to a part of him that would still be there when he left.

The last thing Anton said to her before she surrendered to sleep was, "I could have loved you, you know."

His words made her smile, even though she wished they had more time together. But she promised herself that one day, she'd see him again.

THIRTY

DARYNA

*D*aryna. The name didn't feel like it belonged to her anymore as she placed a scarlet line to her neck.

Back in her cottage, Daryna's chest burst forward from the settee, her head collapsing against her knees. She ran her fingertips along her throat, searching for the cut she'd given herself only moments before. It was gone, the skin smooth. She'd thought that perhaps she would have come back from Torlarah forgetting everything that had happened.

Forgotten Roka.

Wished for it. Prayed for it.

Tears she didn't even know she'd had bottled up, spilled down her cheeks. She was Kezia. She remembered herself, remembered *everything*. That was what she had wanted all along, had yearned for, and now she wished desperately to be rid of it.

Heavy breaths came out in a panicked swelling wave. Lifting her head, she reclined her back against the settee and glanced at Pav who was still passed out. In sleep, he appeared even younger.

She stood from the furniture, tilting Pav to his side so he could lie down. Grabbing the wool blanket from the edge of the settee, she spread it across his body. He'd been sweet the short amount of time she'd known him, and perhaps she really wouldn't have minded having him as a younger brother. But she would never tell him that.

Kezia. Kezia. Kezia. The name repeated over and over and *over* in her head, a taunting mantra. The person she'd become over the past eight years had blended with the one she'd used to be. She took a shaky swallow.

Maryska.

Her sister was dead—by Kezia's hand. Her sister had always rivaled Kezia, even though Kezia had always only wanted to be left alone. So it pleased her dearly that Maryska was gone, for what she'd done to Kezia and everyone else.

Anton—who wasn't dead.

Nahli—who *was* dead.

As Kezia thought and thought about spells and concoctions, perhaps there was something she could do. Wiping away the last of her tears, she stormed out of the cottage into the dark. With a lit lantern, she went inside the barn where Lilac was busy nibbling on hay. It reeked of animal droppings, and she would clean up after she figured out what she needed to do first. She poured the horse more water then grabbed the shovel leaning against the corner of the barn.

Closing the door behind her, she walked with purpose behind the cottage, farther out to where the two bodies were buried.

Kezia reached the two burial spots. Boda's body could stay rotting down in the earth for all she cared. Using all the strength of her upper arms, with a hard and fast strike, she dove the shovel into the dirt that concealed Nahli's body. She pressed on her wooden leg for support while taking her good foot to push the shovel into the ground. The dirt wasn't as firm as it had been the first time she'd dug the two graves, yet she still built up a sweat.

She shut out her thoughts, shut out the wind, shut out the

sound of the shovel going through dirt, and sealed the gate to anything inside of her that was vying to come to the surface and affect her.

The moon gave its final goodbye to the morning as the sun rose and spread its rays on Kedaf. The bright beams offered light but left no hope as Nahli's face was revealed under its caress.

Kezia's shoulders fell, and she had to hold herself back from breaking. She thought that perhaps Nahli would have been whole the way Anton was supposed to be, and she could have figured out something. But she wasn't.

Nahli had already started to decay, and insects had eaten away at her flesh, the smell of rot permeating the air. Kezia threw down the shovel and crashed down to the ground, harnessing her heart for as long as she could.

The blasted organ ruptured with hot lava as she peered down at her leg. It should be the least of her problems, but the wooden appendage bothered her regardless, because it was a reminder of how everything had started. Unstrapping the appendage and tearing it away, she chucked the nuisance to the grass.

"I think you might need that," a male voice said from behind her. One that didn't irritate her as much.

Pav.

"I'm glad you woke," she said, staring forward. "I didn't want to have to bury you out here, too." The words came out softer than she'd intended.

Any other time she could have forced herself to sound nonchalant, as though she wouldn't have cared if she needed to bury him or not. Even before she was Daryna, having a friend was a rarity. And perhaps that was what he was.

Cradling her wooden leg in his hands, Pav moved to sit beside her. "Think of the distance you would have had to hop in order to retrieve this. You have quite the arm." He held the leg up as if it were a gift. "Hopping on one leg more than two times tires me."

Kezia huffed and took the leg out of his hand, then strapped it back on. "I tried to dig up Nahli, thinking Roka could be wrong. But he wasn't."

"No, he wasn't," Pav agreed, sadly shaking his head.

He wrapped an arm around her shoulders. "Don't be hard on yourself. It is what it is. You weren't the one who killed Nahli."

"I know, but I'm still part of the cause."

If only she'd known that Boda was going to kill Nahli, then she could have prevented it from happening. Yet if Nahli hadn't been in the Bone Valley, then would Maryska have still been queen? For one permanent death to save everyone in Torlarah, she knew the outcome was the right one. But it still left so much for Kezia to hate.

"If you think about it," Pav started, "anyone can be the cause of anything. Take the day Nahli dropped off the chicken, for example. If I had chatted longer or talked less to her, she might not have died. Even something as small as that could have affected the outcome. So even I can be part of the blame."

His words didn't soothe her, but she understood his point. "You better hurry and retrieve your brother. He may suffocate underground if you tarry." She shooed him away with her hands.

"I'm glad you still have what I'd consider your humor." Pav smiled, standing. "Wouldn't have wanted all of Daryna to vanish."

Kezia felt relieved that Pav would be able to get his brother back after he went through so much to find him. Not only was Anton part of the group that defeated Maryska, but in a way he had helped with restoring her memory. As soon as Maryska was disposed of, the spell on Kezia had worn off.

She smiled at Pav in return. "Thank you." Either way, she needed to say it. "Don't worry about our bargain. I won't be needing a helper any longer."

"A bargain is a bargain."

"I think your brain or your swordsmanship can find you a better trade. I'm not going to be the one who holds you back."

He clutched his chest and laughed. "Aww, your heart must have grown even more."

"Perhaps." Secretly, she wanted to rip the organ out and bury it as if it were dead too. A part of her wanted the memory barrier back up so she didn't have to remember certain parts. Like *him*...

"I'll invite you to dinner soon. You can meet my sisters."

She nodded as he turned to walk away. But there was one more thing to be said. "Pav, I don't care if you break someone's heart, because those people mean nothing to me. But watch out for your own, it's one of the best I've encountered. If someone cracks it, let me know, and I can brew you something."

"To make them go bald?" He smirked.

"Perhaps even a little worse." And she wasn't jesting about it, either.

For the rest of the afternoon, Kezia busied herself with work around the cottage and cleaning up the barn. She'd brewed herself several cups of tea, but couldn't eat anything because of how hard her mind was working.

Before the light through her window pulled back and expelled darkness, Kezia finally challenged herself to return to the grave to rebury Nahli. She even came up with the notion about waking Nahli with a tonic, but it wouldn't be her, only a rotting corpse who wouldn't be able to speak.

Tearing the shovel from the ground, she held it tightly in her fists. She scooped up the granules of dirt, her hands vibrating as she held it above the hole. Nahli's eyes were closed, but they still seemed to beg Kezia not to cover them in darkness.

The nervousness still dwelled within her because it wasn't something that only belonged to Daryna. It was something she always had to fight. Some days were bearable, and some weren't. And right then, she could feel it rousing.

An image of Roka's face, just before she'd slit her throat in Torlarah, crossed her mind. She knew she wouldn't be able to brew another concoction on her own to go to the afterlife, and that affected her more than she'd have liked.

There was the younger Kezia inside of her yearning to see him again, and yet there were parts of her that loathed him to no end. Everything wasn't his fault—everything was his fault. It was as if she was holding a flower and picking off petals, determining what the right answer would be.

"I love you," Roka whispered beneath the stars. "Do you love me?"

"No," Kezia said, keeping her voice even.

"Lie." He kissed her behind the ear, his hand brushing her bare stomach. And she shivered at his touch, his soft caress.

It was a lie. She thought she could never love anyone, but then there was him. Her body craved his touch, his words. "Show me how much you love me then."

His mouth caught hers, and she felt him hard against her. She wanted them to give each other everything, so she pulled his naked body closer.

Her hands shook at the memory. Before they'd made love under the stars, he'd brought her a tambourine, not just any instrument, but one he'd made. And in that gesture, she'd known what her feelings were.

All along, when Kezia was Daryna, she thought she hadn't remembered anyone, but she had. Because Roka had been the man she'd dreamt about on some nights.

Kezia released the shovel and yelled toward the forest, "Roka!" She hoped there would be no answer—she prayed there would be. "Roka! I know you can hear me."

A rustling from the bushes and a crackling of dead leaves fractured her thoughts. Roka twisted out from behind a tree, which made him appear as if he were floating. Since she'd seen him last, he'd managed to find a shirt. He now wore a blue tunic, paired with the brown trousers and his bare feet. The fronts of his braids were pulled back, so they all swung behind his shoulders as he took steps toward her, his meerkat tail hidden away like when she'd first met him.

Even though she'd called for him, anger rippled to the surface because he'd been *spying* on her. "Were you already there in the forest? Watching me?" she hissed.

He said nothing as he moved toward her, not until he stopped only a few paces from her. "Yes."

"For how long?" She shouldn't have called out to him, and a piece of her had thought he wouldn't really come. But another knew that he would—he always came.

"I think the answer will only cause you more anger." His eyes held steadily onto hers, no longer was he staring at the ground as though he were a child.

"You're a bastard, you know that?" she screamed.

"You have made that quite clear, three times over, I believe. Yell it as many times as you wish. I deserve it," he said, his voice soft.

Was he going to continue keeping count, and next time tell her it was number four? Because there would be a number four! And he did deserve it. No matter how much Maryska illusioned herself to look like Kezia, there was no possible way her sister's personality could have matched hers. He should have noticed that. She would have known if someone was pretending to be him.

"You should have been able to tell that *she* wasn't *me*."

"I know, I should have. It was … it was because I was so happy beyond belief that you were there with me. I only thought you were quieter since you were not used to Torlarah.

252

It is a lot different than up here. You had only been one time before."

That was why the cave in Torlarah had felt familiar, why she knew Maryska's otherworldly smell in her cottage, and how she knew the spell would get her there. Roka had used a different spell than the one she'd conjured when bringing her before.

But quiet? She'd never stayed quiet around him for too long. There was always something she yearned to say to him, whether with irritation or another word she would not think about. Somehow, he always banished all her insecurities when she was around him.

However, she didn't need him for anything. She shoved his chest with both hands—he didn't even stumble backward.

"I hate you!" Kezia screamed, and she meant it at that moment. She shoved at him again. "I hate you! *I hate you!*" Hot tears filled her eyes, and she fell to the grass, too tired to stand any longer.

Roka's strong arms wrapped around her, holding her tight. "I know you do. And you can hate me for as long as you wish, but do not cry over me. I am not worthy of your tears, my darling Kezia." He lifted her chin. "You—only you—are the one woman who has ever made me *feel*. I was only with her because I thought she was *you*."

Kezia absorbed his words, but the thought of his body skin to skin with Maryska tarnished anything she knew they'd had. She wouldn't even know how to get that back.

Before her heart drummed any harder, she twisted away from him, but his hand reached forward and clasped her wrist.

"You don't even know me anymore, Roka," she said. "I've changed. Lucky for you, you were buried away and not even awake, while I had to live alone these past eight years, turning into someone bitter. Once you remembered things, not much time had passed, so you may be the same, but I'm not."

"Kezia, I would take you in any form. Believe me, I've

been affected by Maryska too."

She knew he was, but even though she had her memories again, parts of her weren't fully there. As with her body missing a piece, her brain was just the same.

Back in the traveling caravans, she remembered when she would keep to herself. Her sister never wanted anything to do with her unless Kezia had something she wanted—no matter how minuscule it was.

Kezia had once found a shiny blue stone when she was eight and hid it under her pillow. The next morning it was gone, and she knew Maryska had taken it. Men, women—they all wanted Maryska. Except for one. And even then, she'd managed to take him from Kezia.

She had always preferred spending time with her tambourine, never wanting to be touched by anyone or anything, until Roka.

Now, she hated looking at him more than anything, but she threw her arms around him anyway. She should have expected him to smell like the life and death of Torlarah. But he didn't. He smelled like cinnamon. The familiar scent circled around her, and she closed her eyes, pretending for that one moment that she was back with him at the caravans when he'd asked for her to be his wife.

She'd wanted it more than anything. And he promised her she could have a thousand tambourines if she wished for them.

Then, there had been the argument with Maryska.

Kezia awoke, drowsy, everything unfocused.

"I heard what you plan to do," Mayrska said. "You know I always get what I want."

Her gaze tried to focus on Maryska and just as she saw what was in her sister's hands, the ax slammed down.

She was too unbalanced and lethargic to scream, only air released from her lips.

"I could have taken a finger, or an ear, or even a toe. But I prefer to take something much bigger to use in my tonic for

Torlarah."

"*What?*" *Tears pricked at Kezia's eyes from the throbbing in her leg. She couldn't even move to look.*

Maryska lurched forward and shoved something in between Kezia's lips. She held her mouth closed, forcing Kezia to swallow. She was too weak.

"*Roka shall welcome me home,*" *Maryska purred.*

Those were the last words Kezia heard from her sister before her eyes fluttered shut.

Kezia had later woken, without a single memory, in another territory, and inside a covered wagon that Maryska must have put her in. Her sister had always been ruthless, and she should have known back then that Maryska was capable of anything.

Taking a deep swallow, Kezia now focused on Roka. "You truly can't return Nahli to her body?" she asked, in the hopes that perhaps he secretly could.

"No, it does not work like that." She heard the heaviness of his words, and she was sorry too.

She wept harder, even though she and Nahli weren't friends, yet if given the chance, they could have been. But there was something between Nahli and Anton, and through it all, they'd found each other.

Life wasn't always fair.

Her crying halted as her heart swelled with an emotion that should have made her nervous, but it was the one thing she could do to make amends with herself. It made her think that perhaps her heart wasn't so hardened after all.

THIRTY-ONE

PAV

Pav left Kezia's cottage—who he'd still think of as Daryna from time to time—and ran all the way back to Ionna's. As he passed the blooming trees, he was slightly dazed when he entered one of the corn fields to Ionna's home. He'd returned sooner than expected, not even needing to be gone the full two days.

The things he'd seen were strange and should give him enough nightmares to last a lifetime, but oddly enough, he still found Torlarah interesting. For now, he needed to focus on retrieving Anton's body—alive. He couldn't believe it.

He prayed his sisters and Ionna weren't home, so they wouldn't question him about what he was doing outside with a shovel, unburying his dead—but not really dead—brother.

Once he reached Ionna's home, his luck was intact—no one was outside. Pav hurried to the shed, hoping he wouldn't have to answer any questions before the task was complete. Tool after tool—too many to count—decorated the walls and the floor. He shuffled through endless gadgets until he found the shovel hidden underneath several rakes and brooms. They also needed to be organized, apparently.

Pav ran, perspiration pebbling against his skin, to where

Anton was buried in front of the Sequoia tree. Without any pause, he slammed the shovel into the dirt, a throb running up the length of his forearm.

"Damn, this dirt is hard," he muttered to himself as he pulled the shovel back and pushed in again. Even though Pav needed a good nap, he couldn't let the exhaustion affect him.

"What in all of Kedaf do you think you're doing? You left notes for your sisters as if you were going to be gone and possibly never return. Do you know how worried Yeva is?" Ionna yelled from behind him, her brow furrowing with worry.

She must think me mad. He felt like it as his hands shook. Yet he struck the shovel into the earth again, fishing out more dirt.

"Look, Ionna, I know how this may appear. And I promise I'll explain it to you once I get Anton out of here."

"Pav..." She held up her hands as if she was trying to calm a spooked mare. "Come inside, and I'll go to the market and fetch your sister."

There wasn't time to deal with her questioning.

"I'm going to explain this to you as quickly as I can and once I'm done, you can either help or let me finish." He hadn't meant to sound so blunt, but he needed to unbury his brother.

Anton would wake the following morning, and if he wasn't out of the grave, Kezia would be right—he really would die.

"Go on." Ionna watched him, her expression becoming serious.

Pav nodded. "I went to Daryna's, who really is a witch. She brought me to the afterlife, to a place called Torlarah. We found Anton, who *was* poisoned by Maryska, incidentally also the queen of the place. Anton was all bone—no skin—and was with Nahli and a meerkat. Nahli was the one who gave us the chicken and was then killed sometime after. The meerkat was really the king of Torlarah named Roka. Without going into too much more detail, we defeated Maryska, and Anton was never really dead because someone from Torlarah can't kill a

257

mortal. The mortal has to knowingly sacrifice themselves." He took in rapid breaths after spewing out the words because he felt as if he needed all the oxygen in Kedaf at that moment.

"All right..." Ionna said ever so slowly, a deep crease settling in between her brows. "I think we *really* need to find Yeva."

"Ionna, please!" he shouted with desperation. "If I've never been completely serious in my life, I am right now. If Anton really dies this time, I will never forgive myself, or you, for that matter."

With a loud sigh, Ionna pressed a few fingers to her right temple. "Let me go and retrieve another shovel, and you can explain it all to me in full detail later. But I know what we're going to find below the dirt, Pav, and it isn't going to be pretty." She still didn't believe him, thinking him delusional, but at least she was trying to understand.

Ionna returned as Pav lifted out more dirt to his growing pile. She pushed the shovel in, helping to speed up the process.

"Is Tasha not here?" he asked, wiping a hand across his sweaty brow.

"No, she's at Mrs. Evanko's."

"So, how was that goat stew I made?" His stomach twitched at the thought of food, but that would have to wait too.

"Fabulous, but are we going to casually talk as if we aren't digging up a dead body?"

Pav tilted his head side to side. "I think it's fine, since he isn't dead."

"Are you sure you want to keep going?" She tossed a pile of dark granules over her shoulder.

"Haven't you ever believed in miracles, Ionna?"

"I don't know. I suppose?"

"Then let's just keep going."

After digging for what seemed like his entire lifespan, Pav ceased shoveling and stepped down into the grave to continue.

Using both hands, Pav dug like an animal making a hole to burrow in, until a flash of Anton appeared. He wiped the dirt away from his brother's face. Even though Roka had explained to him that Anton would look the same as the day he was buried, Pav still had images pass through his mind of his brother's body in a decomposed state with half the skin on his face missing. But Roka had spoken the truth—Anton was whole.

"Pav!" Ionna gasped, covering her mouth as she peered at Anton's face. "You were right! He wouldn't look like this if he were really dead." She focused her attention on Pav. "You said he will wake in the morning? What do we tell your sisters until then? I'm not sure if we should get their hopes up just yet."

"I told you so." He smiled. "But I think it would be best to tell them beforehand, since I'm going to put him in my bed."

Ionna leaned on her shovel as though in thought. "This is… I don't even know how to describe it. I'm sorry for not believing you, though. I've just met so many people who have been in denial over death and have done erratic things because of it."

"I understand. It's a hard thing to believe."

In the village, he'd come across townfolk before who weren't able to handle loss. At the market, he'd met a woman who would constantly speak about her infant when she came to Yeva's booth. Pav had told her to bring the babe by one day, and she'd agreed yet still always came alone. Later, he'd found out her infant had died four years before. Out of all the circumstances he'd known of, that had been one of the worst.

Ionna hopped into the hole and helped remove the dirt from Anton's legs. "This is going to be the hard part, getting him out of here," she grunted.

Anton was less muscular than Pav, so he could lift him on his back once his brother was on the ground above. "Go ahead and get out. When I push him up, try and roll him to the grass."

"Easier said than done."

Ionna was right about that. It took him about twenty attempts to haul up Anton's dead-weighted body. Groaning, Pav shoved his brother as hard as he could, praying Ionna would be able to roll him out the first time.

She did.

"Thank the stars, the sun, and the moon," he said, pulling his own sweat-soaked body out of the empty grave. "And the clouds shaped as animals."

Leaving Pav alone with Anton for a moment, Ionna fetched a large pail of water. Together they stripped off Anton's tunic and pants to clean him as best they could before carrying him inside.

As Pav held Anton under his shoulders and Ionna had his legs—because she refused to let him do this by himself—they gently laid his body on the bed to rest.

"What now?" she asked. Her dirty fingers rested against her cheeks, while she stared down at Anton.

"Now, we wait."

THIRTY-TWO

ANTON

I could have loved you, you know. The words he'd whispered to Nahli passed through Anton's lips as his eyes flew open. His body jerked up, and two firm hands grabbed his shoulders before he fell to the side.

Anton thought they were Nahli's delicate hands until he realized the skin was callused.

"You're all right," Pav said. "I didn't leave you buried in the dirt. We're at Ionna's."

A wide grin spread across his brother's face, but Anton couldn't bring himself to mirror the smile. It wasn't even a settee he was resting on, but an unfamiliar bed.

"I'm here. I'm really here in Kedaf," Anton whispered. "It wasn't a dream, was it?"

Pav scratched the side of his face. "Some parts I wish had been, if I'm to be honest."

Memories of the night before with Nahli came to him— them together, kissing, skin touching, him inside her, her gripping him, stealing each other's breaths. He wanted to return, dig a hole through the earth and find his way back to her. But it wasn't that easy, not unless he truly wanted to die. For what Nahli wanted, he would remain in Kedaf.

Pav's smile slipped away. "It will be all right. It isn't as if you'll never see her again. Perhaps it wasn't meant to be."

When will I see her? Years from now?

Anton's eyes narrowed, his lips tightening.

Biting his lip, Pav held up his hands in front of him. "All right, I didn't mean it how it came out. I only meant perhaps—I don't know what I meant—but maybe it wasn't meant to be right now, yet one day it could be. Anyway, I'm glad you're here, and you know who's going to be happy to see you? Tasha. I think she'll miss my storytelling, though." He tapped the side of his chin. "Or perhaps I have the new role of being the nighttime reader."

Anton had to put a hand to his head, while Pav continued to babble on, as everything was still foggy.

Weak and shaking, Anton stood from the bed barefoot, with only a pair of trousers on. As he took a step forward, his knees buckled and his legs collapsed.

Pav caught him just before he smacked into the wood floor. "Careful. Perhaps you should lie back down."

The door jerked open, and Ionna walked in. Her dark irises flew to Anton, a beaming smile spread on her lips, and her sleeves were rolled up like she'd just been out in her fields.

Yeva rushed in past Ionna, her blue eyes wide. She threw her arms around Anton, and he hugged her back with a heavy breath.

"I thought you had lost all your marbles," Yeva cried to Pav then focused on Anton. "I screamed at him for disappearing. And when I found out he and Ionna dug you up, I was horrified beyond belief. Then they showed me your body on the bed, appearing the same as before, and I didn't know what to think."

Anton sank down to the feathered mattress. "I don't know what to think, either."

"You look like you need to rest and eat, so let me get something. Pav told us a story that I wouldn't believe possible."

"Believe it."

Swiftly, his sister nodded, still wide-eyed when she rushed out of the room.

Ionna smiled and clasped her hands in front of her. "I already have a room set up for you if you'd like to stay here with us."

"Thank you." Anton didn't know what he was going to do. Would he stay here? Go back to his old cottage? There were too many pieces shifting around in his head.

She placed a hand on his shoulder, giving him a gentle squeeze. "I'll let you get some rest."

Everything should have been easier now that he was home in Kedaf, and it would have been if he hadn't met her. It should have been elation at seeing his family again, starting his new craft, and finding his place in the world.

But Kedaf wouldn't be as it was before.

The door creaked, and a small-frame of a girl with tangled curly hair entered the room. In her arms she carried a chicken, and Anton held his breath before slowly releasing it. This was the hen—the one Nahli had stolen from Daryna.

Pav plopped down beside Anton. "I told Tasha you might want to meet the chicken Nahli gave to us. What were the chances?"

Hesitantly, Tasha padded farther into the room, quieter than usual. Was she frightened of him?

"Hello, baby bean. I know this is probably difficult for you..." To think a person dead and now alive would frighten almost any adult, let alone a child.

Tasha handed him the hen but didn't sit beside him. "Are you going to go away again, Ton-Ton?"

Anton stroked the black and white feathers of the hen. "No. I'm here to stay. But we don't know how long we truly have, do we?" He patted the bed on the empty side beside him, and she stiffly sat down. "What you need to remember is that no matter where Pav, Yeva, or I are, we love you. That never disappears."

Nodding, she scooted closer to him. "Juju here wants you to read us our story tonight."

Pav pretended to appear offended as he flung his hands to his chest. "But I thought I was the official storyteller now!"

"I wasn't finished yet." One tiny finger flicked up from Tasha's hand. "And then Pav will tell us all a story."

"That's more like it."

Yeva's hurried footsteps thudded across the floor as she entered the room, carrying a bowl of broth in one hand, a glass of water in the other, and a loaf of sweet bread tucked under her arm.

"One of us could have helped you," Pav said, standing and attempting to take the items from her.

"I told Ionna I had it, and, Pav, you still need to rest, too. You stayed up all night in here."

He waved her off. "I'm fine."

Yeva set the broth and water on the nightstand then handed Anton the warm bread. He didn't feel like eating, but he entertained her by taking the bread and placing a buttery piece in his mouth.

"May I talk to Anton alone for a few moments?" Yeva asked Pav and Tasha.

Pav nodded and Anton handed the chicken back to Tasha, giving his sister a kiss on the head. His brother wrapped his arms around Tasha's shoulders and led her out of the room.

Yeva took a seat beside him, meeting his gaze. "You can talk to me."

"You wouldn't understand."

"Pav had no difficulty pouring out the dramatic tale from start to finish with gory details that he could have left out."

"That's Pav, though. Not me."

"But you still always tell me things straightforward."

His shoulders slumped. She was right—she was always

right, and Anton needed to get everything off his chest anyway. They had been through so much together with their mother's suicide, their father's death, and struggling to have food in their mouths. As he told her about the Bone Valley and Maryska, he left out certain parts about Nahli that were too private, but said enough so Yeva would know how he felt about her. The last thing that fell from his lips was why he'd returned, when Nahli hadn't.

Yeva wrapped her arms around him, drawing his head to her shoulder. He wept. Hot tears slid down his cheeks, and he cried like a child. It had been ages since he'd truly wept—not when his parents had died, not when he'd whored himself out to villagers for coin, not even when *he* had died. He always tried to hold it all within, to not affect his siblings, but he was crying for all of it now. All of it, including Nahli.

It felt as though he was nine years old again, with Pav swinging a wooden sword that almost took out Anton's eye, leaving a scar in its wake. Yeva had held him then as he cried while his father stitched him up. Spilling tears over physical things was much simpler than what he was now feeling.

Lifting his head from her shoulder, Anton looked for something to dry his face. Yeva stood, tossing him a shirt from Pav's closet. He rubbed away the physical parts of sadness while his mind continued to writhe inside him.

"We didn't get rid of any of your belongings," Yeva said in a soothing voice. "All your clothing is in here, along with Pav's things. We can move them in the room Ionna set up for you, when you feel like it."

His things… A thought struck him fast and hard. "You remember that satchel in the market I told you I took from the thief? You said you didn't want it, so I kept it."

"Yes, I remember it."

"Well, did you keep it?"

"I did." She peered at him, questioning. "It's in my room. Do you want me to get it for you?"

He nodded a little too quickly. "I'd like to bring it back to Nahli's home."

Her bridge.

Yeva left the room while Anton went to Pav's closet to find one of his tunics. He tossed on a dark blue one and rubbed at his eyes with the heel of his hands, making sure he could hold his internal stitches together.

His sister padded back into the room with the leather satchel in hand. He smiled to himself as he took the bag and pulled it close.

"I wish I could have met her properly," she said. "Not only when she'd brought Juju."

"You almost did that day in the market, if you'd made it to the booth sooner." He smiled, wondering how Yeva would have reacted.

As though reading his thoughts, she laughed. "If she'd been that desperate for herbs, I would have given her some, if you must know."

"I know."

Yeva knew as he did what it was like to struggle, and she was the most generous out of the four of them. That was one thing that he loved and hated about her.

"I'll return a little later, if that's all right?" Anton didn't have to ask her to leave, but he didn't want her to have to worry again.

Pursing her lips, she nodded.

"I promise I'll return."

"We just got you back is all."

Anton grasped both of her shoulders. "I told Tasha I'd read her a story tonight. I'm not going to break what I said."

She tossed her arms around him once more. "Be careful."

Before leaving, he drank down his broth, then told Pav and Tasha goodbye. Worry flickered in both of their eyes, but Anton couldn't sit there a moment longer, cooped up inside Ionna's home. He needed to go outdoors—he needed to see

266

where she'd lived, to give her one final goodbye.

The pale blue sky sat absent of clouds as he walked off the path, stepping over fallen tree limbs. Anton didn't know what he was going to do when he arrived back at Ionna's, most likely spend the rest of his life carving objects to keep his mind occupied. He would help out Ionna with the herbs for his sister to sell, and that would be his life. Before he'd died, or thought he had, his future path had felt like a dream come true, but now he not only wanted that but also something he couldn't have.

Clutching the satchel to his chest, and inhaling the leather of it, Anton headed for the bridge. He passed the tall hills in the distance, then the lake, stopping to glance at the water for a moment to see the sun reflecting off it. Too many lakes reminded him of her, and he didn't want to look or think about it anymore.

Anton stared at the loose gravel trail beneath his feet for the remainder of the way, listening to the consistent pattern of crunches below his boots, the songs of insects, and the crowing of birds.

He held up a hand and stared at his skin. The familiar bones hidden underneath the layers were already becoming a distant memory until it would feel like it had never happened—like *she* had never happened.

When the decaying bridge appeared, directly in his line of sight, Anton lifted his chin higher. Focusing on his destination, he started to pick up the pace toward the open space below the curving and broken wood. He didn't know why he was in such a hurry. Perhaps he thought for a moment she would be there.

His boots pummeled the hardened earth, trampling the tall weeds beneath his feet. When he drew nearer, his gaze caught on a sprawled-out blanket across the ground. Chest heaving, he inched even closer, noticing trinkets, a pile of rumpled clothes, and a pan resting in the corner. Then something recognizable caught his eyes, his tunic. The one he'd worn the day he'd met her—the one she'd taken. Kneeling, he lifted the fabric and brought it up to his face. It smelled of her—honeysuckle—as if she'd worn it.

His grip tightened as he fisted the material, and he threw it down. Taking the satchel strap in his hand, and with emotions flaring up, Anton pounded the bag over and over against the ground. He wasn't going to let himself lose it again like he had in the bedroom, but tears still managed to find their escape.

Anton let out a choking noise and tossed the satchel next to his tunic on the dirt. He released a loud roar—because he needed it, because it stopped him from thinking.

"I'm not sure what my poor satchel ever did to you, but you do know that's my favorite one, right? I don't think I appreciate you whacking it like that," a teasing, familiar voice called from behind him.

Nahli.

Eyes wide, heart screaming, he whirled around. "What? *How?*"

Nahli took a step closer and closer, as he did the same, still too far away, until she finally reached him and he reached her, neither one of them touching. Raven hair hung loosely past her shoulders, brushing her tan tunic.

"I suppose you have Kezia to thank for this."

Kezia. There could have been only one thing that may have possibly happened.

"She went to Torlarah?"

"I would have argued with her not to exchange her life, no matter how much I wanted to come back. But I suspect her decision was a firm one. When I knew her as Daryna, she never would have done anything she didn't truly wish." Nahli paused. "I think she may also have unfinished business with Roka."

"I—I…" He couldn't get the things out that he needed to say. It was as if no words existed, only a vision he couldn't believe was there.

"Don't worry, I won't be attempting to thieve from you

again." She smiled, two dimples forming in her cheeks.

With those words, he clasped her face between his hands and pressed his mouth softly to hers. "You already have. You're a thief who has stolen my heart, and I never want you to give it back."

Nahli's smile grew wider. "Even when I didn't have a heart, you had the ghost of it. Because skeletons, you know, don't have hearts."

"Now you're starting to sound like Pav." He chuckled.

She laughed along with him, so much so that tears beaded against her lashes.

"When I told you I could have loved you, I take back what I said." He pressed his finger to her lips to prevent her from speaking. "Because I already do." There was no reason to wait longer to say it because he knew how he felt. He didn't need a longer amount of time to tell him so. And with life, he didn't know what could happen tomorrow.

Anton slid his finger slowly down her lips, catching on the bottom one.

She nipped the tip of his finger. "I love you too."

"Now what do we do?"

She shrugged. "I suppose we have time to figure it out together."

EPILOGUE

NAHLI

Three years. That was how long Nahli had been living inside the Divine Valley. It was strange to still think that the outdoors had once been covered in bones—that *she* had been bones.

When she'd passed away for the second time in Kedaf, Nahli had feared she'd wake again as bones, or worse, she wouldn't wake up at all. What if she'd come into the Divine Valley the same as the first time, a pile of remains, not knowing she was there?

But she hadn't.

The deep blue sky had opened for her, and she floated to the grassy ground as though she were in a bubble. More than anything over the past three years, she missed Anton, but she knew he'd one day be with her again.

Before she died, she'd grown old and gray. Now, she appeared as she was in her much younger years. She hadn't known it then, but she missed the agility—no longer needing to use a cane with her aching fingers.

After death, she'd found Pav and Ionna, who had been more like the family she'd never had in Huadu. Every morning under the afternoon orb, Nahli would swordplay with Pav and Ionna, challenging one another.

Yeva and Tasha were not in the Divine Valley yet, but she would see them again one day, too. Not only did Anton remain in Kedaf, but so did their children and grandchildren.

At her door came a hard knock, pulling Nahli from her reverie. She had expected it to be Pav, but her brows lifted when she saw Kezia standing before her instead. Even now, she remembered her as Daryna, the woman she'd known but never really understood until the past three years.

Kezia didn't ask if she could come inside as she brushed past Nahli and sank down onto a padded chair. Her deep blue gown wrapped around her tan skin perfectly. Two horns, resembling that of an antelope, sprouted from the top of her head. Like Roka, Kezia could also shift into an animal.

Her hazel eyes met Nahli's. "Today, I have a surprise for you."

"Your surprises don't generally end up being good."

Kezia cocked her head. "What about the one where you got your life back?"

Nahli appreciated that more than Kezia could ever know, but she wondered if the queen had any regrets about it.

Either way, Kezia had chosen to switch places with Nahli. She'd been willing to give up her life by becoming a queen— that had been the only way. If Maryska hadn't gotten between the lovers, Kezia would have already been queen to begin with. And as selfish as it was, Nahli didn't want to think about how that would have affected her life, and everyone else's.

"So only that one time, then," Nahli replied, taking a seat in the chair beside Kezia.

"Roka wants you to meet him in the garden."

"Oh, how secretive," Nahli teased. "Are you the teensiest bit jealous?"

Her gaze shifted to her fingernails, inspecting them thoroughly. "Why would I be?"

Kezia went around pretending she was immune to Roka, but Nahli knew she wasn't. The way her eyes always slid to

Roka when they were in the same room, the way he brushed a finger against her in passing, along her neck, her wrist, her shoulder. Nahli would catch Kezia trying to suppress a smile.

Underneath everything, Nahli believed—whether she had forgiven Roka or not—Kezia was his queen and he was her king, and they were more than just titles.

"Because I know you love him."

Narrowing her eyes at Nahli, Kezia waved her on and led her out into the bright light of the Divine Valley. Laughter, singing, and chatting echoed across the bright green hills, lined with tall, leafy and flowering trees.

A glowing orange orb, like the sun, shone high in the sky. At nightfall, it would ripple and fade to a pale shade of silver.

Once she rounded a hedge into the garden, Nahli stopped in her tracks when her gaze settled on a familiar, beautiful man with not locks of gray, but blond.

Anton.

She rubbed at her eyes because it had been so long since she'd seen him this way. As he talked to Roka, he hadn't noticed her yet. The ruler stood shirtless, as he almost always was, his braids and meerkat tail swaying in sync.

Anton's blue eyes angled to Nahli and froze, then his lips pulled back into a grin.

"I told you I had a surprise for you," Kezia murmured, grabbing the skirt of her dress and strolling away.

She didn't know whether to be thrilled or melancholic—if he was there, that meant he wasn't alive in Kedaf any longer.

Death had slinked its way in and found him.

But she was too excited to see him, period. Nahli ran and leapt into his arms, wrapping her legs around his hips. "I've missed you," she whispered in his ear.

"Not as much as I've missed you."

"I'm sorry you're here."

"I couldn't walk anymore. My health was deteriorating." His lips pressed against hers. "This is more than anything I could have asked for."

"You know I am right here," Roka stated.

Nahli slid down from Anton's hold, but she left her arm around his waist. "Sorry," she said, not meaning it at all.

"How about I chat more with the two of you later?" Roka whirled away, leaving them in their moment together.

Anton cradled her face and drew it closer to his. "Do you remember how I once told you that you were a thief who had stolen my heart?"

"I remember." How could she not? It was one of her favorite memories—one that had stayed with her every day.

A smile spread, lighting up his whole face. "You never stole it—I gave it to you willingly. And I would again and again, as I'm giving it to you now." Anton caressed her lips with his, reuniting them in an intimate dance.

In response, Nahli's heart and bones gave themselves to him as they always did.

What was once the Bone Valley had become a faded, distant memory, but not forgotten, as its pieces remained in everyone and everything within the Divine Valley.

Did you enjoy The Bone Valley?

Authors always appreciate reviews, whether long or short.

Subscribe to Candace's Awesome Newsletter for exclusive content and giveaway!

http://eepurl.com/dhV0yv

Join Candace's Facebook Group: Candace's Pretty Monsters

Also From Candace Robinson

Glass Vault Duology
Quinsey Wolfe's Glass Vault
The Bride of Glass

The Laith Trilogy
Clouded By Envy
Veiled By Desire
Shadowed By Despair

Faeries of Oz Series
Lion (Short Story Prequel)
Tin
Crow
Ozma
Tik-Tok

Cursed Hearts Duology
Lyrics & Curses
Music & Mirrors

Letters Duology
Dearest Clementine: Dark and Romantic Monstrous Tales
Dearest Dorin: A Romantic Ghostly Tale

Campfire Fantasy Tales Series
Lullaby of Flames
A Layer Hidden
The Celebration Game

Vampires in Wonderland
Rav (Short Story Prequel)

Merciless Stars
The Bone Valley
Between the Quiet
Hearts Are Like Balloons
Bacon Pie
Avocado Bliss

Acknowledgments

This story was one I had wanted to share for a long time, and while I love all my stories, this one has a big chunk of my heart. There are so many people to thank that have helped with this process, and because you're reading this now, this is for you, dear reader. Thank you for sticking with me for a story that is more than just bones. You are what breathes life into Anton, Nahli, Pav, Kezia, Roka, and all the other characters of this tale.

About the Author

Candace Robinson spends her days consumed by words and hoping to one day find her own DeLorean time machine. Her life consists of avoiding migraines, admiring Bonsai trees, watching classic movies, and living with her husband and daughter in Texas—where it can be forty degrees one day and eighty the next.

Connect with Candace:

Website: https://authorcandacerobinson.wordpress.com/
Facebook: https://www.facebook.com/literarydust
Twitter: https://twitter.com/literarydust
Instagram: https://www.instagram.com/literarydust/
Goodreads:
https://www.goodreads.com/author/show/16541001.Candace _Robinson or ignore that and just try searching for Candace Robinson!

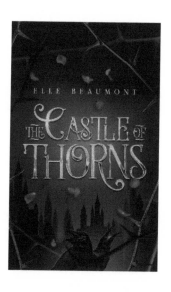

The Castle of Thorns by Elle Beaumont

After surviving years with a debilitating illness that leaves her weak, Princess Gisela must prove that she is more than her ailment. She discovers her father, King Werner, has been growing desperate for the herbs that have been her survival. So much so, that he's willing to cross paths with a deadly legend of Todesfall Forest to retrieve her remedy.

Knorren is the demon of the forest, one who slaughters anyone who trespasses into his land. When King Werner steps into his territory, desperately pleading for the herbs that control his beloved daughter's illness, Knorren toys with the idea. However, not without a cost. King Werner must deliver his beloved Gisela to Knorren or suffer dire consequences.

With unrest spreading through the kingdom, and its people growing tired of a king who won't put an end to the demon of Todesfall Forest, Gisela must make a choice. To become Knorren's prisoner forever, or risk the lives of her beloved people.

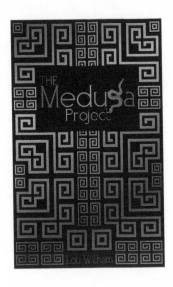

The Medusa Project by Lou Wilham

Everyone takes things that don't belong to them.

From Medusa, it was her reputation. From Poseidon, it was his freedom.

When Poseidon is released from prison, after years of being locked away, the bodies start piling up, and all fingers point to Medusa. Agent Kyrie Alcide of the Perseus Initiative is tasked with investigating the case, and keeping tabs on Medusa. But Kyrie is about to find out that everything in the legend of the infamous gorgon might not be as it seems.

Now, if Kyrie can't discover who the real murderer is Medusa could find herself their next victim.

Lightning Source UK Ltd.
Milton Keynes UK
UKHW011938221121
394396UK00002B/541